PRAISE FOR SUSAN STOKER

FOR *JUSTICE FOR MACKENZIE*

"Daxton's desperation to find Mackenzie is rousing and believable, and readers will have a white-knuckle read until the end . . . pure entertainment."

—*Kirkus Reviews*

"Irresistible characters and seat-of-the-pants action will keep you glued to the pages."

—Elle James, *New York Times* bestselling author

"Susan does romantic suspense right! Edge of my seat + smokin' hot = read ALL of her books! Now."

—Carly Phillips, *New York Times* bestselling author

"Susan Stoker writes the perfect book boyfriends!"

—Laurann Dohner, *New York Times* bestselling author

"These books should come with a warning label. Once you start, you can't stop until you've read them all."

—Sharon Hamilton, *New York Times* bestselling author

FOR *RESCUING RAYNE*

DEFENDING
CHLOE

Rescuing Mary
Rescuing Macie (April 2019)

Badge of Honor: Texas Heroes Series

Justice for Mackenzie
Justice for Mickie
Justice for Corrie
Justice for Laine (novella)
Shelter for Elizabeth
Justice for Boone
Shelter for Adeline
Shelter for Sophie
Justice for Erin
Justice for Milena
Shelter for Blythe
Justice for Hope
Shelter for Quinn (Feb 2019)
Shelter for Koren (June 2019)
Shelter for Penelope (Oct 2019)

SEAL of Protection Series

Protecting Caroline
Protecting Alabama
Protecting Fiona
Marrying Caroline (novella)
Protecting Summer
Protecting Cheyenne
Protecting Jessyka
Protecting Julie (novella)

Protecting Melody
Protecting the Future
Protecting Kiera (novella)
Protecting Dakota

SEAL of Protection: Legacy Series

Securing Caite (Jan 2019)
Securing Sidney (May 2019)
Securing Piper (Sept 2019)
Securing Zoey (TBA)
Securing Avery (TBA)
Securing Kalee (TBA)

Beyond Reality Series

Outback Hearts
Flaming Hearts
Frozen Hearts

Stand-Alone Novels

The Guardian Mist
A Princess for Cale
A Moment in Time
Lambert's Lady

Writing as Annie George

Stepbrother Virgin (erotic novella)

DEFENDING
CHLOE

Mountain Mercenaries, Book 2

Susan Stoker

Montlake
Romance

Published by Montlake Romance, Seattle

www.apub.com

Amazon, the Amazon logo, and Montlake Romance are trademarks of Amazon.com, Inc., or its affiliates.

ISBN-13: 9781542040020
ISBN-10: 1542040027

Cover design by Eileen Carey

Cover photography by Wander Aguiar

Printed in the United States of America

DEFENDING
CHLOE

Prologue

"Come in, son."

Leon Harris opened his father's office door and slipped inside the room he was rarely allowed to enter. Just shy of twenty-five, he had moved back home two months ago after finally graduating with his master's degree in accounting. He wasn't interested in the occupation, but he did like money, so it seemed like it could be a good match. Not to mention, his father had hinted there would be a future in the family business if he got his degree.

"Sit," Ray Harris said, motioning to the large brown leather chair situated in front of his obnoxiously oversize and imposing mahogany desk.

Leon barely kept the sneer off his face, the expensive furniture reminding him of the vast differences between them. He was sick to death of his father controlling his allowance and not giving him the money he needed to live the lifestyle he felt he deserved. Everyone knew Ray Harris was loaded. Why he'd made Leon live on only a hundred thousand a year while he was at school was still a mystery. One that pissed Leon off.

"Good evening, Father," Leon said in a perfectly controlled and modulated tone, none of his anger toward the man leaking into his words.

Ray Harris sat back in his own leather chair, fingers pressed together in front of him as he contemplated his only son. Finally, he took a deep breath and leaned forward, piercing Leon with an intense gaze. "Congratulations on earning your degree. I told you after you graduated high school that if you got your graduate degree in accounting, I would hire you . . . and you'd start on a journey there's no turning back from. My question for you is this: Are you sure this is what you want?"

"Yes, Father," Leon said immediately.

Ray held up a hand. "Not so fast. You have to completely understand what it is we do."

Leon nodded eagerly. *Finally* he was going to be invited into Father's inner circle. The curiosity over the years had been unbearable. He'd seen his father enter meetings that were secured by several bodyguards, both his own and those of the visiting businessmen invited behind the office door. Leon hated not being in the know, and it looked like he'd finally jumped through enough hoops that his father was going to enlighten him. About fucking time.

"A couple years ago, Joseph Carlino approached me and asked if I would join his branch of the Cosa Nostra. Do you know what that is?"

Leon nodded, even though he wasn't sure. The last thing he was going to do was admit to his father that he didn't know something. Smug bastard would use it against him for the rest of his life. It's what the asshole did.

Ray's lip curled, but he didn't call his son out on his obvious lie. "Cosa Nostra is the Mafia. One of the oldest and most well-known divisions. It began in Sicily in the eighteen hundreds. It was brought here to the United States by immigrants and is alive and well in our country today. There are different branches of the organization, and Joseph Carlino is the head of the Cosa Nostra up in Denver. There are several other influential families he works with, and he asked if I wanted to join their ranks, bringing their brand of business here to Colorado Springs."

"And you said yes, right?" Leon asked excitedly. The Mafia was cool as shit, even if they used a stupid Italian name like Cosa Nostra.

His father sighed as if his question was absolutely ridiculous. "Yes, Leon. I did."

"Cool," Leon breathed.

"If you're done acting like an eight-year-old, I'd like to bring you up to speed on what we do."

Leon nodded, but inside he was seething. He hated that his father treated him like he was still a kid.

For the next two hours, Ray Harris told his son details about what the family business involved. He outlined the insider trading, extortion and protection rackets, occasional drug dealing, and blackmailing operations that were the backbone of their family's contribution to the Cosa Nostra, including how money was collected.

When he was done, Leon's mouth was practically watering.

The thought of the amount of money he could get his hands on was almost overwhelming. He'd not only have the kind of lifestyle he'd always known he deserved, but he'd also have power and respect to go with it. "What will I be doing, Father?" he asked, visions of roughing up business owners and suitcases full of money flying through his mind.

Ray Harris leaned on his desk and looked his son in the eyes. "I've told you what we do, but that doesn't mean you'll immediately be in the thick of things."

Leon's eyes narrowed. That didn't sound good. "What do you mean?" he asked.

"I mean don't think it's escaped my notice that you were a fuckup at the university. You skipped classes more than you went to, you paid other students to do your work, and you even slept with, then blackmailed, some of your professors. While that kind of behavior would normally get a student kicked out, you were lucky that the president of the university owed me a few favors. Not only that, but you barely graduated, thanks to your behavior."

Leon sat back in the chair and crossed his arms over his chest. Father had always been a huge stick-in-the-mud. Women were put on this planet to serve men. They were weaker, not as smart. Of course he'd used chicks at school to do his work for him. And the teaching assistants he'd slept with were nothing but whores anyway. "What will I be doing?" Leon repeated, not liking where the conversation was going.

"You're smart, Leon," Ray said. "Your grades don't show it, but I know it as well as you do. But you're going to have to prove yourself to me before I give you access to any of my spreadsheets. It's not only the Harris family name that's at stake here. It's also the Carlinos' and the Smaldones', the two most influential families in the Cosa Nostra. If even the smallest thing is screwed up, we're out. And I don't mean just kicked out. We're dead. Do you understand that?"

"Yes, Father," Leon answered obediently. He'd learned over the years how to deal with his old man.

"Good. Since our money is tied up with Joseph Carlino's, I'm not willing to simply let you loose on the spreadsheets to run amok. You're going to have to prove that some of what you were supposed to learn in your classes stuck. Show me that you inherited some of the same math aptitude as your sister."

At the mention of his sister, Leon ground his teeth. He hated being compared to Chloe. Father was always throwing her successes in his face, and Leon was sick of it. She was five years older than he was, and Father had always treated her like a fucking princess instead of the stupid cunt she was. She was working for some company downtown—he couldn't remember the name—as a financial adviser. She apparently made good money, but Leon didn't give one little shit. He hated the spoiled bitch. Always had. Always would.

"Why don't you have *her* work for the business?" he asked a little snarkily.

Ray slammed his palm on the mahogany desktop, and Leon flinched in surprise. "Don't tempt me, boy," he said in a vicious, low tone. "She's female, that's why. The Cosa Nostra doesn't have women at their helm. But make no mistake—she's twice as smart and can run circles around you when it comes to making money."

Leon cleared off all emotion from his face, checking the old, familiar rage. It had always been this way. *Why can't you be like Chloe? Chloe would know how to do this. Chloe gets all As; why can't you?* He was so sick of being compared to his *perfect* older sister, he could scream.

Ray Harris took a deep breath and steepled his fingers under his chin. "When I married your mother, she was the sole heir to her family's fortune. She was worth millions. But that's not why I married her. I fell in love with her and didn't give a crap about her money. I made enough on my own. Her family lawyer managed the money for her, and it wasn't ever an issue between us. After she passed away, I discovered there were stipulations put in place over a century ago that further protected the almost half-billion dollars she had in her accounts. The money was *solely* hers. Even though she'd married me, I had no legal right to it."

"But . . . when she died, you got it, right?" Leon asked.

Ray shook his head. "No, son. I receive a stipend every month, but the rest of the money is untouchable."

"That's bullshit!" Leon said.

"When Louise passed five years ago, her fortune automatically went to her daughter, but Chloe doesn't receive it until she's thirty-five. Apparently, her ancestors preferred that their women have more time to get married and have children of their own before they inherited."

"That's not fair," Leon said. "What about you?"

Ray shrugged. "I don't need one dime of her family's money."

"So I get *nothing*?" Leon fired back.

Ray eyed his son critically for a long moment before saying, "That's right. You get nothing."

"Thanks for nothing, *Mom*," he murmured.

"Don't speak ill of your mother," Ray chastised. "She set things up so fifty thousand dollars is transferred every month to my account, to be used on Chloe's behalf and to pay for the management of the fund. But you know what I've been doing with it?" Without waiting for an answer, he went on. "I've been giving *you* an allowance, so you could screw around at the university and fuck any woman you want, whether or not she wants *you*. I've been cleaning up your messes and paying people off so they don't press charges against you. I've been paying your drug bill when your dealers come to me complaining that you haven't paid them for the merchandise you've taken off their hands. I've been using it to cover *your* ass, son. But that stops *now*. You're on your own. No more allowance from me. And when Chloe turns thirty-five, I'll tell her about her inheritance. How she uses her money will be up to her."

Everything in Leon's vision went red.

This wasn't happening. There was no way his fucking sister had that kind of money at her disposal, and he had *nothing*. "That's not fair!" he whined again.

Ray shrugged. "Fair or not, it is what it is. Here's the deal. You can have that fifty thousand a month flat-out. But . . . I want to see what you can do with it. Your job is to see how much you can make it grow. If, after one year, you've turned that six hundred thousand dollars into at least two million, I'll welcome you into the family business with open arms. I'll let you have access to and manage the money in the business account." He squinted at his son. "Prove to me that you learned something, anything, in the last seven years while you were at school. Show me that the money I spent was used for more than just fucking, drinking, drugs, and partying. You do that, and you're in."

"I have to live off that *and* invest it?" Leon asked.

"Yes. You won't get another dime from me. You can live here, and you can have your car. But that's it. Everything else is in your hands."

"And if I don't agree?" Leon asked.

Ray put his hands behind his head and leaned back in his chair, looking relaxed and unconcerned. "Then you're on your own completely. No more allowance. No more car. No more living off Harris money."

Leon didn't move for a moment as he and his father stared each other down. The unfairness of it all was almost too much to swallow. He knew his father was trying to light a fire under his ass to motivate him.

But instead, he'd lit another kind of fire.

A dangerous one, which would soon blaze out of control and consume everything Ray Harris knew and loved.

Slowly, Leon stood and held out his right hand toward his father. "Deal."

Smiling, Ray also stood and shook his son's hand. "Make me proud, son."

Without a word, Leon nodded and turned to leave. As he shut the heavy wooden door behind him, Leon dropped the amenable mask he'd been wearing for his father. A snarl curled his lip up, and he glared at the office door.

"Mark my words, Father. Chloe's money is going to be mine. Every penny. Not only that, but I'm going to take yours too. In fact, I'm going to take *everything*. Prove myself to you? Fuck that. I don't have to prove myself to *anyone*. No one tells me what I can and can't do."

And with that, Leon Harris spun around and headed for his suite of rooms on the opposite side of the large mansion, his mind going a hundred miles an hour. He had plans to make. Big ones.

Chapter One

"What'd you find out?" Ronan Cross asked impatiently.

Ro and his friends were sitting in their usual spot in The Pit, the pool hall/bar they frequented. The six of them were all members of Mountain Mercenaries, a group of men who worked for their handler, a man named Rex. The cases they took on were all about saving women and children from the dregs of humanity who wanted to enslave and rape and murder them.

But at that moment, Ro only cared about one woman.

Chloe Harris.

She'd stumbled onto his property in Black Forest just north of Colorado Springs, wearing ill-fitting clothes, and the story she'd told him simply hadn't added up. Ro still would've let it go . . . if not for the large black-and-blue mark on her lower back. Someone had hit her. Hard.

He couldn't let *that* go. He'd spent the last few years doing whatever was necessary to get women out of danger; there was no way he'd let the only one who had intrigued him on a personal level in a very long time disappear from his life like a puff of smoke, especially if she was being abused.

He'd given her his card, knowing he most likely wouldn't hear from her. He also knew, better than most, that battered women rarely reached out until they were at rock bottom, and sometimes not even then.

But he was afraid battered-woman syndrome wasn't the reason she hadn't contacted him. He had a feeling it was because she was being *prevented* from calling him.

How he knew that, Ro couldn't say. But he did.

She said she lived with her brother, Leon Harris.

Him, he knew.

They all did. Anyone who was anyone in Colorado Springs knew Leon. Over the last few years, he'd gone out of his way to throw money at enough charitable organizations that the city leaders loved him. But Ro and the other Mountain Mercenaries knew he was a member of La Cosa Nostra. The Mafia.

He wasn't the big man in charge—that was Joseph Carlino, who lived and worked up in Denver. But during the last decade, Carlino had branched out, inviting other influential families to join his network.

The only reason Leon Harris—or Carlino, for that matter—hadn't been on their handler's radar and taken down was because the group didn't participate in crimes against women. There was no prostitution or human trafficking in their organization . . . as far as Rex knew.

In fact, Joseph Carlino and his main business partner, Peter Smaldone, were well known for loving their wives and children. Not only that, they went out of their way to ensure they were protected, with several bodyguards assigned to each.

Ro had talked to Rex about his suspicions regarding Leon and his sister. His handler had insisted there was no way Carlino would put up with abuse toward women in any way, shape, or form.

But Ro couldn't put Chloe out of his mind. So he'd called in one of his friends. Specifically, Meat.

Hunter Snow, also known as Meat, was their resident computer expert. He could hack just about any database.

"So?" he asked, drumming his fingers on the tabletop in front of him as he waited for Meat to tell him what he'd found out about Leon.

Meat frowned. "I honestly didn't think I'd find much of interest. The man's no saint, that's for sure. He's got half of the mayor's office on the hook for one thing or another, and half of the cops as well."

"For what?" Gray asked.

"The usual. Seems the leaders of this city have a penchant for either visiting ladies of the evening up in Denver or for doing a variety of drugs."

"I fucking hate politicians," Arrow said under his breath.

"Seriously. I wish Lieutenant Joe Kenda hadn't retired. He'd clean up the force without any issues," Black threw in.

"The guy from that TV show? The one who says, 'Well, my, my, my' all the time?" Ball asked.

"That's him. One of the best detectives the Colorado Springs Police Department ever had. Even though he was around in the eighties, when DNA evidence wasn't as much of a thing as it is today, he still managed to close most of his cases," Black explained.

Ro ignored his teammates. He didn't give a shit where someone was sticking his dick or what he was shoving up his nose, and he really didn't care about some fucking TV show. His concern was Chloe. "What else?" he asked Meat.

"How do you know there's more?" he asked.

Ro didn't respond verbally; he simply stared at Meat.

"Fine. There's more," his friend admitted. "Looks like two years ago, Leon Harris started up a new business. You know that strip club on the southeast side of town? That's his."

"BJ's?"

Meat rolled his eyes. "Yeah. Apparently, whoever came up with the name thought they were clever. Anyway, it's Harris's property. A lot of the blackmail pictures seem to come from there. But the interesting thing is, I'm not certain if Carlino knows about the place. He's made it clear on more than one occasion that the Cosa Nostra doesn't dabble in low-class establishments like that. As Rex mentioned, they treasure their women, and likely wouldn't consider disrespecting them by visiting or owning a strip joint."

"So what's the deal?" Ro asked.

Meat shrugged. "Carlino must've either given Harris permission to open the club or is maybe looking the other way for some reason. Or just isn't monitoring Leon's club as closely as he should be. I'm not sure. But from the outside, it definitely looks exactly like what it is—a strip club."

"And from the inside?" Arrow asked, leaning forward on his elbows.

Ro looked around and saw that the rest of the team seemed to be just as interested in Meat's answer.

"I don't know yet. I'm still looking into it. But on the surface, the business is legit. Taxes are paid on time, paperwork was filed correctly with the city to open the joint, and full-time employees have health insurance. I did manage to dig deep enough to find that another building on the other side of town was recently purchased, and a license was approved for a second club." He rolled his eyes. "With the proposed name of the Beaver Den."

"What's with your sudden interest in the Harris family?" Ball asked Ro. "Leon Harris has been on the scene for years, as has his little strip joint."

Ro inhaled a breath and held it for a long moment before exhaling noisily. "About two weeks ago, a woman walked into my garage and asked to use the phone. She was wearing high heels that she couldn't walk in very well and clothes that were way too tight. She was jumpy and nervous and was putting out vibes I didn't like."

"And?" Gray prompted. "What else?"

Ro wasn't surprised that Gray seemed impatient. Ever since he'd hooked up with Allye, he preferred to spend less time hanging out, playing pool at The Pit, and more time at home with his girlfriend. Not that Ro could blame him.

"You know where I live, man. Black Forest isn't exactly on the beaten path. There was absolutely no reason for her to be there, not on foot, dressed as she was. I would've let it go without much thought if it wasn't for the huge bruise on her back. It was easy to spot under the see-through blouse she had on."

Arrow whistled.

"She said her name was Chloe Harris, and that Leon was her brother. She lives with him. And when she was picked up by a chick who looked like she had a permanent stick up her arse, she got an arse chewing of massive proportions. The whole situation didn't sit well with me then, and it doesn't sit well with me now," Ro said.

Meat was frowning. "I knew Leon had a sister, but I don't remember much about her. I'm going to need to look into her. You should've told me about her in the first place," he scolded Ro.

Ro shrugged, not in the least affected by his friend's rebuke. "I wanted to know about her brother, if he was into shady shit. And now I know that he is."

"Owning a strip club isn't exactly shady," Gray commented.

Ro looked at his friend. "Maybe not. But possibly doing it under the radar so Carlino doesn't know about it certainly is. Not to mention the blackmail and other shit he's doing. Look, Chloe seemed like a good girl. You know what I mean. She was nervous and scared."

"But just because she had a bruise and lives with her brother doesn't mean he's the one abusing her. She could have a boyfriend who's knocking her around," Black pointed out rationally.

"It's him. I bloody know it," Ro said without a trace of doubt in his tone.

"Rex has said that La Cosa Nostra is off-limits," Gray reminded him.

"Look, I'm not asking us to do an all-out assault on the strip club. I'm just checking things out."

Gray didn't look convinced.

"Seriously," Ro said. "Meat is going to continue to look into the Harris family and see what he can find out."

"And what are *you* going to do?" Ball asked.

Ro grinned for the first time. "Anyone up for a night out?"

"Let me guess. BJ's?" Arrow asked.

"I haven't been to a strip joint in ages," Ro said. "Thought we could change things up a bit. The Pit gets old sometimes."

The others rolled their eyes.

"If we do this, we're just going for recon," Black stated emphatically. "Before we do anything, we need to bring Rex up to speed and get his input. You know as well as I do that when we signed on with Mountain Mercenaries, we swore we'd never act on our own."

Ro gave a curt nod. "You don't need to remind me. I know what I promised, and I never go back on my word."

"But?" Gray asked, obviously having heard more to Ro's statement.

"We also promised to do whatever it took to make sure no woman is oppressed or held against her will. If we find that Harris is making women—or God forbid, girls—do more than simply take off their clothes, or if he's forcing them to work, maybe by holding something over their heads, I'm going to do everything in my power to shut that shit down," Ro said.

"Agreed."

"Me too."

"Right on."

Ro was pleased when his friends concurred with him.

"I'm in," Black said. "But I have one more question."

"Shoot," Ro said.

"Are you going to lose your shit if this Chloe woman is at BJ's? And more importantly, if she's there, but of her own volition?"

Ro clenched his teeth together so hard, his head hurt. "If she's there, it's not because she wants to be," he said after a second.

"And if she is?" Black pushed.

"If she is, then fine. But if there are underage girls there, or women who *aren't* there of their own free will, I'm going to try to get Rex in on this to take Harris down."

"Even if it brings the Cosa Nostra down on Mountain Mercenaries?"

Ro leaned toward Black. "Yes."

Black grinned. "Good. Just making sure."

Ro relaxed a fraction but was a little annoyed with his friend. He hated when Black did that shit. He did it all the time, loved to play devil's advocate. He knew Black was just as committed as they all were to taking down scumbags who treated women like shit.

But for some reason, the particular innocent woman who'd stood in his shop and bravely looked him in the eye and told him she was fine, when she obviously wasn't, wouldn't leave Ro's mind. He'd stake his life and reputation on the fact that something more sinister was going on with her.

He'd had premonitions in the past—they'd saved his life more than once—but never had they involved a woman. That alone should've freaked him out, but it didn't. Instead, the thought of Chloe Harris being in over her head made him more determined than ever to get to the bottom of whatever was going on.

If her brother was somehow blackmailing her or making her do something she didn't want to do, Ro would make sure she got out from under his thumb. No matter what it took.

Chapter Two

Chloe sat in the back seat of the Mercedes and listened as her brother and his girlfriend, Abbie, talked about the upcoming night. She clenched her hands together so hard she knew she'd have fingernail marks scored into her flesh by the time they got to BJ's.

BJ's. What a ridiculous name for a strip club. But it was quintessential Leon. He'd always thought he was a lot funnier than he actually was.

Chloe had no idea how she'd gotten to this point in her life. Once upon a time, she'd lived a happy, privileged life. She'd loved being a big sister and had adored her parents.

But then her mom was killed. Her dad had never been super affectionate, but it seemed like with the death of his wife, all traces of her loving father had vanished as well. It wasn't that he didn't love her, he just disappeared behind his office door more and more. Work became more important than anything else, including his children.

That was also around the time her brother had begun to hang out with a new group of friends. Young men of questionable character with some less-than-gentlemanly reputations. Chloe had tried to warn him, but he'd ignored her.

They hadn't been close in the intervening years; she'd already graduated from college and gotten a job. She'd thought after her father's death, when she'd lost her job and Leon had invited her to move into the mansion she'd grown up in, maybe he'd matured into a better man than he'd been when he was younger.

But she'd been wrong. Way wrong.

Chloe sighed grimly. What was done was done. She couldn't turn back time; she could only go forward.

"It's time to stop fucking around," Leon told Chloe, shaking her out of her depressing reminiscence.

"What?" she asked, not sure what he was talking about.

"Fuck, would you pay attention?" Leon griped. "Have you heard a word we've said?"

She could only shake her head.

Abbie patted her brother's arm and looked scornfully at Chloe. "I've been training you to work the private rooms for a few weeks now. It's time for you to start full-time."

"Tonight?" Chloe asked, dread filling her.

"You'll get your toes wet, so to speak," Abbie said with a mean chuckle. "Instead of spending half your time in the back with the books and then working the floor, you're going to spend all your time serving . . . and more. You obviously won't dance, because you're the most uncoordinated person I've ever seen. You manage to trip over cracks in the sidewalk, for God's sake. You'll serve drinks, and also start entertaining patrons in the private rooms, starting tonight."

Chloe whole body froze, her nails digging harder into her skin.

The last couple of weeks had been hell. Ever since Abbie had picked her up in Black Forest—after Leon had kicked her out of his car—Chloe had been going through humiliating "training." She'd made a tactical error that day: pissing her brother off badly enough that he'd decided to change her duties at the club.

"I'd really rather keep serving and doing the books. I'm not sure I'd be good at . . . all the other stuff." She tried to make her voice sound compliant rather than angry. It had been getting harder and harder to keep up the biddable-sister role she'd assumed for the last three years as she'd plotted and planned.

"I'm sure if you put your mind to it, sis," Leon said smoothly as he divided his attention between the road and the mirror so he could look at her, "you'd find that you're more than capable of providing acceptable *entertainment* for our guests. I've been patient. You've been living rent-free for years. You don't have to pay for food or utilities or even clothes. You haven't been able to find a job in your field, so I even took pity on you and hired you to work for me. But it's time you realized your free ride is over.

"You've got a good enough body. Even though you're overweight, I've had several men approach me, wanting a taste. It's not like you're married. If you'd tried a little harder with the men I've set you up with, you could've been married with your own family by now. But no. You're still mooching off me—and that shit stops *now*. Your accounting skills are a dime a dozen. You'll do me more good, and make me a ton more money, this way."

Chloe shuddered. She knew what her brother was doing. She'd seen Leon smoothly manipulate so many other people, she recognized his tactics a mile away. "So if I married one of the men you've been pushing at me, I wouldn't have to be a prostitute?"

His easygoing look evaporated at her words. "You've always acted like you're so much better than me and everyone else around you. But news flash—you aren't. It's way past time you were married. You're a disgrace to Mother and Father and the Harris family. I set you up with a perfectly good man the other week. And instead of doing what you should for this family, you insulted him. I had to come retrieve you like you were a child."

Chloe knew she'd gone too far that day, but having the fifty-eight-year-old, twice-divorced "friend" of Leon's try to stick his hand down her low-cut shirt—and laugh when she got offended—had been too much. She wasn't going to take that shit. No way.

The man had called Leon and told him to pick her up. Said things "weren't going to work out" and he "wouldn't marry such a cold bitch no matter how much money was involved."

When Leon had picked her up, he'd been furious. And instead of trying to placate him, which Chloe had gotten really good at over the years, she'd told him in no uncertain terms that the man was a pig, and she was done meeting *any* men Leon wanted to set her up with. He'd gotten so mad, he'd kicked her out of the car right then and there.

Chloe forced herself to pay attention to her brother . . . and not think about the *other* man she'd met that fateful day.

"If you aren't going to help expand the family business by marrying a man from a respectful family," Leon went on, "you'll need to prove your worth another way."

"By getting naked?" Chloe asked incredulously. "How in the world does that expand the family business?"

Abbie turned in her seat as if to say something—but instead she struck out, slapping Chloe as hard as she could.

Chloe immediately put a hand to her face and glared at Abbie.

Leon had begun dating the woman about a year and a half ago. She'd quickly dropped the facade of trying to be friends with Chloe, and her true colors came through. She'd been a willing spy for Leon, just as evil as he was, and she'd kept tabs on Chloe often. Lately, however, her role had changed to that of jailer. Chloe could no longer do anything, go anywhere, without Abbie at her side. Watching. And reporting back to her brother.

"Stop back talking!" Abbie ordered. "You should obey your brother. It would serve you right if he let you out of the car right here and let you fend for yourself."

Chloe winced, knowing they would expect to see fear. But now that she was supposed to work the private rooms at BJ's, she hoped Leon *would* let her out of the car. She'd been biding her time for the last three years, but if she had the chance to escape tonight, she'd take it—even without the full amount of money she'd calculated she'd need to not only survive, but to hide from her insane brother and his girlfriend.

That last time he'd kicked her out of the car, he'd dropped her off in the middle of Black Forest, a sparsely occupied subdivision north of Colorado Springs. She'd walked to what looked like a home-based business, and she'd been able to borrow a phone to call Abbie to come get her, as she knew that was expected of her. Chloe remembered the encounter with the homeowner as if it were yesterday.

Ronan Cross. Ro. He'd claimed he was American, but his delicious English accent said differently.

He'd seen the bruise from where her brother had hit her a few days prior, and he'd been pissed on her behalf. He'd also been respectful, hadn't taken advantage of a helpless woman in the middle of nowhere, and hadn't even glanced at her too-small blouse with her boobs hanging out.

Instead, he'd given her his business card in case she needed help. He'd actually ordered her to call him if she needed anything.

She'd thrown out the card. She couldn't afford to let Abbie or Leon think she was trying to get help from someone, or even that someone might've been interested in her enough to give her his number. But she'd memorized the name of his business: Ro's Auto Body. If she needed help, she'd look up his number on the internet and see if he'd been serious about his offer.

"Go ahead. Stop the car and let me out," Chloe said, hoping against hope that she might piss off her brother enough that he'd do exactly that. Her mind spun with ways she could get away from him. It wasn't exactly how she'd planned, but at this point, it was more important to escape than to continue playing the role she'd been perfecting for so long.

Leon chuckled. "I will. But you won't be wearing a fucking thing when I do. You want that, sis? I don't think so. This isn't really the best neighborhood, and a woman walking around butt-ass naked would be too much of a temptation, I'm thinking. You'd be flat on your back within minutes. I bet you wouldn't think working at BJ's would be so bad, then, huh?"

Chloe knew better than to call her brother's bluff. He *would* strip her naked and force her out of the car and leave her there. *Damn.* She'd have to reassess and figure out another way to get away from him.

She had no idea what had happened to the loving and happy little boy she'd helped raise, but any trace of him had long since disappeared. She also couldn't understand why her brother hated her as much as he did. Whatever affection they may have had for each other when they were little was long gone.

She sat back in her seat in defeat.

"Right, so tonight," Leon went on, "the first half of the night will be spent training, just like the last two weeks. You'll watch what the other girls do in the private rooms and critique their performances. Then, when the club gets busy, it'll be your turn. I expect you to put your best foot forward, sis," Leon sneered. "I know how important getting As is to you. You'll definitely be watched and graded on your performances tonight, just like you've been doing to the other girls. Have no doubt about that."

"And if I don't live up to your expectations?" she asked.

Leon pulled the Mercedes into his personal parking space at the back of the strip club and shut off the engine. He turned in his seat so he could look at her face-to-face for the first time. "This is your training period," he informed her. "I realize it'll take some time to get used to working the rooms, and I'm willing to give you that time. Tonight, it's hand jobs, lap dances, and BJ Specials only. But tomorrow, you're expected to do *everything* the other girls do in those rooms. If you don't, I'll just have to move you over to my other business."

A shiver moved up the back of Chloe's neck, but she refused to ask what he was talking about.

Abbie ran a hand over Leon's arm and looked back at Chloe. "Your brother hasn't told you about this because of your tender sensibilities, but he owns a whorehouse. Men pay him quite handsomely to partake in sex when, where, and how they want it."

Chloe inhaled sharply. "But that's . . . that's illegal, Leon! How could you?" It was a stupid question; she knew he had no scruples, but Abbie had still surprised her.

"How could I?" he asked, one eyebrow rising arrogantly. "Father once said he'd hire me to work for the family business only if I proved myself. I had to triple a set amount of money before he'd allow me to work for him. Well, he died before my timeline was up, but I *still* showed him. I tripled that fucking money and more. And you know how I did it? Not by investing, that's for sure. I did it by selling pussy. That's how. Desperate men will pay anything I want them to, just to get their dicks wet.

"Don't curl your lip at me, sis. You're living in *my* house. How do you think I pay the mortgage? Pay for the food you eat? Pay for the servants who do everything so you don't have to lift a finger? I've let you slide for the last three years, but that's done. Your tits and ass are more valuable to me than your brain. Anyone can add numbers together."

"Don't do this," Chloe pleaded, ignoring the fact that Abbie was sitting there listening. "Just let me go. If you don't need me to do the accounting anymore, I'll just go." She'd hoped that if she went along with the training Abbie had forced her to endure over the last couple of weeks, Leon would eventually change his mind and just let her continue to serve drinks instead of working the back rooms. In the past, her submission had been enough to earn her a reprieve and get Leon off her back for a while. She'd thought maybe the training was just a scare tactic for making him so mad.

But it seemed that he was determined to follow through with his threat this time. The transformation of her job, from accounting to serving and now to whoring herself out, had been three years in the making—but tonight was apparently what Leon had been pushing her toward all along.

Leon laughed. "We've been over this time and time again. You can't go *anywhere*. I'm all that's standing between you and the Mafia, sis. From the first month you moved into the house, you gladly helped both the Carlino and Smaldone families with their investments. They don't let just anyone peek into their finances or see their offshore accounts. Not to mention the little fact that you prepared their taxes for the last two years. Taxes that were most certainly underpaid by millions of dollars because of the under-the-table money we've accepted.

"You're a part of the *family* now. And I have to report to them every week. If I so much as hint that you've gone rogue, or that you want to quit, they'll make their move. They know ways of torturing people that would have you pleading to die before you've been in their clutches an hour. You'll be *begging* them to let you do their taxes, invest their money, or even be their personal bitch. I'm protecting you, Chloe. And you know it."

Knowing her brother the way she did, she had no doubt he'd turn her over to Carlino and Smaldone in a heartbeat if it meant saving his own ass. She would've left Leon's house—and Colorado Springs, for that matter—almost as soon as she'd moved in, if it hadn't been for him threatening to turn her over to the notorious Mafia leaders.

She was scared of her brother, but Chloe was absolutely *terrified* of Carlino and Smaldone.

She should've realized Leon had ulterior motives when he'd asked her to move in after she'd lost her job. They hadn't been close in years, and she hadn't even talked to him in months. But when he'd called her one night, while she was feeling especially down about the way her life was going, she'd caved.

The first time she'd tried to leave, just a few months after moving in, Leon had dragged her back to the house kicking and screaming. He'd told her it was for her own good. That the Mafia leaders would kill her if she left because she already knew too much.

That had also been the first time he'd hit her. It had surprised Chloe so much that she hadn't fought back—she'd just stared at her brother in disbelief as he'd told her about their family's Mafia involvement.

The warnings worked. She'd continued living in Leon's house complacently for a short while, but as his demeanor worsened, she'd tried to leave once more, regardless of the Mafia threat. Leon had once again found her and brought her back to the house.

That time, he'd had her beaten for daring to disobey him.

The broken ribs she'd gotten that night had kept her bedridden for weeks. Not that she likely could've gone far at that point, even if she'd wanted to. Leon had started locking her in her bedroom after her second escape attempt.

Even locks may not have deterred her from somehow finding a way to leave, but while she was still recovering from the beatdown she'd gotten on her brother's orders, she'd been visited by a man.

He'd introduced himself as Peter Smaldone. And he'd done his share of roughing her up as well.

He'd threatened to pull out her fingernails one by one and cut off her ears if she even thought about not doing his taxes and investments anymore. He said that Leon acted on *his* orders, and he was required to keep Chloe with him and working for the Cosa Nostra.

Chloe learned her lesson that night—but she hadn't lost the determination to get away from everything her brother represented.

So she'd pretended to be scared of her brother. She ate what he told her to eat, wore what he and Abbie wanted her to wear, and continued to invest his and the Mafia's money.

But she'd also made a plan—one she knew would take a while to execute, but in the meantime, she got healthy again and learned all she could about her brother's and the Mafia's weaknesses.

She also made a new investment account, under a fake name, and every time she transferred money from one of Leon's accounts into another, she put a minuscule amount in the secret account.

It wasn't enough to be noticed by anyone who might be auditing her work. Since Leon had cleaned out her own personal accounts, she literally had no money to help her get away from him. She'd had to do something.

The account had been accumulating for three years. Three of the longest years of Chloe's life. She'd pretended to be meek and beaten, but inside, her determination had only grown.

Now, enough was enough. The money might not be as much as she'd hoped, but her time was up. She had to escape. Tonight.

Leon leaned toward her and narrowed his eyes. "Tonight's your introduction to how your life is gonna be from here on out, Chloe. You've had enough time to watch and learn. You'll take your own customers into a back room. You'll tease them. Show off your tits. Let them touch if they want. Dance, get them off with your hands or mouth, but nothing more. They'll be so desperate for your pussy, they'll be dying for it. Tomorrow night, you'll work the rooms from the time we open until we close—and you'll do whatever the paying customers want. If my man watching the live feed doesn't think you're giving a customer his money's worth, I'll *personally* escort you across town to the whorehouse, and you can stay there until you've learned your lesson. Understand?"

What else could she do but nod? Chloe's chin dipped, and she hid her face, knowing her fury and hatred would show in her eyes.

Leon grinned. "Good. Get her ready, Abbie," he ordered as he climbed out of the car and headed for the back entrance of the club without another glance.

"Time to go," Abbie said as she opened the back door. "We need to get you changed into a more appropriate outfit."

Chloe didn't want to imagine what was more appropriate than the short shorts and low-cut blouse with the push-up bra she was already wearing.

Feeling cold and dead inside, and more and more worried about what she might be forced to do that night before she could make her escape, she stepped out of the car. She didn't protest when Abbie took her upper arm in an unbreakable grip and marched her toward the door her brother had disappeared into.

Chapter Three

"You good?" Gray asked Ro before they entered BJ's.

They'd decided it would be better if only three of them showed up at the strip club for reconnaissance, rather than all six. Black, Ball, and Meat were standing by, just in case. Nothing was supposed to go down tonight, but the others had offered their assistance anyway.

Gray, Ro, and Arrow were standing next to Gray's Audi talking quietly before approaching the seedy-looking club. There was a neon-pink sign that said BJ's high above the concrete building, and the parking lot was packed with cars, from beat-up old junkers to high-end luxury vehicles. It was a popular place, which was both good and bad.

"I'm good," Ro declared, answering Gray's question.

"There are cameras all over this place," Arrow warned. "It's undoubtedly how they keep their eye on the women in the club, and it's also a great way to get footage to blackmail clients. So watch yourselves. Don't do anything that'll put us or the Mountain Mercenaries in a vulnerable position."

Ro and Gray nodded.

"Tonight's play is to just get the lay of the land. See if we can tell if anyone looks like they're being coerced to be here, and take in the state of the dancers. See if they look coked out or healthy. We'll report back to Rex and let him decide if we're going to take this further. Got it?" Gray asked.

Arrow nodded but Ro hesitated.

"You worried about seeing the sister?" Gray asked.

"Yeah. You didn't see her that day," Ro said. "Something was wrong. And if she's here, something is *really* wrong. This is not her kind of place. If I had to guess, I'd say she would never be caught dead in a sleazy strip club if she had any say in the matter."

"We'll cross that bridge if we get to it," Gray told him. "Just keep your cool if she's in there. Okay?"

"No promises," Ro declared honestly.

Gray sighed. "Before you do something crazy, talk to us, all right? You know we'll have your back."

"If I can, I will," Ro agreed.

"Guess that's about as good as we're gonna get, huh?" Arrow joked. "Come on, let's do this. The sooner we go in, the sooner we can get the fuck out of here. I can't stand these places."

"Then why'd you volunteer to come?" Gray asked.

Arrow looked his teammate in the eye and said, "Because this is important to Ro. I haven't seen him this intense about something in a very long time."

Ro took a deep breath. He *had* been intense about finding information on the Harris family. After his brief and memorable meeting with Chloe, he couldn't have done anything differently. He wasn't surprised that his friend had noticed there was more to his inquiry than simple curiosity. Chloe had gotten to him. She was a mixture of vulnerability, bravado, and bravery that struck a chord in him, opening up feelings he hadn't felt in a very long time. Ro wasn't sure if he was excited about that or wary.

"Come on," he said succinctly. "It's time."

The three men walked toward the front door and, after entering, were met by a large man acting as a bouncer. He looked them up and down, then nodded to let them pass.

They went down a short, dark hallway and pushed aside a black curtain to enter a huge room. The music was moderately loud, and the bass was heavy. Ro could feel it pounding in his chest as they looked around.

There was a large stage at the back of the room, with three women dancing in various stages of undress. One woman was completely naked and writhing against a pole. Men were holding up cash, obviously waiting for her to complete her routine and come closer to the edge of the stage to collect the tips.

Another woman was wearing a G-string but had already removed her top. Her tits were large, obviously fake, and she was bent over the edge of the stage, letting men stuff cash into her panties and cleavage as she pushed her boobs together.

The third woman wore a pair of boy shorts and a bra. She was dancing to the music, but it was obvious her heart wasn't in it. She turned her back to the audience and shook her arse, making the men cheer in approval.

Tables were set up throughout, and Ro could see several women performing lap dances. A bar stretched along the left side of the room, with two scantily clad bartenders behind it concentrating on pouring drinks. A man stood with his arms crossed at the entrance to a hallway next to the bar, obviously guarding it from uninvited guests.

Everywhere Ro looked, he saw women in skimpy clothes serving alcohol to the men filling the room.

Ro's eyes quickly scanned the place, looking for Chloe. He didn't see her, which both worried and reassured him.

"Come on. There's a table over there," Arrow said, pointing to the far corner of the room to the right of the door. It was easy to see why it wasn't a popular spot. It was far from the stage and the action going on there, and it was fairly dark.

But for the three men who quickly made their way to the table, it was perfect. Their backs could be against the walls so no one could sneak up behind them, and they could see the entire room without having to turn around. Not only that, but the corner muffled the music significantly, allowing them to hear each other talking without too much difficulty.

"How'd Allye feel about you coming out here tonight?" Arrow asked Gray.

The other man grinned. "She actually encouraged me to come."

"Seriously?" Ro asked. He couldn't imagine any woman wanting her man in a strip club, looking at other women's naked bodies.

"Yup. She said it was the equivalent of a girls' night out. Said as long as I looked, but didn't touch, she'd reap the benefits of me getting hot and bothered by looking at boobs all night."

"She's somethin' special," Arrow commented.

"That she is," Gray agreed. "Now, what's the plan?"

"Sit and observe for a while," Ro said. He opened his mouth to say more, but they were interrupted by a woman wearing a bikini top so small, they could see her areolas peeking over the top edge of the minuscule fabric. She was wearing nothing else but a pair of panties, sheer enough that the black hair underneath was clearly visible.

"What can I get for you?" she asked in a monotone voice.

Ro's eyes narrowed. For someone dressed so provocatively, she certainly wasn't doing anything to try to entice them.

"Rum and Coke," Arrow said.

"Whatever's on tap," Gray added.

"Newcastle Brown Ale," Ro said. He got a blank look from the waitress. "It's a British beer, love." When she didn't respond, Ro sighed. "Whisky on the rocks."

The waitress looked relieved and nodded at him. She turned on her five-inch heels and headed for the bar to put in their orders.

"What do you wanna bet we're gonna get the most watered-down shit we've ever tasted," Arrow said dryly.

"Not a bet I'd take," Gray said.

Ro didn't answer; his attention was on the women around the room. There were a lot, but the men still outnumbered them two to one. Onstage, the naked woman had finished her dance and collected the bills littered around her. She'd been replaced by a tall, slender Asian woman who had worn a kimono when she'd first walked onstage, but had quickly stripped it off. She was wearing a set of pasties over her nipples and thong panties. She was currently showing off how flexible she was, and had the men cheering and practically throwing money at her.

The amount of flesh on display did nothing for Ro. He enjoyed the female form as much as any heterosexual male, but he wasn't there for pleasure. He dreaded finding Chloe, but at the same time hoped he'd see her tonight. The clothes she'd been wearing two weeks ago were the only reason he thought she might be there. He couldn't imagine why else she'd been wearing the skimpy outfit she'd had on.

He eyed the waitress who was returning with their order. When she leaned over the table to set down the drinks, her tits threatened to pop out of the bikini top she was almost wearing.

When she was done, she put the tray under an arm and leaned on the table with her hands. The position was provocative and sexual and would've been extremely hot—if not for the stressed look on her face. "Are you boys new here?"

"Sure thing, beautiful," Arrow replied for the group.

"Welcome to BJ's. Where your pleasure is my pleasure," she said in an almost bored tone. "Anything you need, all you have to do is ask. Feel free to walk around, and know that all the servers accept tips, just as the dancers do. We have private rooms in the back, where you can get to know any of the women better. If you're interested, just talk to the object of your affection. She'll let you know the price for what you want."

She looked over her shoulder then, and Ro couldn't help but follow her line of vision.

31

He stiffened when he saw Chloe following a man out of the guarded hallway.

She was looking at the ground and shuffling along behind the man as if embarrassed, rubbing her bare arms and frowning.

Ro shifted in his seat, ready to get up and rush over to her, but Gray put a hand on his arm, halting him.

The waitress looked back at them and straightened. "Your regular waitress should be here soon to see if you need anything else, but I'm available for hire in a back room if you're so inclined." And with that parting shot, she winked, then turned and headed straight for Chloe.

"What. The. Fuck?" Arrow bit out. "Did she just tell us that we could have any woman here for a price?"

"Sounded like it to me," Gray said.

Ro didn't respond, instead keeping his eye on Chloe. The waitress walked up to her and bent her head to have a short conversation. Chloe nodded and went to the bar to pick up a tray. When she turned her back, Ro glanced at what she was wearing. Compared to most of the servers, it was downright nunlike. But that made her all the more intriguing, and he saw several men ogling her arse as she turned to face the bar. She was still showing way too much skin for Ro's taste . . . and her own, as well, it seemed.

Her heels were a modest three or so inches, whereas the other women were wearing anywhere from four to six. With the added inches, Ro estimated she'd be just about the same height as he was. Chloe had on a short skirt that came to the middle of her thighs. She wore a corset top, which made her waist look small but her tits look way too large for her frame. They were sitting high on her chest and definitely on display. Her shoulders were hunched, as if she was trying to hide herself from the men leering at her, but it was no use. There was no hiding the abundance of flesh that had been pushed up on her chest.

She was way curvier than their previous server; her corset didn't quite cover her belly, and a tiny pooch was on display as she made her way reluctantly to their table. Every step made the skirt she was wearing ride up her curvy thighs, until she was almost flashing them by the time she arrived.

She looked uncomfortable and miserable, and Ro wanted to throw his arms around her to shield her from the stares and lust of the men in the room and spirit her away.

Forcing himself to stay seated, he waited to see what she would say or do when she came up to their table. He was eager to see if she'd pretend to not know him, or if she'd acknowledge that they'd met before.

She walked up and stopped where their previous waitress had stood. But she held the tray in front of her, as if shielding herself from their gazes, and kept her eyes on the floor.

"Welcome to BJ's. Where your pleasure is my pleasure," she said in a shaky voice. "I hope you're enjoying your drinks. Anything you need, all you have to do is ask. There are private rooms in the back, and it would be my pleasure to show you the excellent hospitality BJ's is known for . . . if that's your desire."

She waited, and Ro swore she was holding her breath. He was furious that she and the other waitress were basically whoring themselves out, but he didn't act on that anger. Now wasn't the time or the place.

"Chloe?" he asked quietly, wanting to reach for her, but not wanting to upset her any more than she was already.

At the sound of her name, her eyes came up for the first time and met his, flaring wide. He could barely see them in the dim atmosphere of the club, but he thought they were a dark brown. She obviously wasn't wearing the purple contacts she'd had in when he'd first met her. She had heavy makeup on her face, and her straight black hair was swept back into a messy bun at the nape of her neck.

She opened her mouth to speak, but abruptly closed it.

"Don't panic," Ro told her quickly. "Me and my friends are here to see if you need help. If not, if you're cool, then we are too. But if you don't want to be here and need assistance, all you have to do is say the word, and I'll make sure you're safe."

She continued to stare at him with eyes as big as saucers. He saw she was gripping the tray so hard her knuckles were turning white. She looked away from him to Gray and Arrow, then her eyes came back to him. "Why?" she asked.

"Because in my world, *no one* hurts a woman. She doesn't have a fist-size bruise on her back, and she definitely doesn't wander around Black Forest without a purse or a way to call for help, wearing clothes too small and heels too high."

She flinched at that and took a deep breath. "I . . . I can't . . . I don't know . . ."

"Stop panicking," Gray ordered, and her eyes swung to him. "First things first. Are you okay? Are you safe?"

Chloe licked her lips and looked to the side, but neither nodded nor shook her head.

"Okay, that answers that. Is it just your brother who's watching you?" Gray asked.

They got a little head shake at that.

"When do you get off work?" Arrow asked.

"Three."

Ro looked at his watch. It was one thirty. She still had another hour and a half to go. "Do you have to go in the back room with anyone who asks?"

She nodded her head.

Ro leaned forward and ordered, "Look at me, love."

She looked at him, and he was stunned at the hope and fear he saw in her eyes. It made him want to take her in his arms and lead her out of there without another word. But he knew they'd never make it to the door. Not if she was being watched by more than her brother. "You tell anyone who asks that I've already paid for your next session in a private room."

The hope in her eyes died, and all that remained was the fear . . . and a hint of anger.

Ro hated seeing the fear, and he understood why she'd be upset at what she assumed she was being made to do, but he didn't have time to explain, as the waitress who'd served their drinks approached the table. She leaned into Chloe and said something into her ear. Ro couldn't hear what it was, but Chloe's lips pressed together in agitation.

She turned to the other woman and blurted, "He's already said he wants a session." Chloe gestured at Ro with her head.

The waitress nodded. "I'll tell Abbie," was all she said, and she turned to head back to the bar.

"The woman who picked me up from your house is also watching," Chloe said softly.

Ro understood what that meant. He wasn't sure if this Abbie would recognize him in the dark bar, but he pulled the old ball cap he'd thrown on at the last moment lower on his forehead, just in case. The last thing he wanted was for Chloe to suffer for associating with him.

"So, um . . . sessions start at fifty dollars for a lap dance, and depending on what you want, they go up from there," Chloe said, not looking him in the eyes as she recited the price for time in a back room.

The rage rose inside Ro until he felt as if he were going to burst, but he controlled himself. Barely. He heard Gray growl under his breath and saw Arrow sit straight up in his chair across from him. None of the men of Mountain Mercenaries liked it when women were taken advantage of or abused, but they *really* didn't like it when they were obviously scared and unwilling, as Chloe was.

Ro picked up his whisky and downed it, then stood without looking at his teammates. He held out his hand to Chloe and said, "I want as much time as I can get, love. Let's go."

Chapter Four

Chloe stared at Ro's hand and swallowed hard. She hated herself right now. Hated her life. Hated her brother. All she wanted to do was turn back the clock and go back to when she was working for Springs Financial Group and was relatively happy.

She'd been racking her brain all night, trying to come up with a plan on how to get out of working the back rooms and how to escape, but she hadn't been able to think of anything that would work yet. She knew Abbie was watching her like a hawk, and Leon had his minions everywhere. They'd never let her simply walk out and disappear.

"Chloe?" Ro asked.

Taking a deep breath, knowing she didn't have a choice, Chloe put her hand in his.

The feel of his calloused hand closing around hers should've made her feel sick to her stomach, considering what she was about to do, but instead she felt instantly protected. Which was just stupid, considering he was taking her to one of the back rooms.

She'd thought about him a lot over the last couple of weeks, and had even considering calling him, maybe asking him to come to the house on some pretense. She'd beg him to take her out of there, and of course he'd say yes, and they'd ride off into the sunset.

But this wasn't a fairy tale, and that never would've worked anyway, as Leon would've had his henchmen grab her and hurt Ro in the process.

Yet somehow, here he was, standing in front of her, holding her hand as if she'd conjured him up.

Of course, he hadn't thrown her over his shoulder and spirited her out of the club, as she'd dreamed, but instead was taking advantage of one of the private rooms.

They stood there for a heartbeat, holding hands, and it was as if the rest of the club simply disappeared. Then she was jostled by a man walking by, and it shook Chloe out of her stupor. She turned and headed for the back hallway. The one she'd just come out of. The one where she felt like she'd left the old Chloe behind, and had become someone she didn't even know or like anymore. Didn't *want* to know.

The bouncer at the hallway—Chloe thought his name was Dan—halted them, as was protocol. He was the one who handled the exchange of money; the girls were never allowed to touch what they made. Of course they weren't. They might steal some of it, enabling them to get away from the club and Leon.

"Payment's due up front," Dan told Ro in a no-nonsense tone, holding out his hand.

Chloe tried to drop Ro's hand, but he wouldn't let go.

"No problem. How much?"

"Depends on what you want," Dan replied.

"I want as much time as I can get," Ro said, again without looking at Chloe.

She didn't like that Dan was arranging what she would and wouldn't do, but it wasn't as if she really had a choice. If it wasn't him, it would be Abbie. Or Leon. Her life was no longer her own, and it sucked. Big-time.

Dan eyed Ro, then turned a lust-filled gaze to Chloe. She shivered. As the "new girl," she knew a lot of the workers wanted their chance at having her. Abbie had oh-so-considerately explained that employees usually got first dibs on the newbies, to "train" them, although Chloe was an exception.

"Thirty minutes. Tops," Dan said. "It's fifty bucks for a lap dance for ten minutes, with no touching. If you want the BJ Special, you get fifteen minutes for a hundred. You want more than that, it's another hundred every five minutes."

Without blinking or throwing a fit at the cost, Ro dropped her hand and reached for his wallet. He opened it and counted out four hundred-dollar bills, and held them out to Dan. "Thirty minutes it is, then."

As soon as Dan took the money and his wallet was back in his pocket, Ro took Chloe's hand back in his. She knew he wasn't doing it out of affection, only to make sure she didn't run off on him, but it still felt good.

The money disappeared into Dan's pocket, and he crossed his arms over his chest again. "All the rooms are monitored for the safety of our employees."

Ro nodded. "What else?"

"What else what?"

"What are the rules?"

"Rules? There *are* no rules. Other than to use a condom and have fun," Dan said with a smirk. "Room four at the end is open."

Every muscle in Ro's body seemed to tense, but he simply nodded, and as soon as Dan stepped out of the way, Ro was towing her down the hall at a fast clip, keeping his head down so the cameras couldn't pick up his features. He threw open the door and pulled Chloe inside, shutting the door with a definitive click.

"No lock. At least that's somethin'," he said with a grimace.

Chloe shivered. She hadn't even thought about that. If a client got overzealous and locked them in, no one would be able to help her . . .

if Abbie or the perverts watching up in the video room would even bother trying.

When Ro didn't move, she looked at him. He was gazing around the room, taking it in. There wasn't much to see. A small five-by-eight-foot room with a leather armchair in the middle of it. No rugs on the floor, no pictures on the walls. There was a small table against one of the walls with a container of disinfectant wipes on top and a small trash can beside it. A tiny window high up toward the ceiling provided a little light from the parking lot.

The light fixture hanging in the middle of the room had an extremely low-watt bulb, giving only enough light for the cameras to make out features and pick up what was happening. Chloe supposed it was meant to be soothing and romantic, but instead it was simply creepy.

Without a word, Ro walked to the chair, still holding her hand, and turned. He met her gaze and sat slowly. He let go of her hand once again, and for some reason, Chloe felt as if she'd been abandoned. Ro spread his legs apart and reached out and pulled her to him. Her shins hit the leather of the chair, and she winced.

He opened his mouth to say something when the music started. It wasn't soft and seductive either. It was loud and harsh. Music that was more appropriate for some sort of BDSM dungeon than a private room in a strip club called BJ's.

Ro's eyes didn't stray from hers. They were intense and piercing and, in the dim light of the room, seemed darker than they were. "Where's the camera, love?" he asked. "I don't want it to look like I'm searching it out."

Chloe blinked and licked her lips. "Above the door," she said in a tone just loud enough to be heard over the music, but not loud enough to be picked up by the camera.

"Good. Your head is blocking it from my view," Ro said as he nodded and gazed into her eyes. His hands were resting on her hips, but they weren't squeezing her uncomfortably, and they weren't roaming inappropriately. She'd take that as a win.

"I'm supposed to make sure you're fully on tape at some point," she admitted.

"I'd expect nothing less. Don't worry about it," he told her.

Chloe stood between his legs awkwardly. She knew she was supposed to be swaying to the music, stripping, something, but she was caught in his gaze. What she really wanted to do was throw herself into his arms and beg him to get her out of there.

"Dance, love," he said with a small squeeze of his fingers. "Since we're being watched, you need to make sure they don't suspect anything."

Chloe didn't know exactly what he meant about suspecting anything. She had no idea what his plans were, but she knew he was right. If she didn't want Abbie or, God forbid, her brother, barging into the room and at the very least, embarrassing her—and at the most, forcing her to perform some sort of sex act in front of them—she had to get on with it.

Without another choice, Chloe did as Ro ordered. She swayed her hips and brought her hands up to her hair, trying to look seductive, but having a feeling she just looked stupid instead.

Ro's hands moved up from her hips and settled on her sides, between her corset and the waistband of her skirt, and she jerked. His fingers were chilly on her overheated skin, and she sucked in her stomach, trying to hide the small belly she knew was showing in the skimpy outfit.

"Relax. Don't think, just move," Ro said.

Relax? As if. But she did her best to dance to the music pounding in through the speakers.

And through it all, Ro didn't take his eyes from hers. He didn't ogle her cleavage. His hands didn't roam up and down her body like the last guy's had.

"That's it. You're doing fine." His voice was low and gravelly. It was soothing. Everything he'd done since she'd met him was calming. He'd asked to see her bruise a couple of weeks ago, didn't demand it. Yes, he'd held her arm firmly, but he hadn't hurt her, not like Abbie did when she grabbed her, or like her brother when he hit her.

He'd held her hand gently in the club, and so far hadn't grabbed her boobs and demanded she dance while he jacked off. Chloe shivered at the memory of her last time in a private room. Luckily, the man hadn't wanted the BJ Special . . . but that's what Ro had paid for.

She swallowed hard at the thought and stared down at the man sitting in front of her. Ro's eyes stayed glued to her face, but Chloe used the time as she danced to take him in. He was wearing a pair of black jeans that clung in all the right places. He had quite the impressive bulge between his legs, which scared the shit out of her at the moment. Any other time, she might've been intrigued, but considering he'd just paid four hundred dollars to have her to himself in a private room at a strip club for thirty minutes, she wasn't exactly thrilled.

A pair of scuffed and dirty black boots were on his feet. Chloe could tell a lot about a man by looking at his shoes. Leon wore only black or brown loafers. They were always polished and buffed—by one of the members of the paid staff at his house, of course. If shoes were a metaphor for life, it was all a facade. Her brother's loafers might be clean, but that didn't mean *he* was. Leon, as she'd learned, was as dirty as they came. He just had others do most of his dirty work, including clean his shoes, so he didn't have to.

But Ronan Cross's shoes were broken in. Comfortable. She would bet everything she had that he'd never even thought about doing something as silly as polishing and buffing the beat-up leather. That he thought the more broken in his shoes, the more comfortable.

"A little more hip action, love," Ro said, bringing her out of her silly musings. She nodded and put a bit more effort into her dance as she continued to examine the man in front of her. He wore a white T-shirt and a black leather jacket. He sported a five-o'clock shadow, and his lips were pursed together tightly at the moment. His nose was slightly crooked, as if it'd been broken in the past. He had long eyelashes and high cheekbones, which would've made him look like a pretty boy if it wasn't for the too-long light-brown hair that fell over his forehead beneath the cap.

Drawn back to his eyes, Chloe decided that they were his most interesting feature. They were blue, but changed colors depending on his surroundings. Right now, they were dark blue because of the lighting, but weeks ago they were lighter, more a dark sky blue than the midnight blue they seemed to be at the moment. She could see an ocean of emotions in them but couldn't really decipher any of what she was seeing.

Shaking her head at her inane thoughts when she should be thinking about how in the hell to escape her personal nightmare, Chloe closed her eyes and tried to forget where she was. What she was doing. Namely, dancing suggestively, practically in the lap of a stranger.

"Here's the deal," Ro said in a voice too low to be overheard by the camera over her left shoulder. "I came tonight to make sure you were safe. My friends and I did some research on your brother. And what we found wasn't good. I can help you, Chloe. Help you find a place of your own, get a job away from here. You don't have to do this. Not for money, and certainly not for your brother."

Chloe squeezed her eyes shut even tighter to keep the tears from falling. She wanted to scream "Yes!" and drag Ro out of the room and right out the front door. But she couldn't. Leon wouldn't allow her to leave. Not now. She knew too much.

"Twenty minutes left. Get on with it, girl!" a voice from a speaker over the door boomed.

Chloe started so badly she would've fallen if it wasn't for Ro's hands at her waist. She recognized Abbie's voice, and her eyes popped open, and her breathing sped up. She knew what she was supposed to be doing, but she didn't want to. Not now. Not ever.

"Come here," Ro coaxed, pulling her toward him with unrelenting strength.

Chloe's hands came up and landed on his shoulders as he pulled her up and onto his lap. She had no choice but to straddle him. Her knees were on the cushion next to his thighs. Her short skirt rode up, and Chloe knew if he looked down, he'd be able to see the bright-red thong Abbie had forced her to wear.

Blushing and breathing hard with anxiety, Chloe hovered over Ro's lap, trembling.

"Swivel your hips, love," Ro said, still not looking anywhere but at her face. "Dance on my lap like you were just a second ago."

Without thought, she did as he asked, swaying to the music a little stiffly, but swaying nonetheless. His hands helped, pushing her down to rest on his lap, then pulling her up and rotating her hips.

Chloe's brows furrowed in confusion. She glanced down toward their laps for confirmation, then looked back up at him. "You're not hard."

It was a stupid thing to say. She knew men were sensitive about that sort of thing. The last thing she wanted was for Ro to get pissed at her, especially when so far he was being downright gentle compared to the last man she'd been with inside a private room. But instead of being upset, he grimaced.

"If you think I'm going to get turned on right now, you're daft."

She loved the British words that appeared in his speech every now and then, but she was still confused.

"Don't look at me like that, love," Ro said, even as he ground her down on his lap once more. "If I was on the pull, I wouldn't come to a strip club."

"On the pull?"

His lips quirked into a half smile, but he got serious almost as quickly. "Looking for sex. If I wanted sex, I wouldn't come to a strip joint . . . no offense. And as beautiful as I think you are, there's no way I can get hard—not when I see the terror in your eyes."

"Oh . . ."

"Reach up and take your hair out of the bun," Ro ordered.

Without thinking, Chloe reached up and removed the band, letting her hair fall in waves around her shoulders. It should've made her feel better, more concealed, but it only increased her nervousness.

Slowly, Ro moved one hand up to her head and grabbed a fistful of hair, pulling her head back. He leaned forward, and Chloe inhaled sharply as she felt his lips on the side of her neck.

"Shhhhh, this is all I'm doing," Ro reassured her. "Just giving whoever is watching a show. That's it, keep moving on me."

Chloe tried to relax but couldn't. She mechanically moved her hips on his lap, and grabbed his biceps, digging her nails in as she waited for what he was going to do next.

Ro moved his mouth up to her ear, and she felt the warm air from his breath waft over the sensitive skin there, making goose bumps shoot down her arms.

"Yes or no—are you here of your own free will?" Ro asked.

Chloe stiffened. She wanted to say no so badly, but she also didn't want the man under her to get hurt if she did. Leon wasn't in the best shape, but he had a lot of friends, especially here at the club. Men who wouldn't dare disobey him if he told them to rough up Ro. She'd made up her mind to escape tonight, but could she risk Ro's life by involving him?

And if she didn't, could she get away on her own?

She had so many questions, but no clear answers.

"Yes or no, love?" he asked again, but Chloe felt as if her mouth were full of cotton balls. She couldn't swallow or say anything.

She felt Ro sigh, but he didn't press. He said, "Okay, it's showtime. I'm going to make it look like I'm pushing you to your knees. That way, they'll get a decent shot of me on camera. Undo my pants but stay up on your knees, so the camera can't see exactly what you're doing. I'll put my hands on your head, and you pretend to give me a blow job."

Chloe jerked involuntarily. No, she didn't want to do that. She *couldn't* do that, no matter what he'd paid.

"You can do this, Chloe," Ro said as if he could read her mind. "Pretend. That's all this is. Undo my pants, but don't pull down my drawers. It's a show, love. That's all. Trust me."

When she still hesitated, he said, "Chloe. It's either this, or the real thing with another man who wouldn't give a shit about your feelings."

"And you give a shit about my feelings?" The question came out without thought, and Chloe winced. If she ticked him off, he could hurt her, could make her do exactly what she didn't want.

She opened her mouth to apologize, when the man under her smiled.

Holy. Hell. She'd never seen Ro smile before—and it took her breath away. The grin transformed him from a hard-ass, somewhat scary-looking man, to an extremely hot one, in a bad-boy kind of way.

"I give a shit," he said after a moment. "Trust me, love."

At his words, Chloe took a deep breath and nodded. What choice did she have? This was the best offer she was going to get. Any other man would force her to take his cock down her throat.

"So brave," Ro murmured. "Here we go."

And with that, she felt his fist tighten in her hair, and he used his upper-arm strength to lower her gently to her knees between his legs. She did as he requested and stayed upright, blocking his lap from the view of the camera.

With shaking hands, she undid the belt at his waist, and it took three tries to undo the button of his jeans because she was shaking so hard. But she finally got it and went for the zipper.

She got it halfway down before Ro said quietly, "That's enough."

Chloe wasn't sure where to put her hands. She'd given a blow job before, but she and her boyfriend at the time were both naked and in bed. Ro was a stranger, and she was so out of her element it wasn't funny.

Without a word, Ro took her hands in his and placed them on his thighs. Chloe curled her fingers and held on as she felt his hands grasp her head.

"Yes or no, love?" Ro asked.

Knowing he hadn't forgotten his earlier question, Chloe bit her lip in indecision and stared at his lap. He *still* wasn't hard. She'd undone his pants and was practically breathing on his dick, and he didn't have an erection. He was built, there was no doubt, but he truly wasn't getting off on what they were doing. That went a long way toward increasing her trust in the man.

"Here we go," Ro muttered, and she felt him put pressure on her head, pushing her down toward his lap.

Knowing time was running out, and she had to do this, Chloe closed her eyes and pretended to give Ro the BJ Special.

She bobbed her head up and down in the best imitation of a blow job she could manage, her hair hiding Ro's lap. She'd never given a man a blow job this way before—on her knees while he watched every move she made—and wasn't sure she was doing a good job of faking it. It was a little daunting; she'd always preferred to have her partner lying down. But she couldn't deny, if this were real, there might be something almost empowering about Ro watching her as she pleasured him.

At one point during the fake blow job, she felt one of Ro's hands make its way to her ass and squeeze. Her skirt was still up around her hips, and she knew she was giving the pervert behind the lens—and Abbie—a great view of her bare butt, but that was honestly the least of her worries at the moment. She felt proud that she only jumped once at the feel of Ro's calloused palm on her bare skin before trying to ignore how possessive his hand felt.

After several minutes, Ro murmured, "Okay, love, big finish."

She would've smiled if she weren't the one in this situation. He jerked his hips and moaned. Loudly. Knowing that moan would be heard by the camera, Chloe stopped moving her head. She brought a hand up to her mouth and pretended to wipe it.

Looking up at Ro, she blinked at the admiration she saw in his eyes. It had been a long time since she'd seen anyone look at her with something other than disgust, contempt, or lust.

"Close me up."

Without taking her eyes from his, she fumbled with his jeans and belt. When she was done, Ro put his hands on her waist again and hauled her up from the ground and back onto his lap. She was straddling him once more as he ran a hand over the side of her head and asked, "Are your knees okay? I know the floor had to be bloody hard."

Frowning, Chloe licked her lips. "They're okay."

"Rubbish. But I'll let it slide for now." He brought his other hand up, and then he was cupping her face, his fingers twined in the strands of hair around her ears. "Yes? Or no?" he asked once again.

Chloe hesitated. She had no idea what Ro would do if she admitted she wasn't there of her own accord. She knew her brother. He might be an ass, but he had a lot of people on his payroll. People in his household who didn't come to her aid when he hit her. People he paid a lot of money to keep tabs on her. People who wouldn't hesitate to restrain her if Leon said the word.

And people like Peter Smaldone and Joseph Carlino, who would torture Ro for helping her. She had no idea what this . . . mechanic . . . would be able to do to help her.

But the thought of having someone in her corner, making her feel not so alone, was too much to resist. She hadn't trusted anyone in a very long time, but hadn't Ro just proved that he could be trusted? At least a little bit? She knew he could be buttering her up at the moment, only to throw her under the bus later, but she had no other options.

Throwing caution to the wind, Chloe took a deep breath and whispered, "No. I'm not here of my own free will."

The expression on his face didn't change. The only way she knew he heard her was the way his fingers tightened their grip on her head for a split second.

Then he dropped his head and very gently brushed his lips against hers.

Chloe jolted at the touch of his lips. It felt as if an electrical current had zapped her. It was crazy, because his kiss had been light and not at all sexual. But the second she felt his touch, something between them changed.

He stared at her, and she felt his rough hands at her sides once again. She should've been embarrassed that she was sitting on his lap practically naked, her skirt rucked up to her waist. But she wasn't. She felt . . . safe.

"You smell so bloody good," Ro whispered.

Chloe knew she was blushing. Men had been praising her tits and ass all night, but Ro's whispered confession was more complimentary than anything she'd ever heard.

"Lilacs. It's my lotion. My mom bought my first bottle when I was a teenager. It reminds me of her."

Ro closed his eyes and leaned into her for a second. She felt his nose brush against the sensitive skin behind her ear once again and heard him inhale.

She shivered.

He pulled back and his lips parted, but they were interrupted before he could say a word.

"Time's up!" Abbie's voice boomed through the room. "Let her go, sir, before we have to send Dan in there to force you."

Chloe felt Ro's hands drop from her body, and he held them out to his sides. She awkwardly climbed off his lap, tugging her skirt down as she stood in front of him.

Ro slowly stood as well and nodded at her corset. "You'll want to fix that before we go back out there."

Looking down at herself, Chloe saw that one of her boobs had finally escaped the corset. She was flashing Ro.

Swiftly bringing a hand up to her chest and stuffing herself back into the material as best she could, she tried to control her blush. When she looked back up at Ro, she suspected he hadn't taken his eyes from her face the entire time she'd been fixing her wardrobe malfunction.

Any other guy would've taken advantage of the free peep show. Not Ro. She had a feeling he wanted to save her the embarrassment of having other men stare at her. Chloe knew no one else would've said a word, just enjoyed what she didn't know she was showing them.

"Thanks," she said softly.

"You're welcome. Come on, time to go." Then Ro took her hand and led her to the door, opened it, and they walked back into the loud club. Together.

Chapter Five

Ro hated to leave without a word to Chloe, but he had less than an hour to get ahold of Rex and the others and come up with a plan. He looked back once before he went through the black curtain into the short hallway at the front of the club and saw her watching him leave with disbelief in her eyes.

That look nearly gutted him.

He'd wanted to tell her that she wouldn't have to spend another night in that hellhole, but he didn't get a chance. As soon as they'd appeared out of the hallway, Dan had told Chloe the stag party that was taking place needed another server for last call. She'd been whisked away before Ro could reassure her in any way.

He'd gone back to the table where Gray and Arrow were sitting and told them it was time to go. Without any questions, they'd immediately stood and headed out with him.

Ro kept quiet until they reached Gray's Audi. The second they were inside, he pulled out his phone and called Rex.

"Talk to me," their handler said by way of greeting.

"There are definitely women there against their will. And they're offering more than lap dances. On the surface, it looks on the up-and-up, but I think with just a little digging, it'll be easy to expose it as a sex-trafficking setup."

"You know we need more than that," Rex said. "As much as I want to bust in there, that's not going to make this thing go away. Harris'll just go quiet for a while and resurface later. We need to play this smart."

"He's forcing his own sister to whore herself! She told me that she was there against her will. We need to get her and the others out."

"Not without hard evidence," Rex repeated. "It sucks. I get it. But an asshole like Harris isn't making the kind of money he is just with that club. If we move now, we'll never save the women in any other places he operates like that club—or worse."

"If Chloe was your sister or wife, would you be telling me the same thing? Would you be telling me to be patient? No, you bloody wouldn't!"

"That was out of line," Rex said in a low, pissed-off voice.

Ro took a deep breath. He knew Rex was right, it was just hard to hear. "I apologize. But Rex, I joined this group to save women from having to go through things like this. As of right this second, Chloe hasn't been forced to service some punter. By this time tomorrow night, I'd bet everything I have that won't be the case anymore. I understand where you're coming from, I do. I absolutely don't want to do anything that will hurt the reputation of the Mountain Mercenaries . . . but this is personal. Chloe isn't some nameless, faceless, persecuted, and abused woman. She's flesh and blood to me, and if the look in her eyes was any indication, she's at the end of her rope. I'm her last chance."

Rex was silent for a long moment before he said quietly, "If you can get the sister out without making Harris shut down his entire operation, then I'll support you. But that's a big if, Ro."

"I can do it."

"Do I want to know how?"

Ro smiled then. "I'm going to take a page from the arsehole's own playbook. Stay tuned for more info." Then he hung up.

Gray was pulling away from the club as he asked, "What's the plan?"

"The plan is to call the others. Our faces are all over surveillance cameras at that place."

"But Ball's, Meat's, and Black's aren't," Arrow concluded.

"Exactly," Ro said with satisfaction.

All three men nodded as Ro looked back down at his phone and dialed once more.

Chloe was both disappointed and angry. She'd gone out on a limb and admitted that she needed help. She'd thought for sure Ro was going to do something to get her out of the club . . . what, she had no idea, but surely between the two of them, they could've thought of something.

But instead, he'd walked out of the restricted hallway, then left.

Once again, she was on her own—which she was used to, but for a second she'd had the hope that maybe, just maybe, she'd have someone on her side for once.

Abbie and Leon had been full of praise for her first night in the private rooms and the way she'd "played hard to get" for the clients. Apparently, there was a waiting list for her services the next night, which made Chloe sick . . . and desperate.

She'd been willing to do just about anything to get away from her brother and Abbie before tonight, but now she realized it was do-or-die time.

Chloe knew once she got back to the house, her chances of escaping were almost nil. Even with Leon and Abbie thinking she was scared of her own shadow and too submissive to try to escape again, they'd still be on the lookout, just in case.

Her big plan before tonight had been to crawl out her window, even though it was on the second floor, and creep carefully through the grounds surrounding the house to the street. There, she'd avoid any cars and walk into the city. It wasn't much of a plan, but it was the best she could come up with.

Abbie'd had the great idea to replace all her clothes with slutty shorts and skirts, low-cut blouses and lingerie, but Chloe had hidden a few items, including some jeans and T-shirts, under a loose board in her closet. There was no way she was going to let Leon or his girlfriend dictate how she could dress in her spare time. When they locked her in at night, she put on her comfy pajamas and planned.

Leon had also cut up her driver's license, but thankfully hadn't known about the passport she'd gotten a couple of months before she'd moved in with him. She kept that hidden with her clothes as well, knowing she'd need it to claim the money she'd been squirreling away.

She had no car; hers had broken down—or so it appeared—and Leon had promised to take it to the shop before he'd shown his true colors. Instead, he'd informed her the mechanics couldn't fix it, and he'd sold it to them for scrap metal.

Chloe was well aware she'd gotten herself into this situation, and regardless of Leon's threats to sic the Mafia heavies on her, it was time to get herself out. She'd have to be extra careful to cover her tracks so no one could find her.

Feeling desperate, Chloe looked down at herself. She'd been allowed to change back into the shorts and blouse she'd been wearing when she'd arrived at the club earlier. She wished she had on a pair of her jeans, but her secret hiding spot had ultimately been for nothing. She couldn't risk going back to the house.

Not having her identification would be even tougher, but she couldn't shake the overwhelming feeling that her best shot at getting away was before they arrived home.

Abbie and her brother were ignoring her, happy to discuss how the night had gone and how much money they were going to make off her.

"Did you see the interest she got? Her waiting list is twenty men deep," Abbie crowed.

"We'll get there an hour early tomorrow so the staff can have their shot before we open," Leon informed his girlfriend. "Make sure you move the chair in the room too. The images we got tonight sucked because her head was blocking the guys' faces most of the time. We need better angles if there's any chance to use the video for blackmail."

"Sure thing. I'm also thinking of upping her fee. She's new and not used as hard as the others. We can use that to our advantage," Abbie said.

Chloe clenched her teeth but kept her head down. She knew in a minute or two, Leon would have to slow down to take a turn, and that was going to be her best chance. She purposely hadn't put on her seat belt when they'd left BJ's for this reason. She was desperate enough to throw herself out of a moving vehicle to get away from her evil brother once and for all.

It was going to suck. It was possible she'd break a bone . . . or two. But as long as she protected her legs so she could run, she'd endure any amount of pain to get away.

Abbie was talking about limiting Chloe to BJ Specials for at least a week, so they could tease the patrons a bit more before allowing her to "go all the way," when Leon suddenly exclaimed, "What the fuck?"

Chloe felt him stomp on the gas suddenly, pinning her body momentarily against the seat. She'd already been tense as she'd prepared to throw open the car door and tuck and roll, but Leon speeding up definitely hindered her plans. There was no way she'd be able to survive jumping from the car while it was moving as fast as it was.

But she didn't have time to turn to discover what Leon had seen, or what he was trying to outrun before something hit the back end of the Mercedes. Chloe's body was thrown forward, then violently to the side as the car spun. Her head smacked against the passenger window, hard enough for her to see stars.

The car continued to spin in a circle, and Chloe heard Abbie screaming, then the sound of metal crunching and glass breaking.

The car came to a stop, and everything was silent for a moment. The hiss of steam rising from the front end of the Mercedes, where it had hit a tree alongside the road, was the only sound.

Then Abbie started screaming again.

Before Chloe could see what was wrong, or throw herself out of the car and run, the door next to her opened, and a hand reached into the car and latched onto her arm. She was being forced up and out of the car before she could get her thoughts in order. She got a glimpse of a very tall man wearing a mask before he swung her up and over his shoulder and headed for a huge Hummer behind her brother's wrecked car.

Chloe felt a strong arm band around her thighs, holding her in place securely. Her head was hanging down over the man's back, and she tried to shake it to clear her senses, but all that did was make her head throb.

"What are you—"

Leon's voice was suddenly cut off, and Chloe propped herself by using a hand on the man's extremely hard ass to look up. She saw another man in a black mask standing next to the driver's door of the Mercedes, and just as Abbie screamed yet again, another man stuck his hand through the passenger-side door, cutting off her screech.

Fear spiked through Chloe. What was the saying? Out of the frying pan, into the fire?

She didn't want to be with her brother or Abbie anymore, but she didn't know the men who had run into their car. Shit, what if these men were working for Carlino or Smaldone? Maybe they'd found out about her siphoning Leon's money into a separate account, and they were here to make her pay?

Panic made her squirm in desperation. Why couldn't everyone just leave her alone? What had she done to deserve this life?

"Calm down," the man holding her said, even as his arm tightened even more around her thighs.

But Chloe couldn't calm down. She knew if these three men got her into the Hummer, things could go from bad to worse. Pushing herself up, she arched her back and tried to throw herself off the man's shoulder.

He swore and stopped by the back door of the large all-terrain vehicle.

When Chloe's squirming didn't make the man lose his grip, she twisted and wrenched the mask off his head, seeing only that he had blond hair. At her actions, he abruptly dropped his shoulder and put her on her feet, spinning her around to face the Hummer.

Chloe didn't have any weapons, so she used what she *did* have. Namely, her teeth. She turned her head and bit his arm, making sure to grind down to do as much damage as she could.

"Ow!" the man complained, loosening his grip on her long enough for Chloe to wrench free. She landed on the ground on her hands and knees. Hard. Momentarily stunning herself. Her head hurt worse than anything she'd ever felt before, but she tried to ignore it. She had to get away.

"Oh shit, grab her, Black!" one of the other men called as Chloe sprang to her feet to sprint away from her captor.

A man with hair as black as midnight—she could see him clearly, now that he'd taken off the mask he'd been wearing—snatched her around the waist, then immediately changed his grip until he'd clamped his arms around her torso, trapping her own arms by her sides. He was about the same height as her, now that she'd lost her heels in the scuffle, around five-nine. Chloe immediately threw her head back, trying to break his nose so he'd let her go.

At the last second, the man avoided her maneuver and swore. "Fuck."

"We need to get out of here," the third man said.

"I know," the guy who held her, Black, said grumpily. "I'm workin' on it. If Ball hadn't dropped her, we'd already be on our way."

Chloe hadn't heard Leon mention anyone named Black or Ball when he'd threatened her with the Mafia, but that didn't mean they weren't affiliated with Carlino and Smaldone.

"Don't hurt her, or we'll get our asses kicked," the third guy warned as he pulled off his own mask and shoved it into his back pocket.

"Don't hurt her? She bit me!" growled the first guy, sounding disgusted.

"I'll do it again if you get near me!" Chloe threatened. She was being forced to march back toward the Hummer. She couldn't get her arms free of Black's hold. She tried going limp, but that just made it easier for the man to carry her closer to the vehicle.

Chloe wasn't an idiot. She knew the statistics. If you got in a car with your captors, the odds of you making it out alive went down exponentially. She had no intention of getting into the car with these kidnappers. No way. No how.

"The other two won't be out long. We only gave them enough to stay unconscious while we got out of here. You're sure there aren't any cameras around here, Meat?"

Chloe didn't recognize the third man's name either. Meat . . . She tamped down her imagination before it tried to come up with awful reasons behind their nicknames.

"Nope. We're in the clear," Meat told his buddy.

"Bring her here," the one she'd bitten ordered. Ball. His name was Ball.

She looked up at him and saw he was holding a syringe. The sight of it made her fly into a full-blown panic. "No, get away from me!" She kicked her legs and shook her head wildly from side to side, making the pain pound that much harder, but she couldn't let them knock her out. There was no telling where she'd end up if they did. What they'd do to her when she was unconscious.

"Shit, she's bleeding," Ball said, his brows furrowed in concern.

"Probably hit her head when we did the PIT maneuver," Meat said. "Ro'll take care of it. Come on, Ball, do it."

Chloe could barely make out their words over her thrashing panic. Joe? Who was Joe? What would he take care of? Was he with the Mafia too? She struggled even harder, trying to get out of the man's grasp.

Meat came up beside his friend and clamped a hand on her upper arm, and between him and Black, they held her absolutely immobile as Ball came closer with the needle.

"This isn't going to hurt," Ball said as he reached for her arm.

"Fuck you," Chloe spat. "It's not *your* arm you're about to stick."

"True," he said, chuckling.

The laughter infuriated Chloe. All the pent-up frustration and fear she'd felt for the last few years, and especially in the last two weeks, came spewing out her mouth as she felt the needle pierce her skin. "I'll never stop fighting! If you get near me, I'll bite off your dick, you asshole. You're kidnapping the wrong woman. Why can't men just leave me the fuck alone? What the fuck did I do to *any* of you? Nothing!"

The man the others called Ball pulled the needle from her arm and took a step back. He looked shocked at the words she was shouting at him. *Good.*

"What gives you the right to drug me? To kidnap me?" She began to feel dizzy already but fought the pull of whatever Ball had drugged her with.

"I'm tired of being told what to do! What to wear. Why are men such bullies? I'm gonna turn you and your Mafia friends in to the police, and you'll wish you never followed Joe's orders . . ."

Chloe's eyes closed, and she was so tempted to keep them shut. She was so tired. Tired of being scared. Tired of being bullied and pushed around.

"Who's Joe?" Black asked from behind her.

The question made her lids pop open once more, but everything was blurry because her eyes wouldn't focus. Her anger slowly leaked away, leaving behind pure and unadulterated fear. "Oh shit. Please, just let me go! I won't turn you in. I was kidding. I just want to leave. I was going to get away tonight . . . disappear. I won't tell about the investments. Don't do this. Please . . . I'll give you everything I've taken if you let me go. All of it. Every penny!"

Chloe felt herself being shuffled forward. Someone had opened the back door of the Hummer, and she was lifted into another man's arms and placed gently on the back seat. She wanted to scoot across to the other side and open the door and run away, but she couldn't get her body to obey her brain's commands.

"You want to go back to your brother's house?" Black asked. She knew it was him even with her blurry vision. He was standing in the open door, reaching across her and clicking the seat belt into place.

"No," Chloe answered immediately. "Just drop me off on the side of the road somewhere. That was my plan anyway. I'll figure out where to go once I wake up."

"We're not going to leave you on the side of a road, Chloe," Meat said from her other side.

Chloe rolled her head in his direction. He was sitting next to her on the back seat, and when she looked at him, he placed a folded-up cloth on her forehead. She winced at the momentary pain it caused.

"Sorry about that."

Chloe's brows knit together. She was so confused. Why was he being nice? Trying to stop the bleeding on her head? She recalled what he said. "Leaving me would be better than taking me to Joe or back to my brother to whore me out."

"Who's Joe?" Ball asked from the driver's seat.

"I don't know," Chloe whispered. "You said Joe would take care of me. Your boss. I don't want him to. Please . . ."

"Shhhhh," Meat said soothingly. "You're okay. Everything's going to be okay."

"Easssy for you to sssay," she slurred.

Her eyes closed again, and she felt as if she were floating. Whatever they'd given her was powerful stuff. She couldn't fight it anymore.

Despair settled over her, like the fuzzy blanket she'd used to cover herself on her couch before she'd lost her job. She'd loved that blanket. She wondered what had happened to it.

Within seconds, she wasn't thinking anything anymore. Her body slumped over, unconscious and vulnerable to whatever the three men had planned for her.

"What the fuck took you so long?" Ro barked as soon as Ball pulled into his driveway in Black Forest. He hadn't had a lot of time to plan the liberation of Chloe from her brother, but his teammates were ready when he'd called them from the club.

Meat had done some quick research and figured out the route Leon would likely take back to his house, and had found an area where there weren't any surveillance cameras. Ball was the best driver out of the three and was the natural choice for doing the Pursuit Intervention Technique, otherwise known as the PIT maneuver. Black went along to assist in the takedown of Leon and his girlfriend. All in all, the entire thing should've only taken a few minutes. But the Hummer had rolled in about ten minutes later than planned. And every minute that had gone by had made Ro sweat all the more.

He reached for the handle to the back seat but stopped short when Ball climbed out of the driver's seat and said, "There were complications."

Ro looked through the window and saw Chloe slumped over, being supported by Meat. But more alarming, he saw that the cloth the other man held to her head was soaked bright red with blood.

"Bloody hell," Ro swore, and opened the door. He had Chloe's seat belt off and was striding toward his front door with her in his arms before anyone had time to explain anything else, not that he gave them time to explain as they followed him into his house.

Arrow held the door open as Ro entered. He went straight for the sofa and gently laid Chloe down. His eyes roamed her body, checking for other injuries. He hated the ill-fitting shirt she was wearing, and her shorts had ridden up and were so tight, he could clearly see the outline of her sex through the material.

"Gray, go get a pair of sweats and a T-shirt from my room," Ro ordered without taking his eyes from Chloe's chest gently rising and falling.

"Not sure that's the best idea," Gray warned. "She's not going to be happy if she wakes up and realizes you changed her clothes."

Ro had knelt next to the couch, and he turned then, keeping one hand on Chloe's arm, needing the connection as he faced his friend. "You think she's going to be any happier waking up wearing these skimpy clothes and having us gawking at her?"

Gray tilted his head in acknowledgment. "You've got a point."

"And you're still standing there," Ro returned.

Gray smirked but turned on his heel and left the room.

"What the fuck happened?" Ro asked no one in particular as he turned back to Chloe. He gently lifted the cloth and swore at the gash it revealed.

"Did the PIT as planned," Ball said. "Although that jackoff Harris is obviously a shit driver because he panicked and sped up, then jerked the wheel. That's when we think she hit her head on the window. We were there within seconds and got Harris and the girlfriend locked down."

"Did he see you?" Arrow interrupted to ask.

"No," Black said. "We had masks on. They won't remember much of what happened when they wake up anyway."

Meat came in from the nearby kitchen and handed Ro a clean cloth. Nodding his thanks, Ro replaced the bloody one and put pressure on the gash to stop the flow of blood. He didn't think it would need stitches . . . maybe some skin adhesive, though. He and his teammates had used plain ol' superglue before, but the medical glue was better. Head wounds bled like a son of a bitch. Intellectually, he knew that, but it didn't help the feeling of helplessness at seeing *Chloe* bleeding.

"Your Chloe is one hell of a fighter," Ball said. "I had her and was bringing her to the Hummer so we could get the fuck out of there, and she bit me. Fucking hard, I might add."

Ro stared up at his friend in disbelief. "She *bit* you?"

"Yup. On my arm. Surprised the fuck out of me, and I dropped her. She tried to run, but Black got her. Even tried to head butt him. Let's just say she wasn't happy in the least that we were snatching her. Thought we were taking her to someone named Joe. I know it wasn't in the plans, but we had to sedate her, Ro. She was panicking way the fuck out."

Ro sighed and looked back down at Chloe. He was seeing her for the first time not scared or nervous. She looked relaxed and serene lying on his couch. Of course, she was bleeding and thought she'd been kidnapped, but she was with him and finally safe. Her arsehole of a brother couldn't whore her out the next night at his bloody strip club. Ro knew he had to be okay with that. Okay with scaring her.

"Joe?" he asked, remembering what Ball had said.

"We were confused too," Meat said. "She was going on and on about Joe. Even begged us to leave her on the side of the road so she wouldn't have to go back to her brother, and so Joe wouldn't do whatever he was going to do to her either. It took a minute, but when she was out and we were on our way back here, I realized I'd told Ball that you would take care of her bleeding head. I think she just misheard me and thought I said Joe."

"Bloody right I'll take care of it," Ro said under his breath.

"Here are your clothes," Gray said, entering the room with a pair of Ro's sweatpants and a T-shirt.

"You need anything else from us?" Arrow asked.

Ro stood and looked at the five best friends he'd ever had. He'd been a member of the SAS, Special Air Service, the elite special forces unit in the British Army. He'd worked with other men he'd called friends. He'd saved their lives and they'd saved his. But he hadn't found his "place" until he'd been hired by Rex and begun work as a Mountain Mercenary. Working to help rid the world of arseholes like Leon Harris, who thought nothing of abusing, manipulating, and blackmailing women, was Ro's calling.

Fighting against religious zealots when he was in the British Army was one thing, but most of the time the things he'd done for his country were political, and he'd felt removed, both emotionally and physically, from the results of his actions. Not so with saving women and children. He saw firsthand what they went through, how they'd been treated, and how grateful they were to be freed from their oppressors.

Working with Gray, Arrow, Black, Ball, and Meat was different from working with the men in his old platoon. They *knew* each other. Inside and out. He didn't have any siblings by blood, but these five men were his brothers. In every sense of the word.

"I'm good," Ro told Gray.

"She's going to be pissed when she wakes up," Meat warned. "She wasn't happy about being sedated. Not in the least. You're going to have your hands full."

"I've got this," Ro said firmly.

"Seriously," Black warned. "She—"

"I'm not going to have her wake up to a bunch of men telling her she can't leave."

"Fine, but the last thing she should do is run. And she will," Ball warned. "You didn't see her tonight. She was freaked out. *Beyond* freaked out. She's at the end of her rope. Desperate. If you turn your back on her, she'll bail. Guaranteed."

Ro eyed his friend. "Then I'll just need to convince her that I'm on her side and would never hurt her."

Ro and Ball stared at each other for a long moment. Finally, Ball simply shook his head. "Don't say I didn't warn you," he said.

"Noted," Ro replied.

"You want me to call Rex and tell him what went down?" Arrow asked.

"Yeah. But wait until tomorrow. I'll talk to Chloe and make sure she's good, then I'll call and update you. *Then* you can call Rex. You know he'll want as much info as possible and will be royally pissed if we don't have it when we call to update him."

Arrow chuckled. "True that."

"Thanks. I appreciate it," Ro told him.

Arrow brushed off his thanks. "Whatever, asshole."

Ro grinned. "Thanks for everything, guys. I mean it."

His thanks were greeted by middle fingers and eye rolls. Yeah, it was safe to say he loved this group of men.

"If I don't hear from you by ten, I'll call," Arrow said.

"If you want me and Allye to come by, just let me know," Gray added.

"I'll keep digging into Harris to see what I can find to use against him," Meat offered.

Black and Ball lifted their chins in their semblance of goodbyes, and suddenly, Ro was alone with Chloe.

He kneeled by her side again and leaned down and gently kissed the cloth over her forehead. "I'm sorry, love," he whispered. "You're free now. And I'm going to make sure you stay that way. He won't touch you again . . . and neither will any other arsehole."

Then, he stood and headed for the bathroom and his first-aid kit.

First things first. Get her wound closed up. Then he'd worry about changing her clothes and getting her settled in bed. Even though he was pissed off on Chloe's behalf, and it had been one hell of a long night, Ro felt more settled and at peace than he'd ever felt before. Simply because Chloe was there.

Chapter Six

Chloe groaned and brought a hand up to her head. It hurt, but not as much as she sometimes hurt after Leon hit her. Cracking her eyes open, she realized it was way past the time she usually got up. She never slept this late. Even when she got home in the wee hours of the morning after working at her brother's strip club, she'd still gotten in the habit of getting up early. It was safer to be up and awake before Leon crawled out of bed. She'd learned that the hard way. The couple of times he'd woken up before her, he'd stormed into her room, dragged her violently out of bed, called her a lazy bitch, and told her to get her ass downstairs and start working.

At that thought, Chloe quickly sat up—and immediately regretted it.

The room around her spun like crazy, and she had to close her eyes to stop the feeling of nausea. When she had herself under control, she cautiously cracked her eyes open . . . and stared around her in dismay.

Where was she? She didn't recognize the room at all. All she knew was that it wasn't her bedroom. Looking down at herself, Chloe saw she was wearing clothes that weren't her own, as well. Her heart rate increased, but she forced herself not to panic. She needed to figure out where she was before she leaped out of bed like a crazy person.

Frowning, she tried to remember anything about how she'd gotten there, wherever "there" was. She had some disjointed feelings of being scared after being at BJ's, but nothing more than that.

Just then, the door to the room opened, and Chloe looked in that direction. The second the man stepped through the door, everything that had happened last night clicked into place.

Immediately, she began to hyperventilate, and she scooted to the opposite side of the bed to get as far away from him as possible.

She had no idea what was going on. But she remembered being with this man at the club, then him leaving, then being in the back seat of her brother's Mercedes and the car accident. She remembered being kidnapped and the men drugging her. Now she was here. Wearing clothes that were too big for her, even if they were comfortable, in an unknown man's bed.

And she knew the man standing in the doorway. Ronan Cross. He'd said to trust him. That he'd help her. She also knew that he was somehow involved in what had happened last night. Had he been the one to arrange her kidnapping? Was he in the Mafia too? Shit!

"You're okay, love," he said in a soothing tone. "Slow your breathing, or you'll make yourself pass out."

"Who are you?" she gasped.

"You know who I am. I'm Ronan. Ro."

Chloe shook her head. "No, your real name. Are you Joe? Did you kidnap me? Were those other men working for you? Are you in the Mafia too? If you've got a beef with my brother, you're going to have to bring it up with him."

"Oh, I've got a beef with that tosser all right, but I'll deal with him later."

Ro's English accent was beyond sexy, but Chloe couldn't think about that right now. She swung her legs over the side of the bed, her body still twisted to keep Ro in her sights.

"Don't get up," Ro said quickly. "You were injured last night."

"No shit," Chloe retorted icily. "Your thugs crashed into our car!"

"Chloe," Ro said sternly, stepping into the room and setting the mug he'd been carrying on a small table next to the bed, "don't."

But his warning came too late. Chloe had already stood up and was backing away from him. She knew the second she stood that she wasn't going to make it very far. The room spun, and her head immediately began to throb once more. The edges of her vision got dark, and she knew she was going to hit the floor.

But before she did, she was caught up in Ro's strong arms. He picked her up and placed her back on the bed. She felt him sit at her hip, but she refused to open her eyes. She felt the sobs well up from deep inside her, and she did everything possible to keep them in, but it was no use.

She was scared, in pain, and confused. She didn't know what was going on, where she was, or what was going to happen to her.

Before she could process what he was doing, Ro turned her gently onto her side and snuggled up behind her. One arm went under her neck, and the other clamped around her waist, holding her to him. Not one inch separated them. She could feel his warmth against her back, and it felt good. That confused her all the more.

She cried then. She couldn't hold back her tears if her life were at stake. She cried because she'd been kidnapped the night before. She cried because of what her brother and Abbie had made her do at the club and what they were planning on having her do every night for the foreseeable future. She cried because all she wanted was her mom, and that was impossible. She cried because her brother was an asshole and his girlfriend a bitch of the highest order.

Throughout it all, Ro held her as if she was the most precious thing in his life. He didn't interrupt her or scold her for crying. He simply tightened his hold, and it felt as if his arms were the only things holding her together. That without him there, she'd break into a million pieces and float away.

Eventually her sobs tapered off to the occasional sniff, and she lay defeated in Ro's arms, wondering what in the hell was going to happen to her next. Things couldn't get any worse, could they?

"I'm not going to hurt you," Ro said from behind her. "Last night was fucked up. All of it. I went to BJ's to see if I could find you. I didn't expect to go into that private room with you, but I'm not sorry I did it. I know if it wasn't me, it would've been someone else, and I couldn't let that happen."

"Why?" Chloe asked. "Why are you doing this?"

"Because the moment I saw that bruise on your back a couple of weeks ago, I couldn't get you out of my mind. I didn't like the thought of someone hitting you. Marking you. My team and I have been researching your brother."

"Why?" she repeated, feeling like a two-year-old.

Ro chuckled, and Chloe tried to ignore how she could feel his chest moving against her back and how the low sound seemed to settle in her belly.

"Because he's not a good guy, love. I don't think that's a big news flash for you. But it's more than that. I had a feeling something was dodgy about your entire situation."

"Dodgy?"

"Sorry, suspicious. I didn't like it then, and I don't like it now. When I saw you last night, and how scared you were, there was no way I was leaving you there. But I think you'd agree that I couldn't just walk out of the door of that strip club with you."

Chloe shook her head. No, even though she'd fantasized about him doing exactly that. It never would've happened.

"So I had to figure out how to get you away from your brother another way. I admit that things didn't go quite as planned. Your brother's a shitty driver, and he swerved at exactly the wrong time; you slammed your head against the window."

"I was going to jump out when he slowed down to take a turn."

"Seriously? You could've been hurt!" Ro exclaimed.

Chloe shrugged. "It was either escape then or not at all. Did you have Leon killed?" she asked, her eyes fixed on the window across the room. She wasn't sure what answer she wanted to hear, and that made her feel even worse. What kind of person did it make her that a part of her hoped he *had* killed Leon?

"What?"

"Did you kill him and Abbie?"

Chloe felt Ro move behind her, and she stiffened when he turned her onto her back. She looked up at him—and was surprised to see the expression on his face. She expected anger that she'd asked, maybe even shock. But she didn't expect to see disappointment.

"No, love. We didn't kill them. That's not the kind of men we are. I can't deny we've dispatched people in the past, but it's not usually what we set out to do. I'll admit the thought did cross my mind when I realized he was going to force you to have sex with the patrons of the club, but he's still alive and kicking; at least he was when my friends left him last night."

Chloe refused to apologize for asking, even though the words were at the tip of her tongue.

He sighed, then went on. "We sedated them. I figured your brother wouldn't exactly let you go out of the goodness of his heart, because it's obvious he doesn't have even a drop of kindness inside that shriveled-up black heart of his. You weren't supposed to fight back," he said with a trace of humor. "Ball said you took quite the chunk of flesh out of his arm."

Chloe also refused to feel bad about what she'd done. "He was kidnapping me. What was I supposed to do?"

Ro reached up and brushed a lock of hair off her forehead. "I think they were expecting you to be grateful."

His fingertips felt soft and soothing against her skin, but she concentrated on their conversation instead. "Grateful to be kidnapped?"

Ro winced and shrugged. "I didn't have a lot of time to plan, love. It was the best I could come up with. But they weren't supposed to drug you. You have to believe me on that."

"Then why did they?" she asked.

"Because they had to get out of there, and they knew you wouldn't stop fighting them, which, since I'm being honest, I approve of. You didn't give up, and that makes you strong as fuck. And in case you're wondering, I admire women who can stand up for themselves. Besides, you were bleeding."

Chloe brought a hand up, but it was caught in Ro's large fingers before she could touch the bandage on her forehead. "I used some glue to close it up. You'll have a small scar, but nothing huge. I know it probably still hurts, and I brought you some painkillers with coffee. You can't get it wet for a couple of days because water will dissolve the adhesive, but I can help you wash your hair if you want."

Chloe stared up at him in disbelief. "I need to go," she whispered.

"Go where? Back to *his* house?"

She shook her head so forcefully, she winced at the pain it caused. "No. I'll never go back there willingly. There are things that I wouldn't mind having from there. My passport, mementos of my mom and dad, but if it means getting caught by Leon again, I'll do without. But I still need to go. Get out of town. The state. *Go!*"

Ro immediately shook his head. "You're not going anywhere," he said.

"So I'm a prisoner?"

"No. Last night, you told me you weren't at BJ's of your own free will. And you're right, if you go back to your brother's house, you probably won't get another chance to escape again. But you also can't just go gallivanting around without any kind of ID. And what about money? You won't get far without it."

Chloe's eyes filled with tears again, and she didn't even try to keep them from overflowing and leaking down the sides of her face into her hair. Man, she hated crying, but she felt so overwhelmed, and she couldn't have stopped the tears for anything. She needed the emotional outlet. "I've got money. Well, sort of. I don't know that I can get it without my passport."

"I'll help you, Chloe. I'm helping you now," Ro said gently. "I swear to God, you won't come to any harm while you're with me. Your brother's a bloody wanker, and I don't want you within a hundred miles of him. He doesn't care who he hurts and who he uses. But I have more questions than I have answers at this point."

"Like?" Chloe asked.

"Like why did he have you move in with him in the first place? He already had someone doing his taxes, so why move you into that position? He works with the Carlino and Smaldone families up in Denver. Do they know about the club he runs? It's not their usual kind of business. Your brother is also making quite a bit of money, and from what Meat has been able to discover, there's no way it all comes from BJ's. So where is it coming from? We're talking tens of thousands of dollars a month, love, not a few extra grand. And why you?"

"Why me what?" Chloe had a lot of the same questions Ro did, but she wasn't going to admit it at this point. She wanted to trust him. To believe that she was safe, but it was really hard for her to trust anyone. To be fair, Ro hadn't hurt her. Yeah, he'd had her kidnapped, but she'd been about to jump out of a moving car, for God's sake. He'd almost done her a favor. She needed help, and he was here, telling her he'd do whatever he could to keep her safe.

She needed to trust *someone*. But after last night, she just wasn't sure if that person was Ronan Cross.

"Why would he try to turn his own sister into a prostitute? Why force *you* to work at the club when there are so many other women he could employ? It doesn't make sense. And things that don't make sense bother me."

Ro slowly brought his hand to the side of her face and used his thumb to wipe away her tears. "You aren't a prisoner here, Chloe. But it's not safe for you to leave just yet either."

She winced and turned her head to the side, dislodging his fingers and breaking eye contact. But he wasn't having it. He forced her to look back up at him. "I care about you," he admitted in a soft voice. "I don't know why, but I do. Please, promise that you won't go leaping out one of my windows and running to the road to try to hitchhike out of here. Give me and my friends a few days to find out more information. I'll share everything I learn about your brother with you. If you decide that you don't want to stay after hearing all the facts, I'll drive you wherever you want to go."

It had been so long since anyone had looked at her with anything other than contempt, she drank it up like a thirsty sponge. "Okay."

He smiled, but it wasn't a happy smile. "Are you agreeing with me simply to agree?"

"No. I'm doing my best to trust you, to believe in you. But it's difficult after the last few years and what I've been through."

"I understand," Ro said, sitting up on the bed, giving her some badly needed space in the process. "Take the pills, Chloe. They'll make your head stop hurting. I'll call Allye later. She's my friend's woman. She can bring you something to wear. It'll make you feel better to have another woman to talk to, I think."

"It will?"

"Won't it?"

Chloe stared at Ro for a long moment. She couldn't read anything sinister in his gaze, but that didn't mean she trusted him one hundred percent either. This morning, he was wearing another pair of jeans with a gray T-shirt. It had the logo of some sort of pool hall on the front. He wasn't wearing any shoes, and the sight of his bare feet seemed extremely intimate. She slowly propped herself up with her back to the headboard. She brought her knees up and clutched them tightly, wrapping her arms around them.

"I thought the same thing about Abbie once," Chloe said when Ro didn't say anything further, simply waited patiently for her to explain her comment. "I was wrong."

Ro held her gaze and said, "A couple months ago, Allye Martin was kidnapped off the streets of San Francisco. She was supposed to be taken to a man who had bought her because he liked her unique hair and eyes. To make a long story short, the man didn't succeed, and we managed to save her from that fate. She's the last person you need to be afraid of, Chloe. Her experience wasn't like yours, but she's been through hell just the same."

"I was excited when Leon told me he was moving his girlfriend into the house," Chloe shared. "I thought having another woman around would loosen my brother up and make him less . . . grumpy. But Abbie turned out to be even meaner than Leon. Of course, I didn't realize I couldn't trust her until I'd already blabbed to her that I was desperate to get out of the house. She ran straight to Leon and told him, and he tightened his already obsessive watch on me. I also think it was probably Abbie's idea to have me start working at BJ's in the first place."

Ro took a step back toward the bed, but when Chloe flinched, he stopped in his tracks, even taking a step backward to give her space. "Allye is not like that, love. I realize my word alone won't make you believe me, only time will do that, but I'll say it again. You are *not* a prisoner here, Allye is trustworthy and a good woman, and I will never, ever hurt you."

Chloe wanted to believe him, but she couldn't. She'd been hurt too many times in the past five years to be able to take anyone at their word. It'd take time for her to trust him.

Ro sighed, then nodded at the cup of coffee with his head. "Take the pills, Chloe. The bathroom is through there"—he used his head once again to indicate a door next to him—"and I'll be downstairs waiting for Allye and Gray to arrive. Take your time, and don't get that wound on your head wet." And with that, he turned and left, shutting the door gently behind him.

Chloe released a sigh of relief. It wasn't that she thought Ro was going to start smacking her around or anything, but there was something about him that made it hard for her to breathe.

She sat on the bed for several minutes, running everything that he'd said that morning through her head. Slowly, she started to remember more and more details from the night before as well. The one thing that stuck out most was how, the entire time she was with Ro in the private room, grinding on his lap, practically naked, he hadn't gotten aroused. Not once. Even when she was on her knees in front of him and had brushed against his dick as she'd undone his pants, he hadn't gotten an erection.

That could mean he was gay, but she didn't think so. Chloe believed him when he'd told her there was no way he could get it up when it was obvious she was scared out of her head.

A little glimmer of hope flared in her belly, but she ruthlessly squashed it. She didn't know nearly enough about Ro, or his friends, to blindly trust them. Her brother had killed that ability in her. She'd planned to escape on her own, and maybe that was still her best course of action.

She swung her legs over the side of the bed and cautiously stood, wavering for a moment before getting her balance. Her head throbbed as she walked around the big bed, keeping her hand on the mattress to make sure she didn't fall. She picked up the cup of coffee and cautiously smelled it. It smelled like . . . coffee. Not that she would know what a drugged cup of coffee would smell like anyway.

Ignoring the pills he'd put on the side table, she shuffled her way toward the bathroom. If she was going to be expected to talk to some strange woman later, she needed to empty her bladder and see for herself how bad the cut on her head was. She had to get on with her life and face what awaited her. Whatever it was *had* to be better than servicing men against her will at BJ's. Right?

Chapter Seven

"Thanks for coming," Ro said as he opened the door to Gray and Allye. Surprisingly, Arrow was also standing on his front porch.

"You're welcome," Gray replied.

"I can't believe you didn't call me last night," Allye complained as she shuffled inside.

"How's she doing?" Arrow asked.

Ro closed the door behind his friends and followed them into the main living area. The first time he'd walked into the house, he'd fallen in love with it. It wasn't huge, but the living area had floor-to-ceiling windows. The view was nothing but trees, and that was the reason he loved it. The house was surrounded by pine trees, and he loved opening the doors and windows in the fall and spring and letting the smell of pine fill his space.

There were three bedrooms on the upper level of the house, but it was the view, and the huge outbuilding he could turn into his garage, that had sold him. Working on engines soothed him. Made him forget the things he'd done in the past, forget some of the awful things humans could do to each other. When he was elbow deep in an engine and trying to figure out how to put it back together, he didn't have to think about anything else.

Gray went into the galley kitchen and straight to the coffeepot. Arrow settled onto the couch. Allye stood in front of him with her arms crossed and tapping one small foot on his hardwood floors impatiently.

"She's okay," Ro said, answering Arrow's question. "I made sure to wake her up every hour or so for a while last night. She woke up about half an hour ago, we talked, and she's doing her morning thing right now," Ro told his friends. What he didn't tell them was that he'd been so worried about her, he'd sat in a chair next to his bed, watching her sleep. That every time she'd moaned during the night, he'd put his hands on her, and she'd calmed down immediately. He didn't tell them that the clothes she'd worn were at the bottom of his rubbish bin next to the house.

He didn't admit that her distrust of him this morning was a blow he wasn't sure he'd recover from anytime soon, or that the ten minutes he'd held her in his arms was the closest he'd felt to another human being in his entire adult life.

"How's her head look?" Arrow asked.

"Okay. It's going to bruise pretty good, but the adhesive is holding . . . unless she decides to ignore my advice and gets it wet this morning," Ro told his friend.

"I'm going up there," Allye announced.

Gray caught her by the arm, halting her movement toward the stairs. "Hang on, babe. What does she know?" Gray asked Ro.

"Not much," Ro admitted. "She was still a little knackered this morning. She wasn't happy, so I skipped telling her about us for the moment. I wanted her to settle in a bit so she'd be more likely to listen later."

Allye sighed and rolled her eyes. "*Boys!* Look, she doesn't know any of you, and she wakes up in a strange house not knowing what the hell is going on. She's not going to 'settle.' If I were her, I'd be trying to figure out a way to get the hell out of here."

Ro's eyes went to the stairs, and he actually took a step toward them, the urge to check on Chloe and to make sure she was still there flashing through him, when Arrow's hand grabbed his arm. The other man had gotten up from the couch and approached him without Ro noticing. He'd been so focused on getting to Chloe that he hadn't even heard his friend move.

"Allye's right," Arrow said. "She has no reason to trust you. Or us. Give her some space. Let Allye go talk to her."

Ro hated it, but knew his friends were right. "Her brother's girl-friend was abusive," he warned Allye. "Was a spy for her brother. She's not likely to trust you just because you're female."

Allye's lips pressed together, but she nodded. "Okay. Thanks." She turned to Gray. "Will you get me two cups of coffee? Things might go better if I arrive with caffeine."

"I already brought her a cup," Ro said as Gray turned back to the kitchen.

"That's fine, but she might need more," Allye replied.

"Be careful with her," Ro said softly. "She hasn't had an easy time lately."

Allye nodded. "I will. Does she know about Mountain Mercenaries?"

Ro shook his head.

"Can I tell her?"

Allye's question was deeper than she probably realized. When they were hired, Rex warned them that they weren't to go around telling everyone who they worked for and what they did. Of course, they all had "normal" jobs, but that wasn't what Rex was talking about. He made it clear that the only time they could tell a woman who and what they were was if they were in a serious, committed relationship.

Ro and the others had taken that to heart, and, as far as he knew, Allye was the first woman to know details about the Mountain Mercenaries. That they were more than a group of friends who hung out at a pool hall and shot the shit.

Gray walked up to Allye just then with two mugs of steaming coffee in his hands. Without missing a beat, Ro said, "Yes. It might go better if she heard about the team from you than me, anyway."

Knowing he was admitting to Arrow and Gray that he had a deeper interest in Chloe than simply wanting to help her get away from the abusive situation she'd found herself in, Ro didn't give a shit.

"Thanks," Allye told him and Gray at the same time. Gray handed the mugs off to her and kissed her on the forehead before she turned to make her way to the stairs.

The three men watched Allye head upstairs—carefully, so she didn't spill any coffee. When she disappeared from their view, Gray said quietly, "You've got a steep mountain to climb, my friend."

"I know," Ro told him. "But I have a feeling she'll be more than worth it in the end."

Arrow clapped him on the back in support. "Come on. We need to talk about what happened last night and what our next steps are."

"I called Meat before we left; he said he was checking into some things and that he'd see us at The Pit later," Gray said.

"Team meeting?" Arrow asked.

"Yup."

Ro didn't respond, just followed his friends into his living room. His mind wasn't on the details of the previous night or on Gray and Arrow's conversation about Leon Harris. He was wondering how Chloe was, and if she was scared by Allye's appearance in his bedroom.

Chloe hadn't done much more than use the bathroom, brush her teeth, and stare at herself in the mirror above the sink. Her straight hair had more kinks in it than she'd ever seen before. She had makeup smeared on her face from crying, and of course there was the large bruise on the side of her forehead. She'd peeled the white bandage off and was surprised at how good the wound looked. Just as he'd said, Ro had used some sort of glue on it and had put a small butterfly bandage over it as well.

She had dried blood in her hair but none on her skin at all. She wondered if Ro had cleaned her up. Chloe looked down at herself and also wondered where her own clothes had gone. She was certainly more comfortable in the T-shirt and sweats than the skimpy clothes Abbie had been making her wear, but the thought of how she got into the clothes was a bit worrisome, and something she pushed to the back of her mind. She couldn't go there right now.

Chloe dropped her head and propped herself up on the counter with her hands. She wanted to trust Ro; she just wasn't sure she could. He was bigger, taller, stronger, and obviously had more connections than she did. But being with him had to be better than being back at the house with Leon and Abbie. She'd been working toward this moment, escaping her brother, for what seemed like forever, and now that she'd done it, she didn't know what to do next. Nothing had worked the way she'd planned. Was she just someone else's captive?

Exhausted, Chloe stood in front of the mirror, feeling as if she were ninety-eight years old instead of thirty-four.

"Hello?" a feminine voice called out at the same time a knock sounded on the bathroom door.

Chloe started so badly she jerked backward and promptly tripped over her own feet. She cried out as she fell, arms pinwheeling to try to keep her balance. But it was no use—she landed on her ass and couldn't keep the "Ow" from escaping her mouth.

The bathroom door opened, and a pretty woman with brown hair looked into the small space. "Oh my God. Are you okay? I'm so sorry! I didn't mean to scare you."

Chloe stayed on the floor, scooting backward on her sore butt until her back hit the side of the tub. She brought her knees up and wrapped her arms around her legs protectively.

The woman put the mugs she'd been holding in one hand on the counter and went down on her knees on the floor in front of Chloe. To her credit, she didn't reach for her or crowd her.

"I'm such an idiot," she said. "I should've known better than to scare you. Are you hurt? Do you need me to go get Ro?"

Chloe shook her head firmly but carefully. The headache she'd woken up with was still prevalent, since she'd refused to take the pills Ro had left for her.

"I'm Allye. Like the space between two buildings, but the *y* comes before the *e*," the woman said in a way that made Chloe think she'd explained how to spell her name many times before. She then shifted so she too was sitting on her butt. She leaned back against the cabinet under the sink and mimicked Chloe's posture, bringing her knees up and holding her legs.

Chloe eyed her critically. Her first glance had been correct—she was pretty. She had brown hair with a striking white streak running from the top of her head down to the tips of the strands. She also had two different-colored eyes, which made her all the more unique. She looked to be just a little shorter than Chloe but was much skinnier than Chloe had ever been. The woman was lithe and graceful, and she reminded Chloe of some of the dancers at the club.

"I'm dating Gray. You might remember him from last night. He said that he met you at BJ's."

Chloe stared at Allye in confusion. "You knew he went to a strip club last night, and you were okay with it?"

Allye chuckled. It wasn't a mean laugh, as she'd gotten used to hearing from Abbie and Leon, but open and friendly. "Oh yeah. First, it was business. He was there because Ro wanted to check on you. Second, I trust him. He'd never cheat on me."

"That's what they all say," Chloe said bitterly.

The humor left Allye's face, but she didn't drop her gaze from Chloe's. "He really wouldn't. Gray is the most honorable man I've ever met. For some weird reason, he loves me, and not a day goes by when he doesn't remind me. I'm not an idiot, I know men cheat. They do it all the time . . . but not Gray. He'd break up with me if he really wanted to be with another woman that badly. It's not in his DNA to be dishonest."

"He sounds too good to be true," Chloe said, feeling jealous of the other woman.

Allye smiled. "Oh, he's not perfect, trust me. I could tell you lots of stories about messy kitchens, acting before thinking, and other annoying habits of his, but the point is that I trust him. Implicitly. And you can too."

"I don't even know him," Chloe shot back, feeling confused. She wasn't comfortable talking with Allye. Once upon a time she wouldn't have hesitated to befriend the warm, obviously amiable woman, but she'd learned her lesson the hard way with Abbie.

"You'll get to know him," Allye said breezily. "I'm super excited to meet you, though. I thought Gray was going to be the only one of the group to find a woman for a really long time."

Chloe stared at Allye blankly, having no idea what she was talking about.

Reaching up for the counter, Allye grabbed one of the mugs she'd carried into the bathroom and offered it to Chloe. "Coffee? I didn't know how you liked it, so it's just black, but I can get Gray to bring up some creamer and sugar if you need it."

Chloe had finished the first cup Ro had left for her and immediately reached for the mug. She loved coffee. Had at least three cups every morning, and since it was way later than she usually got up, her body was craving the caffeine. "Black is fine," she told Allye. She took a tentative sip.

Allye reached back up to the counter, retrieved the other cup, and took her own sip. "Hmmmm. I swear I don't know how Ro does it, but somehow his coffee always tastes better than the stuff I make. He claims he doesn't do anything different, but I think he has to be adding a secret ingredient to the beans or something."

Chloe agreed. She'd been so desperate for the first cup, she hadn't really tasted the smooth brew, but now that she was thinking about it, the coffee did taste different than normal. Better.

The two women drank their coffee in silence. When it dragged on too long, Chloe began to feel nervous. She should get up. Should say something. But she was practically paralyzed, wondering what Allye's real purpose in being there was.

Before too long, the other woman said, "So, I need to tell you something."

And there it was. Chloe stiffened. She *knew* she was probably working with the kidnappers. Knew she couldn't trust any of them. Leon probably owed them money, and they were holding her hostage until he paid them or something. Or maybe they were part of the Mafia and were going to kill her to make some point, or—

"Ro and the others are part of a group called the Mountain Mercenaries," Allye said.

Chloe blinked. Her thoughts had been cut off by Allye's announcement, but it hadn't been what she'd thought the other woman was going to say at all, and she had no idea what she was talking about. "What?"

"My man, Gray, and Ro, and the others, they're all part of a group called the Mountain Mercenaries. Their boss, Rex, calls them and tells them when and where their missions are, and off they go. They're the good guys, Chloe. I promise."

"But . . . mercenaries aren't *good*," Chloe stammered. "Aren't they hired by anyone who needs something dirty done? Like killing people?"

Surprisingly, Allye giggled. She put a hand over her mouth and laughed until Chloe got a little annoyed.

"I'm sorry," Allye finally responded. "I'm not laughing at you. I told Gray the exact same thing when he told me what they were called. The name is badass, I admit, but it doesn't really fit them. They're more like vigilantes. You know, like when a father confronts a man who raped his little girl and blows him away? They might do stuff that's not exactly legal, but they do it because it's the right thing to do. They fight for the underdog. For people who can't fight for themselves. Rex concentrates on abuse against women and kids. He can't stand it, for some reason. The guys go wherever they're needed, both in the country and outside of it. It doesn't matter. They'll do whatever it takes to help kidnapped, abused, and persecuted women. It's a calling for them."

The coffee in her hand forgotten, Chloe stared at Allye in disbelief, but the other woman didn't even seem to notice.

"That's why Ro couldn't forget about you when you showed up here a few weeks ago. He saw that bruise on your back and did what he could to find out more about your situation. He went to BJ's to check things out. Gray said he was hoping like hell you weren't there. But you obviously were. His natural next move was to get you out of that situation."

"He had me kidnapped," Chloe said.

Allye stared at her. "He did?"

Chloe nodded.

Allye shook her head. "No, that's not right."

"A big Hummer crashed into my brother's Mercedes, and before I knew what was happening, I was thrown over a huge guy's shoulder, a needle was shoved in my arm, and I was thrown into the car and driven away. Now I'm in this house, I don't even know where I am, I'm wearing someone else's clothes, and I have no idea what's happening."

Allye reached out toward Chloe, and she instinctively pulled away. The other woman froze and slowly drew her hand back.

"I'm sorry how that all went down," Allye said softly. "But it was probably the only way to get you to safety."

There was a lot of truth in the other woman's words, but Chloe didn't want to admit it. Being kidnapped had actually saved her from having to throw herself out of the moving car, where she'd probably have ended up injured even worse. She shook her head. "I told him I wanted to go, and he wouldn't let me. I'm being held against my will, and I'm scared. Will you help me?"

Allye eyed her for so long, Chloe had no idea what was going through her head. "I met Gray when he showed up in the doorway of the boat I was being held on. I was snatched off the streets of San Francisco and dumped into a boat and taken out into the middle of the Pacific Ocean. Okay, it wasn't the middle, but it felt like it. I was bought by a guy who wanted to keep me for his personal entertainment. That boat sank under us, and me and Gray had to swim for miles before Black picked us up. I would've died then, but Gray wouldn't let me. Refused to let me give up.

"Then, a month later, I was snatched again. But this time I almost didn't make it out. If it wasn't for Gray, Black, Ro, and the others, I would've ended up a statistic. Forced to dance for; have sex with; and serve a psychotic, crazy, perverted man for the rest of my life, or until he got tired of me and sold me to someone else who would've done the same thing. Ro is a *good* man, Chloe. You just have to give him a chance to prove it."

Chloe's hopes sank. Allye seemed nice, but she was obviously brainwashed. She didn't see the bad side of her boyfriend. Didn't want to admit that he and his friends weren't the angels she wanted to believe they were.

"You don't believe me," Allye said with a sigh. "I suppose I can't blame you." Then, instead of continuing to try to convince her, she slowly pushed herself to her feet.

Chloe looked up at her, dreading whatever was coming next. She placed the now-empty mug on the tile at her side and gripped her legs tighter.

"I hope I'll get to talk to you again later, Chloe," Allye said. Then she turned and left the bathroom, closing the door behind her with a soft click.

Staring at the door in disbelief, Chloe didn't move. She figured it was a trick, that Allye would be back with reinforcements. But when a minute went by and she heard no one entering the bedroom, Chloe slowly inched her way over and reached for the knob. She locked the door and resumed her position on the floor next to the tub.

She knew the lock wouldn't hold Ro back for long, not with the way he was built, but it might give her some time to protect herself if he was playing her.

Ro turned toward the stairs when he heard someone coming down. Allye appeared—and she looked absolutely furious.

"What's wrong?" Gray asked, jumping to his feet when he saw her.

Allye brushed off Gray's hands and walked straight to Ro. He'd stood at the same time as Gray, and even though she was six inches shorter than he was, Allye didn't hesitate to poke him in the chest. "You have a problem, Ro."

"Me? What?"

"That woman is scared to death! She thinks you kidnapped her and are holding her against her will."

Ro sighed. "I know. I've told her that I did it for her own good."

"Well, she doesn't believe you."

"I know!" Ro repeated. "That's why I sent *you* up there. To reassure her. To convince her that I saved her from her brother."

Allye turned to Gray and said in exasperation, "She was shocked that I trusted you to go to that nasty strip club and keep your dick in your pants."

Gray merely shrugged. "Can't say I blame her for that. There aren't a lot of women who would like their men going to a titty bar."

Allye huffed out a breath, the group silently considering their predicament for a few tense minutes before she turned back to Ro. "You have to prove to her that she's not being held against her will."

"I would if I knew how. She doesn't believe a word I say to her," Ro complained.

"Then you have to show her," Arrow interjected. "Actions speak louder than words."

Ro faced his friend, his fists clenched at his sides. "She'll run."

Arrow shrugged. "Maybe she will. But if you don't let her see that she's not a prisoner, she'll bolt the first chance she gets anyway."

Ro ran a hand through his hair and began to pace. "You didn't see her last night," he told his friends in agitation. "She was freaked. She didn't want to go anywhere near that fucking back room. But she knew she had no choice. I did my best to keep my eyes on her face and not on her body, to show her that she could trust me. I thought by the time that bloody timer went off that she did. Black and the others were just supposed to stop the car and snatch her away from those arseholes. She wasn't supposed to get hurt, and they weren't supposed to drug *her*."

"But they did. And now you have to deal with the results. Shit doesn't always happen the way we want it to—you know that, Ro. Why are you throwing such a fit about it now?" Arrow asked.

Ro turned to Arrow and actually took a step toward him before realizing what he was doing and stopping himself. "Don't tempt me to kick your arse," Ro warned.

"You can't kick my ass," Arrow returned. "Besides, you don't want to kick *my* ass, you want to kick your own for not doing whatever that woman upstairs needs in order to trust you." His voice gentled. "This is the only way, man. You can't be around her twenty-four seven to make sure she doesn't bolt, and she can't fully trust you until you show her that she can. That she isn't a prisoner. Words are cheap, and you know it."

Ro growled low in his throat and wanted to hit something. But he refrained, barely. He looked Arrow in the eyes and admitted, "I like her.

There's just something about her that grabbed me by the bollocks the first time I saw her and wouldn't let go. She was scared last night, there's no doubt, but she was also angry. I could sense her strength from what little I've seen of her, and I only wanted to get her free of her brother so she could be the woman I feel is dying to break free. I've made a shambles out of this entire situation, but I did it so she could be *free!*"

"If you love someone, you have to let them be free, otherwise they'll never come back," Allye said softly.

Gray chuckled next to her and put his arm around her shoulders. "That's not exactly how the saying goes," he told his girlfriend.

Allye shrugged off his touch and declared, "I don't care. Ro knows what I mean. Look, she's not stupid. If what you said is true, that her brother was forcing her to do stuff at that nasty strip joint, she's not going to go running back to him. But the longer you keep her here and make her *think* she's being held captive, the harder it will be to get her to trust you."

Ro knew his friends were right, but the thought of walking out the door and leaving Chloe vulnerable killed him. He wanted to keep her safe. To make sure her brother couldn't get his hands on her again. And he couldn't do that if she was running around the city on her own.

Bowing his head and rubbing the back of his neck, Ro sighed. "Okay. The others are going to The Pit, right?"

"Yeah. I think Meat said he wanted to meet there around noon."

Ro looked at his watch. They had about thirty minutes to get there, then. "Gray, can you give me a lift?"

"Of course."

"Wait for me outside. I'll be right there," Ro told his friends.

Arrow and Gray nodded, and Allye gave him a big hug. They left without another word, knowing what he was about to do was extremely difficult for him.

Taking a deep breath, Ro made preparations to show Chloe she could trust him, even though it went against everything he'd devoted his life to for the last five years.

Chapter Eight

Chloe quickly ran back toward the room she'd woken up in and eased the door shut. She sat on the edge of the bed and waited for whatever was going to happen next.

Her heart was beating a million miles an hour. She'd learned the best way to get information while living in her brother's house was to spy on him. It wasn't like he was going to tell her anything, and most of the time, the risk was worth the punishment if she got caught. She'd learned to act scared and submissive around him, because that was what he wanted her to be. It had worked well enough to fool Leon, but she wasn't sure it would work with Ronan.

After Allye left the bathroom, Chloe had sat in the locked room for only a minute or two before forcing herself up and tiptoeing to the bedroom door. She was surprised it was unlocked, but quickly took advantage of their screwup and quietly stepped into the hall. She'd heard the others talking downstairs and had sat on the top stair, out of sight, listening to the end of their conversation.

"Please, please, please," she begged quietly. "Leave me alone so I can get the hell out of here." She didn't know what she was going to do about her passport, or getting clothes that fit, but she'd figure that out later. The important thing was escaping. Her goal was the same, even if now she had to escape Ronan's house instead of Leon's.

Within a few minutes, she heard the heavy tread of footsteps on the stairs.

Chloe did what she could to try to keep her facial expression neutral. The last thing she wanted was for Ro to guess she'd spied on him and his friends.

There was a knock on the door, and Chloe frowned, wondering why he didn't just come inside. This was his house; he had every right.

When he knocked again, Chloe said, "Come in."

The knob turned, and then Ro was there. He stood in the doorway, not coming toward her. Not crowding her. "I need to go out for a while," he told her.

Yes!

Chloe wanted to jump up and down, but she merely nodded.

"I know you don't trust me, but you are *not* a prisoner here. You're at my house. The same one you stumbled on the other week. We're kinda far from any other houses, but both my nearest neighbors are friendly."

Chloe's brows came down at that. Why was he telling her about his neighbors?

"You didn't have any shoes on when you arrived last night. They probably came off somewhere between your brother's car and the Hummer. Mine won't fit you, but if you stuffed some socks into the toes of my boots, they'd probably do in a pinch, at least until you can get some that fit. I'm going downtown to meet with my teammates. We're going to be talking about your brother and what the bloody hell is going on.

"You're safe here, Chloe. He doesn't know where you are—at least we don't think so, not yet. I didn't have a lot of time to make plans last night, and I apologize for how things went down. I didn't mean to scare you, but I also knew we had to wait until you were away from the club and Harris's goons before we rescued you. If I'd had more time,

I would've come up with something that wouldn't have scared you so badly. I left some things for you downstairs. I . . ."

He hesitated then, and Chloe found herself leaning forward, wanting to get up and reassure him in some way, which was crazy.

"I hope you'll decide to trust me. I meant what I said. I will never hurt you, and I'll do everything in my power to keep anyone else from hurting you as well. But as my friends told me downstairs, trust isn't something that can be taken. It has to be given. I hope you'll take some time to relax. Take some pain pills." His eyes went to the pills still sitting on the table next to the bed. "You'll find quite the variety in my medicine cabinet, in their original containers; you can choose what you think will work best for you. Find something to eat, watch the telly, do whatever you want. I'll be back later, and I'll bring you up to speed on what Meat has found out about your brother. Then we can discuss what our next steps are."

And with one long, last look at her, a look she couldn't interpret, Ro shut the door.

The click of the latch sounded loud in the silent room, and Chloe held her breath, waiting to hear him lock it from the outside. When nothing happened, she cautiously walked over and turned the knob. It opened immediately. She frowned at it in confusion.

From downstairs, she heard Ro walking around, the click of another door, then silence.

Chloe went back to the bed and sat. Waiting. For what, she didn't know. But she figured this was a trap. No way would Ro leave her by herself in his house, even if his friends had warned him that she didn't trust him.

Hearing an engine outside, she quickly went to the window and looked out. She saw a black Audi driving down the driveway, a beat-up old pickup truck following close behind it.

It took another ten minutes of nothing but silence for Chloe to get up the nerve to leave the bedroom. She walked as quietly as she could to the top of the stairs and listened for any sign that Ro, or one of his friends, had stayed behind to see if she'd try to run. To catch her in the act and punish her. When she didn't hear anything, or anyone, she slowly walked down the stairs.

At the bottom, she looked around. The living room was empty. As was the kitchen. She was about to head to the front door when something caught her eye. Turning, Chloe stared at the dining room table. Or rather, what was *on* the table.

Looking around once more, and seeing no one, Chloe went toward the table. There was a note next to various objects. Picking it up, she read:

Chloe,

I wish my word was good enough to get you to trust me, but as my friend, Arrow, told me, I need to earn your trust instead of demand it. I get that you're uneasy, and I'd be uneasy if I were in your shoes too. For the record, I want you to stay. You'll be safer here with me than on your own. I want to help make sure your brother can't get to you again. But I understand if you don't believe me. If you need to bolt.

I've left the keys to my McLaren for you. Take it. It's worth quite a bit of money if you sell it, which would help you get out of town. It's a 650S. Don't take less than 100K for it. I bought it for more than that, but that's at the low end of what you should get. I recommend you go to Bob's Auto Sales. I know, it's a ridiculous name, but Bob is a friend of mine, and he's been wanting to get his hands on the McLaren for years. He'll do right by you, and he'll pay in cash.

I admit the car isn't exactly inconspicuous, though; if you'd prefer, there are two vehicles in my garage right now that I've just finished work on. An Accord and a Kia. The keys are on hooks inside the garage door. Take either one. I'll deal with the owners and tell them it was stolen, but you should have enough time to get out of town and exchange the plates before that happens.

I'm also leaving all the cash I've got on hand. I'm sorry it's not more.

I don't have clothes that'll fit you, but feel free to take whatever you can use of mine. T-shirts, boxers, whatever.

I just went to the store a couple of days ago, so I've got plenty of food. There's a bag you can use inside the front hall closet. You can get quite a bit in there to tide you over until you get somewhere safe.

I also left a couple of throwaway phones that can't be traced. I've got them for work; sometimes the women we help need a way to remain undetected for a while to get away from their abusers. Take them.

This is not a joke and not a trick. The only thing I've ever wanted was for you to be safe. If you aren't here when I get back, I wish you the best of luck. If you ever need my help, though, I'm here. You can call me, and I'll come to you, no matter where you are.

I hope to see you soon.

Ro

PS. I know you were on the stairs earlier, and in case you didn't understand Allye's reference, here's the full saying:

If you love something, set it free.

If it comes back, it's yours.

If it doesn't, it was never meant to be.

Chloe stared at the note for a heartbeat longer, then lowered it to look at the pile of stuff on the table. Three phones, still in their packaging, a set of car keys, and a pile of cash.

Without touching any of it, she looked around and headed for a door. Discovering a pantry filled to the brim with food, she shut it and went for the next door.

It took three tries, but she finally found what she was looking for. The garage.

She opened the door and stared at the fancy, sleek sports car sitting there. It was black and definitely looked expensive. She'd never heard of a McLaren, but looking at the vehicle, she could imagine that it was worth at least the hundred thousand Ro said Bob would pay for it. A hundred thousand dollars would last her a really long time. And it could get her far away from Colorado Springs and her brother.

Instead of rushing back inside the house to grab the keys and take off, however, she clicked the button to open the automatic door and winced at how loud the motor was. Squinting at the bright Colorado sunshine, Chloe walked outside and looked to her left. She remembered finding this driveway a couple of weeks ago, after Leon had forced her out of his car as punishment. She'd walked along the empty road for at least a mile before she'd come upon Ro's drive. There was another building off to the left of the house. The mechanic's shop. She walked over to it and saw, just as he'd said, a Honda Accord and a Kia in the garage. A pegboard with two sets of keys was hanging on one of the walls as well. He hadn't lied.

Swallowing hard, Chloe wandered back to the house through the garage and pushed the button to shut it. She went back into the dining room and stared at the money, keys, and phones.

Still holding the note, she headed into the living room, sat on the couch, curled her legs up under her, and tried to think.

She had no idea how long Ro would be gone. She should be stuffing shit into one of those bags he talked about and getting the hell out of there. But . . .

Her eyes drifted to the note again. To the postscript.

If you love something, set it free.

She knew Ro hadn't wanted to leave her by herself.

Knew he didn't want *her* to leave.

But trusting him took a giant leap of faith she wasn't sure she had in her. Not since the person she should've been able to trust most in this world, her own flesh and blood, had sold her out. Literally.

But everything Ro had done since the day she'd met him had been for her benefit.

He'd let her borrow his phone. He'd been concerned about the bruise on her back. He'd come looking for her at the club after he'd found out her brother owned it. He'd given Dan four hundred dollars to take her into a private room so she didn't have to *service* someone else. He'd had his friends take her right from under her brother's nose. He'd doctored her head wound. He'd invited more friends over to try to make her feel better.

And finally, he'd left her alone. Given her everything she needed to get out of Colorado Springs and away from her brother, once and for all.

He knew there was a good chance she'd be gone when he got back, but he'd still done it.

All to prove to her that she could trust him.

Tears pricked her eyes, but she stubbornly held them back.

She didn't want to leave. It had been a long time since she'd had someone on her side. And she found that she liked it. A lot.

The thought of taking off and being on her own wasn't a pleasant one. Of course, that was her plan all along, but after being the recipient of Ro's concern, and that of his friends, she suddenly wasn't as fired up to head out into the big bad world by herself.

And the thought of Leon somehow finding her and dragging her back to his house, or BJ's, was terrifying. Chloe knew many of the women who worked at the strip club weren't there by choice. She'd seen the bleak and desperate looks in their eyes. It was obvious Leon was holding something over their heads. Had somehow coerced them into doing what he wanted.

Chloe thought about the whorehouse he said he ran. For the first time, she wondered if *those* women were there of their own free will. She doubted it.

Suddenly feeling sick, she leaned over and took deep breaths to keep from throwing up. Did she want to end up like them? Absolutely not.

Remembering how open and friendly Allye had been, Chloe reluctantly admitted to herself that she was nothing like the women at the club. She wasn't being coerced by her boyfriend. Or Ro. Chloe wanted to trust her. Wanted to trust that the Mountain Mercenaries was a real thing. She recalled how the three men last night had tried not to hurt her during the kidnapping. Even after she'd bitten the guy holding her, he hadn't hit her. Hadn't retaliated. Chloe knew if she'd done that to Leon or one of his thugs, they'd have beaten the shit out of her.

Opening her eyes and sitting up, Chloe looked around Ro's house. He had an expensive television, and the sofa under her was good quality, but nothing was pretentious. Ro himself had been cautious and easy with her. Hadn't yelled at her. Hadn't forced her to do anything, even take the pills he'd left for her.

Remembering how gently he'd held her as she'd cried was the tipping point. Ro hadn't mocked her or even seemed impatient with her tears. Leon always sneered at her when she got upset. Told her to suck it up and quit acting like a baby.

She might regret her decision. Might look back at this moment and want to kick her own ass. But she was going to stay. Try to trust Ro and his friends. She would leave later if she thought Ro was playing her.

The decision made, Chloe felt as if a ten-ton weight had been lifted from her shoulders. She could suddenly breathe easier, and life didn't seem as hopeless as it had even twenty minutes ago.

Ro had done that. By leaving her alone, trusting her in his house, with his stuff. Trusting her not to up and leave the second his back was turned.

Once she'd made the decision to stay, some of what Allye had told her truly sank in. Mountain Mercenaries. It was a catchy, cute name for a group of men who didn't do anything remotely cute. If what Allye had said was true, they'd saved her from a life as a sex slave. And who knew how many other women they'd saved as well? She should be thanking her lucky stars she'd wandered into Ro's garage. If she hadn't . . .

No. She wasn't going to go there.

She was safe now.

For the first time in a really long time, Chloe relaxed. Completely. She didn't have to worry about who was watching her and what they'd report back to her brother. She didn't have to worry about Leon barging into the office and demanding an accounting of how she'd spent every minute of the last hour . . . or hurting her if he didn't like the answer. Didn't have to worry about him bringing random men home and telling her she was going out on a date. Didn't have to worry about accounting, money, or the Mafia.

She could just be.

With that in mind, Chloe pulled the blanket off the back of the couch and curled up on her side on the extremely comfortable cushions. She stared out the large picture windows, watching the trees sway in the slight breeze, and quickly fell into a deep, relaxed sleep for the first time in a really long time.

Two hours later, Ro stood in front of his door, scared to enter. And he was a man who wasn't scared of anything. He'd faced down thugs with knives and guns, even terrorists with bombs. But standing there, wondering if he'd enter his house to find it empty, was terrifying.

Taking a deep breath, he pushed open the door, then quietly closed it behind him.

The first thing he did was look to the dining room table. The money and other things he'd left for her were still sitting there.

Ro closed his eyes in relief and let out the breath he hadn't known he'd been holding.

"Chloe?" he called out.

There was no answer, so he went immediately to the stairs and up to his room. The door was ajar, and he peeked inside. No Chloe. The bathroom door was also open, and the light was off. He stood in the doorway for a long moment, confused.

Suddenly not so sure she'd decided to stay, Ro spun and ran back down the stairs. He went straight to the door to the garage and opened it. He stared at his beloved McLaren, still sitting in its parking spot. He clicked the button to open the garage door and impatiently waited for it to lift. As soon as it rose high enough, he ducked down and strode out onto his driveway. Arrow had already left, but he didn't care about his friend at the moment.

He looked toward his work garage—and furrowed his brows in confusion at seeing both the vehicles he'd been working on still there.

If Chloe hadn't taken his money or his cars, where was she?

Ro went back inside his house, pulling out his phone to call in reinforcements. He'd said he would let her go, but there was no way he could live with himself if she was wandering around in his baggy clothes, with no money or phone. She'd be easy pickings for her brother to catch her.

Just as he went to hit Rex's number, he stopped and stared at his couch.

Chloe was there. She was curled under the blanket he usually had thrown on the back of his couch. All he could see was a bit of her black hair.

Clicking off his phone and putting it back in his pocket, Ro collapsed in the chair next to the sofa and simply stared at his guest in relief.

She hadn't left.

Not only that, but she was sleeping.

Sleeping.

He knew better than most that women who were on the run, or abused, rarely slept soundly. They were jumpy and on edge, making deep sleep an impossibility.

But the fact that Chloe had slept through him calling her name, opening and closing doors, and generally being not so quiet as he searched his house for her said a lot.

How long he sat there, watching her sleep, Ro couldn't say. It was his phone ringing that finally made him move. He quickly fished it out of his pocket, but not fast enough to avoid it disturbing Chloe.

Even as he was bringing the device up to his ear, she pulled down the blanket as she opened her eyes. She didn't wake up like most people did . . . slowly and somewhat confused. She woke up on edge and alert.

That was familiar. Too familiar.

"Hello?" Ro said into the phone, not breaking eye contact with Chloe.

"Leon Harris is pissed way the hell off," Rex began. The program he used to disguise his voice made it sound a bit computerized, but the emotion was still easy to hear. And his handler was *not* happy.

Ro winced and dropped his gaze from Chloe's. "Rex," he said by way of greeting.

His handler didn't give him a chance to say anything else. "I'm glad you managed to get his sister out of there, but have you seen the news?

He's got every fucking reporter at his house, and he'll be appearing on a live breaking-news segment in ten minutes."

"Does he know where she is?" Ro asked, not caring about anything else at the moment. He watched Chloe's eyes get wide at his question, and she quickly sat up, clutching the blanket to her as if it could protect her from her brother. And that enraged Ro.

"I have no idea. My contacts say he's currently investigating everyone who even spoke to his sister last night, trying to figure out if he can make a connection between her disappearance and the club. He's upset that she's been snatched, but his actions seem more angry than worried."

Ro hadn't heard Rex this agitated in a long time. "Not surprised. I haven't talked to Chloe about everything she's been through, but I have a feeling her brother made her life a living hell. Meat made sure there were no surveillance cameras at the location of acquisition," he told his handler. "Eventually, he might figure out who I am, but he'll have no proof that the Mountain Mercenaries have done anything."

"This isn't going away," Rex said. "And if he does eventually recognize you from your private session with Chloe, your house is the first place he'll come looking. That girlfriend of his has even *been* to your house. If they make the connection, you can't stay there. And attention on you means attention on the team, which isn't good. We're only able to do what we do because it's kept on the down-low. If a sex tape featuring one of my operatives is plastered all over the internet, and he's a suspect in a fucking kidnapping, that's not going to go well for the Mountain Mercenaries."

Ro leaned forward and grabbed the remote, clicking on the telly. He felt bad that Rex was upset, though ultimately, Chloe was the important one here. But if he had to quit the team in order for them to remain viable, he would.

As soon as the thought went through his mind, Ro stilled. Would he really quit the team because of a woman?

He looked over at Chloe. She was staring at him with big brown eyes. The bruise on the side of her forehead looked obscene on her pale skin. She looked worried, but he could see the fire in her eyes at the same time. The determination not to go back to being at the mercy of her brother.

At that moment, he realized that yes, he would. He would quit Mountain Mercenaries for her. She deserved a life without having to worry about anything other than annoying drivers, getting to work on time, what to make for dinner, and other normal, everyday inconveniences.

He wasn't in love with her, nor was she with him . . . but that didn't negate the fact that there was something about her that made him want to slay all her dragons. Ro had the sudden thought that if he was ever going to love anyone, let them in on all the shit he'd done and seen in his life, it could be her.

"The club was dark, and I did what I could to keep my face obscured the entire time. If I'm recognized, I'll make arrangements for us to stay somewhere else. Hey, the reporter's on. I'll call you back," he told Rex, then hung up without another word. Ro knew he'd pay for that later, but he wanted to hear what Harris was going to say. What he was up against.

Moving to the couch next to Chloe, Ro made sure to keep a couple of inches between them. He might want to haul her up against him and reassure her that she was safe, but he'd pushed her enough for one day. Ro also wanted to thank her for staying. For trusting him. But they had other things to worry about at the moment. Besides, it might be better to let it go. She'd decided to stay; he had to assume that meant she trusted him. At least a little. He could work with that.

"What's going on?" she asked quietly.

Ro found a station that featured a reporter standing outside of Leon Harris's house and stopped searching for the press conference. He turned to Chloe. "Looks like your brother isn't happy that you disappeared. He's using the press to help find you."

Chloe paled as she clenched her teeth, and Ro wanted to kick his own arse. He took a risk and put a hand on her blanket-covered knee. "He's not going to get to you."

She shook her head. "He's going to give it his best shot. You don't know him."

"I know arseholes just like him. And I'm telling you, love, between me and my friends, we're going to outsmart him and keep you safe."

"Maybe for now," she conceded. "But what about in a week? A month? A year? I can't stay hidden here in your house forever. He holds grudges. He's never going to forget. I need to get out of town, just like I planned. Maybe go to Mexico, or better yet, Timbuktu."

Ro frowned. She was right. In the short term, he could keep her hidden, but Harris lived in Colorado Springs. If Chloe wanted to stay, she would still be at his mercy. Every time she went to the grocery store, or a hairstylist, or even to whatever job she eventually got, she'd be looking over her shoulder to see if her brother was watching and waiting to grab her. The best option would be for her to move, maybe go into the witness-protection program.

The thought of never seeing her again didn't sit well with Ro at all.

Not responding to her comment, because he didn't have an answer for her, Ro turned back to the telly. A pretty blonde reporter smiled into the camera. Her hair blew in the slight breeze, and she looked like she was standing at a charity event rather than outside the house of a man who was worried about his missing sister.

"Thank you for joining us. As you probably know, Chloe Harris, sister to entrepreneur and philanthropist Leon Harris, has been missing for almost twelve hours. The police chief will speak in a moment and update us about what's being done to find Ms. Harris, but first, we'll hear from Mr. Harris himself."

Ro narrowed his eyes as Chloe's brother came out of the front door of his mansion and stood at the top of the steps with his girlfriend, Abbie. He looked impeccable, wearing a gray suit with a white shirt and gray tie. His hair was slicked back, and he looked as debonair and suave as ever . . . not like a grieving sibling. Abbie stood at his side wearing a low-cut white dress. Her hair was perfectly in place, and her makeup had been applied with a heavy hand. They held hands as Leon began to speak.

"My sister is missing. We were coming home from a night out last evening, and we were in a car accident. When we regained consciousness, Chloe was nowhere to be seen. Her purse was in the car, and there seemed to be signs of a struggle. We contacted every hospital in the area, and even some in Denver, to no avail. It's my belief that someone purposely caused us to wreck and kidnapped my sister. I can't believe this is happening, and I'm so scared for her. I have personally put up a fifty-thousand-dollar reward for information leading either to her safe return, or to whoever took her away from her loving family."

Leon looked into the camera then, and Ro felt Chloe shiver next to him. Without thought, he moved closer and put his arm around her shoulders. She seemed to unconsciously melt into his side, gripping his shirt tightly in her fist. Her attention was on the screen, but she was holding on to him as if he were the only thing between her and the monster in front of her . . . and it was likely he was.

"If you have my sister, please, let her come home. All I want is Chloe back. She's an important part of this family, and we miss her fiercely. She's vulnerable, and of late, hasn't been well. She needs her family and her medications. I'll do whatever it takes to get her back home where she belongs. Thank you."

Ro looked down at Chloe. "You need medication?" he asked. He hadn't even thought that she might have some sort of disease or medical issue.

She shook her head. "No. That's bullshit. He's lying."

He didn't doubt her for a second. She answered him automatically. He clicked off the broadcast, knowing Rex and the others would keep him updated on whatever information the police had. He was confident, for the moment, that it wasn't much. Black, Ball, and Meat had been careful at the scene, he was sure of it. Even with Chloe fighting them, there would have been negligible hard evidence.

"What next?" Chloe asked, looking up at him.

"Information," Ro said immediately.

"What?"

"Information. We need it. We can't fight Harris without it." Ro hadn't moved his arm after comforting her, and he realized he enjoyed having her close. "Your brother's press conference will force us to move quickly, and me and the team need as much information from you about your brother as possible."

She opened her mouth to speak, but he talked over her.

"But not today. For the rest of the day, you're going to do nothing but relax. If you want to take a nap, no problem. You've got to be hungry. I'll make us something here in a bit. I want you to get comfortable with me. And I didn't have time to say it earlier . . . but thank you."

"For what?" she asked.

"For staying. I know that wasn't an easy decision, and I'm going to do everything in my power to make sure you don't regret it."

He saw her swallow hard, but she didn't respond.

"I think Allye is going to come over again later . . . at least that's what she told me earlier. She also told me that you couldn't wear my clothes for the rest of your life, and she's right. I gave her some money, and she's going to get you some things to tide you over. When you're feeling up to it, I'll set you up with my laptop, and you can order some things online. We could go to the store and grab some necessities, but I think it's best for now if we lie low, especially since the entire city will be on the lookout for you. Hopefully you can find whatever lilac stuff you use online, and we'll have it overnighted. I'll help you wash your hair later too if you want, but you'll have to make do with my shampoo for now."

Ro stopped when he realized he was babbling. And he never babbled. "If that's okay with you," he finished lamely.

"The lilac stuff I use?" she asked when he'd stopped talking.

Shrugging a little self-consciously, Ro said, "Yeah. It was one of the first things I noticed about you. That you smelled like lilacs."

"Oh yeah, I remember you commenting on my lotion before. My mom gave me a bottle when I was sixteen. I've never used anything since."

"I like it," Ro told her, and watched in fascination as a slight blush spread over her cheeks. Wanting to ease her embarrassment, Ro went on. "So we'll take it easy today. I can tell your head hurts because you're squinting. I can put my team off for a while, but tomorrow we'll probably need to meet with the rest of the guys and start figuring all this out."

"I'm going out on a big limb with you," she told him. "I've been trying to get away from my brother for years. Waiting until I had enough money. Waiting for the perfect moment. I realized last night that my time had run out, and I'd planned to do whatever it took to get away on my own. But then you showed up and offered to help me. I admit, I assumed you'd decided it was impossible when you left without a word. Then I was upset when I thought I'd been taken from one prison to another, but . . . I'm trying to trust you. To believe that you don't work for the Mafia and you aren't just fucking with my head. But you should know, if you're double-crossing me, I have money stashed away that I will eventually get to, and I'll be out of here in a heartbeat. Got me?"

"I got you," Ro said, holding back a smile. "But I'm not fucking with you. I'm sorry you thought for a second that I offered you help, then went back on that promise."

"Fair enough. I'll do what I can to give you information about my brother in return for your help in getting out of this mess."

"Deal." Ro slowly lifted his arm from around her shoulders and stood. "But not right this second. I'm going to start something for us to eat. Do you have a preference?"

Chloe bit her lip, then took a deep breath and asked, "A hamburger?"

Ro loved that she looked him in the eye as she said that. Most people wouldn't think twice about the request, but he knew it probably wasn't easy to ask for what she wanted. Most of the women he'd known who had been abused and beaten hadn't dared look any of the team in the eye when they were being rescued or transported to a safe house. They'd been timid and scared out of their minds. But Chloe had found the strength to look him in the eye and was learning to be honest about her needs. She continually intrigued and impressed him.

"You got it, love. One American hamburger coming right up." He wanted to touch her. So much so that his hand actually twitched, but he held back. Instead, he nodded at her, then turned his back and headed into the kitchen. On the way, he scooped up his car keys, the phones, and the cash he'd left for her and placed them all in the decorative bowl in the middle of the table. He didn't want her using them, but he also didn't want her to feel trapped.

He never wanted her to feel trapped again.

He knew he had to deal with Rex. And get with Meat and the others and set up a meeting for the next day. They'd talked today but hadn't gotten very far, because all they had were questions and no answers. Hopefully Chloe would be able to fill in some of the blanks.

Chapter Nine

Chloe wiped her mouth and sat back in her chair with a sigh. The burger Ro had made was absolutely delicious. She was stuffed, but she'd forced herself to eat every bite. Abbie's latest thing was to not allow her any carbohydrates or sugar. All she'd been eating was salad and grilled chicken.

Abbie had regularly taken great delight in telling Chloe she was a fat cow, and that she needed to lose weight. She'd claimed she was helping her so she could attract a man and get married, but Chloe knew she and her brother were embarrassed by the way she looked.

Until Abbie had come into her brother's life, Chloe hadn't thought twice about her weight. Oh, she knew she wasn't exactly skinny, but she was happy with her body. Her mom had been built much as she was, and Chloe loved that every time she looked in the mirror, she saw her mother's features and hourglass figure.

She worked out at least three times a week and loved taking hikes in the mountains with her friends. Well, with the friends she had before she'd been fired from her job. The bottom line was that while she wasn't considered slender by society's standards, Chloe hadn't had any issues with her body.

Until she'd started working at BJ's and her brother constantly tried to set her up with his friends. He told her they'd be more interested if she lost weight. If she looked more like the dancers at the club. Then

Abbie started in on her. When that didn't work, they began withholding food. The cook would make delicious-looking pasta meals for Leon, but she'd be stuck with the same salads.

So asking for a big juicy hamburger had felt awesome. She didn't have to sneak around to eat what she wanted. And the way Ro looked at her, as if she was perfect exactly the way she was, went a long way toward making her feel like her old self once more.

"Good?" Ro asked.

"Delicious," Chloe told him, then yawned.

Chuckling, Ro stood, gathered their dishes, and made his way into the kitchen. "Why don't you go lie down for a bit?" he suggested.

"I don't know what's wrong with me. I usually only get like four or five hours of sleep a night. I had a lot more than that last night. I should be wide-awake."

Reentering the dining room, Ro said, "It's the stress. It really takes a toll on the body. Do you want to nap upstairs or down here on the couch?"

"Whichever will be less in your way," she responded.

"No," Ro replied. "Your days of having to watch what you say, what you do, and what you eat are over. You tell me what *you* want, and I'll adapt."

Chloe thought about his words. He was right. She might've told him what she wanted to eat for lunch, but she'd fallen right back into old habits when he'd asked where she wanted to sleep. She'd gotten so used to conceding to Leon and Abbie in order to make them less suspicious of her and what she might be planning. She automatically deferred to others when asked questions.

"The couch," she told him definitely.

"Good girl," Ro said.

His praise made her feel ridiculously good.

For the first time since she'd woken up, Chloe realized that she could be in trouble of another kind. She was beginning to really like

Ronan. He was the complete opposite of her brother, thank God. A little rough around the edges; his hands had grease under the nails, he wore boots and jeans, and he was anything but the put-together, suave gentleman her brother projected to the world. But he was ten times—no, a hundred times—the man her sibling was.

In less than twenty-four hours, he'd managed to restore her faith in humanity, something she never would've imagined. He'd helped rescue her from a life as a sex slave, tended her wound, given her a way out if she wanted it, fed her, and promised to try to keep her safe. It was more than she'd had in a very long time.

"Do you want me to get a blanket and pillow from upstairs?" he asked.

Chloe shook her head. "No, thanks. The blanket on the couch will do."

"Okay, but if you get cold, let me know. Allye should be here in a few hours. After you see what she's brought, if you need anything else, you can shop online or make a list, and I'll send Arrow or someone out to get whatever you need."

"Okay." Chloe was too overwhelmed to say anything else.

"Oh, but before you lie down . . . write down the name of the lilac lotion. I'll see if Allye can find that and bring it over with whatever else she's bringing."

"It's okay. I can use something else," she said shyly. "There's no need to go to the trouble."

Ro took a step toward her, and the intense look in his eyes almost made her take a step back, but at the last second she held her ground.

He reached out a hand and brushed her hair back from her face. She shivered at the feel of his rough fingers along her cheek.

"I'd like to say that I'm doing it for you . . . but I'd be lying."

Swallowing, Chloe stared up at Ro for a long moment. She liked his gentle touch. Finally, she nodded.

"Thank you," Ro said, then he turned and grabbed a pad of sticky notes and a pen and held them out to her. She quickly wrote down the name of the lotion she'd used her entire life and handed it back. Seeing the satisfaction in his eyes made her feel warm and gooey inside. She hadn't felt butterflies like she had in her stomach right this second for a really long time.

"Go on, love. Close your eyes for a while," Ro suggested. "I'll be outside in the garage if you need me. I'm expecting a drop-off in about an hour."

"A drop-off?"

"Someone's bringing their car by for me to look at it."

"Oh. Okay."

"Thank you for staying," Ro said softly, an intense look in his eyes.

"Thank you for letting me stay."

And with that, Ro backed away from her. He held her gaze until right before he went around a corner and disappeared.

She let out the breath she didn't know she was holding and whispered, "Do *not* fall for him, Chloe. Just don't."

Then she turned and headed for the couch she'd woken up on not too long ago. Trying to put the press conference and her brother's acting job out of her mind, Chloe lay down and closed her eyes. Within minutes, she was dead to the world.

Chloe was woken up later by a hand on her shoulder. Without pause, she leaped up from what she thought was her bed and lurched away from whoever it was who'd woken her.

"Easy, love," came a calm voice.

She blinked, and reality hit her all at once. Taking a deep breath, she tried to pretend she hadn't just massively overreacted. "Oh, hi, Ro."

"I'm not going to hurt you," he said. "You're safe here. I'll say it as many times as you need to hear it to believe it."

Chloe was surprised to realize she'd hurt his feelings. "I'm sorry," she said softly. "Whenever Leon or Abbie woke me up, it didn't go well for me."

Sighing, Ro ran a hand through his brown hair, mussing it even more than it had already been. "No, *I'm* sorry. I should know better than to touch you like that to wake you up. I did that to Arrow once, and he almost killed me."

"Seriously?"

"Yeah. He pulled a knife and missed my jugular by about an inch. Luckily, I have quick reflexes."

"Wow."

"Anyway, I'm sorry to wake you, but it's been three hours, and Gray and Allye are on their way over. I thought you might want to get cleaned up before they arrive."

"Three hours?" Chloe asked in disbelief. "Holy crap."

Ro chuckled, and the sound made her toes curl. "As I said, stress can be exhausting."

"I guess so."

"I came in to see if you wanted help with washing your hair. It's still too soon to get that cut wet. It'll take at least another night to let the adhesive do its thing."

"Oh, um . . . I guess. But I'm not sure how—"

"I've got a chair on the back deck that I think will work. It's not too chilly outside, so I thought we could do it out there. I can't promise that I'll not make a mess, so I figured it would be easier outside."

"Sounds logical." Chloe looked down at the oversize T-shirt she was wearing. "Should I keep this on?" .

She tried not to blush when Ro's gaze went to her chest. She was fairly well endowed, and she wasn't wearing a corset at the moment, like she had at the club, so her boobs weren't exactly perky. But she should've known Ro wouldn't make her feel uncomfortable.

"Yeah, I think that's fine. Allye would've been here by now if she hadn't insisted on stopping at the mall to find you some more stuff." Ro shrugged. "I'd originally asked her just to bring some of her own clothes for now, but she refused for some reason."

Chloe stared at Ro in confusion. "Her own clothes?"

"Yeah. She's a dancer, and Gray says she has drawers and drawers of leggings and tank tops and stuff. I don't know why she didn't just bring some of those things to tide you over until you could pick out your own clothes. You're almost the same height and all."

Chloe didn't know if Ro was being purposely obtuse or if he honestly thought she would fit into the slender woman's clothes. He didn't give her a chance to comment further.

"Anyway, she'll probably have something that'll work better than my T-shirt, but I figure you want to get this done, so we'll make do. Come on, let's do this."

Chloe followed behind Ro, trying not to notice how good his ass looked in his tight jeans as he led them out onto the porch at the back of the house. It overlooked a small clearing of grass, and more trees as far as the eye could see. She inhaled deeply, loving the smell of the pine and fresh, clean air.

She sat where he indicated and lay back.

"Scoot all the way up," Ro requested, and Chloe did so. Flipping her hair over the end of the chair, she rested the back of her neck on the bar at the top. Ro settled on a stool he'd obviously placed at the head of the reclining chair earlier.

"Close your eyes."

She did. Warm water from a bucket was slowly poured over her hair, and it felt heavenly.

The next ten minutes were the most amazing and life-changing moments she'd ever experienced. She'd never had someone do this kind of thing for her. Before moving in with Leon, she'd dated. She'd even showered with a serious boyfriend in the past, but he hadn't taken the time to wash her hair.

Feeling Ro's hands gently massage her scalp and rub the shampoo through her strands felt strange, but right at the same time. He didn't rush; he didn't dump too much water on her. It never got into her eyes, and she could tell he was being super careful around the wound on the side of her head.

"What was up with the violet contacts you had in when I first saw you?" Ro asked as he washed her hair.

"Abbie thought they made me look exotic." She shrugged. "But they hurt like hell, so I pretended to lose one of them. Not having to wear them was totally worth not getting to eat for a day and a half." She'd said the last without thinking, and it wasn't until she realized that Ro's fingers had stopped moving on her head that she opened her eyes and looked up at him.

He looked extremely pissed off. Like he was on the verge of losing his shit.

"It's okay, Ro," Chloe said quietly. "It wasn't that big of a deal. I'd rather they discipline me that way than hit me. Besides, it's not like I was gonna starve. I have plenty of fat stored up." She patted her thigh as she said it, wanting to make him smile.

But he didn't smile.

"It's not okay," he said. "I fucking hate that they dared to raise their hands to you. And you are perfect exactly the way you are. Anyone who says differently is an arsehole."

Chloe didn't know what to say to that. It was a hell of a compliment.

After a moment, Ro took a deep breath and concentrated on washing the soap out of her hair once again. A few minutes later, he said, "Okay, love, I think that'll do it."

Chloe opened her eyes, and before she had time to sit up on her own, he was there with a hand on her back, helping her. He'd also wrapped her hair up in a towel so it wouldn't drip down her back.

"Thank you," Chloe told him once she was sitting upright.

"You're welcome."

Chloe turned her head to look at Ro for the first time—and gaped at what she saw. He was soaked. From his chest to his knees, he was drenched. "Oh my God, I'm so sorry!" she exclaimed.

"For what?" he asked, his brows furrowed in confusion.

"For getting you so wet."

He grinned, and Chloe's heart about flipped over in her chest. The smile completely transformed his face. He was usually serious and intense, but the small upward tilt of his lips made him seem lighter, more approachable.

"It's not your fault, love. I overestimated my ability to wash your hair and stay dry. But it was worth it."

The way he said those last five words made Chloe blush for some reason. Once again, he stared her right in the eyes and didn't let his gaze stray. It reminded her of the night before, when she was practically naked on his lap, and he respected her enough to do his best not to embarrass her.

Licking her lips unconsciously, Chloe saw the first break in the iron control he always seemed to have around her. His gaze dropped to her lips, and she saw his nostrils flare as he inhaled. Just as quickly as he'd dropped his gaze from hers, it returned, but this time his pupils were a bit more dilated than before, and she could see some sort of emotion in his eyes.

The spell between them was broken when the watch on Ro's wrist vibrated. He broke eye contact to look down at it. "Allye and Gray are here," he announced. "Go ahead and go upstairs. I'll send Allye up, and you two can look through the clothes. Okay?"

Feeling off-kilter yet again, Chloe simply nodded. She didn't understand what was going on between them. They'd only known each other for a short time. She shouldn't be as attracted to Ro as she was. And it was more than his sexy accent—it was how he treated her. With respect. With care. As if she was truly important to him.

Maybe it was because she hadn't been treated like anything more than an employee, an unwanted one at that, for so long. Maybe it was because of her situation. But whatever it was, Chloe knew she had to tread carefully. The last thing she wanted was to fall in love with Ro. He was doing a job. That's it. He might be attracted to her, but it was a situational thing. That was all.

Chloe stood and silently cursed when she swayed and Ro took hold of her elbow to steady her. Goose bumps broke out where he gripped her, and she actually leaned toward him before catching herself.

"Thanks," she said softly without looking at him before turning and heading inside.

As Allye entered his house with several bags in her hands, Ro tried to get himself under control.

Washing Chloe's hair had been a mistake on his part, but he hadn't been able to resist. He wanted to touch her hair and see for himself if it was as silky as he remembered. It had been. The truth was, he hadn't even noticed the water dripping onto his lap when he was rinsing her hair because he'd been staring at her face.

Chloe's eyes had been closed, and she'd had a small smile on her lips. She'd looked serene and relaxed, something he hadn't seen from her since he'd met her. Then his eyes had strayed. He'd forced himself to avoid looking directly at her body as much as possible since they'd met. In the strip club, it had been a matter of respect. She'd been practically naked, but because she hadn't wanted to be there, it seemed too much like rape for him to take advantage of looking at what she wasn't freely offering.

The night before, when she was unconscious, he'd removed her clothes and put her into his, but again, he'd tried to keep his touch clinical, and did his best to preserve her modesty as much as he could.

But as Chloe lay in the lounge chair on his back deck, her head back, relaxed and happy, he couldn't stop himself from looking her over. She had the exact kind of body he loved. Lush and curvy. Why her brother thought she needed to lose weight was beyond him. Her breasts were large, and even wearing his extra-large T-shirt, they strained against the fabric. Her nipples had puckered because of the water he'd poured over her hair, and Ro'd had an immediate fantasy of running his wet, soapy hands down her chest and pinching those nipples, making them stand up even farther.

It was inappropriate as hell—and for the first time, his dick had gotten hard around her. She didn't help the situation when she moaned as his fingers massaged her scalp while he worked the shampoo into her hair.

There was no denying it. Ro wanted Chloe. She was beautiful, yes, but it was more than that. It was her strength. Her determination. Her trust. Those traits got to him more than beauty every time.

"You have it bad," Gray said, clapping his hand on Ro's shoulder.

Ro jumped. He'd forgotten his friend was even there, and that *never* happened to him.

"Whatever," he growled. "I'm just trying to figure out what the fuck is going on."

The smirk didn't leave Gray's face. "Riiiiiight. Just like I was only giving Allye a place to stay while we tried to catch that asshole Nightingale."

"On that note, I'm going upstairs," Allye said, grinning. "That okay?"

"Sure. She just headed up there. Don't scare her," Ro warned.

Allye rolled her eyes. "I won't. I learned my lesson the first time."

"You need help with those bags?" Gray asked.

Allye shook her head. "Nope. I got it. Thanks." She turned on a heel and headed for the stairs. Her arms were full of bags from several different stores. Ro hoped that she'd been able to find the lilac-scented lotion he'd asked her to buy. It was weird how freaking captivated he was by the way Chloe smelled, but he couldn't get it out of his mind.

Forcing himself to think about something other than Chloe naked and changing clothes or smoothing lotion all over her body, Ro turned and headed for the couch. He picked up the blanket Chloe had used and folded it, the faint scent of lilacs making him anxious to see her again.

Hating how obsessed he was getting, he asked harshly, "Has anyone talked to Rex lately?"

He knew Gray wanted to give him more shit, but he dropped the subject of his new houseguest and said, "Yeah. Meat did."

"He still pissed?"

"Yup. But Meat calmed him down enough for him to give us until tomorrow to contact him with a plan."

"A plan," Ro mused. "Do we *have* a plan?"

Gray winced. "I was hoping you'd have some idea of where to go next."

"I spent three hours this afternoon thinking about the entire situation—"

"Out in the garage?" Gray asked.

Ro nodded. "You know I think best when I'm working on an engine. As I was saying, I thought about this all afternoon, and we're missing something. Something big. There has to be a reason Leon hates his sister as much as he does. It's just not natural. Most men go out of their way to protect their sisters. Obviously, not all siblings get along, but why the intense hatred Leon has for Chloe?"

"Hmmm," Gray replied. "We'll have to figure it out tomorrow when Chloe tells us what she can."

"I hate that we have to put her through this," Ro said. "The last thing she needs is to relive her time with that arsehole."

"I know, but if we don't figure it out, she'll always be vulnerable," Gray returned. "Not to mention the second she steps foot outside this house, she's gonna be recognized, and anyone she's with is going to be hauled downtown and have to answer questions. Harris has everyone convinced his sister was kidnapped. We've got to deal with that too. That's Rex's main concern at the moment."

Ro ran a hand through his hair in agitation. His pants and shirt were still wet, but he didn't want to disturb the women upstairs in his room to get a change of clothing. "I know. She can't go home, but somehow we need to make it clear that she's all right and not in danger."

"You look like you could use a drink," Gray told him.

"More like an entire bottle," Ro returned.

Gray clapped him on the back, and they headed for the kitchen.

Chloe stared at all the clothes on the bed. Allye had arrived with a dozen bags in hand and told her she'd picked up a "few things" to tide her over.

"A few things?" Chloe asked in disbelief.

Allye laughed. "Ro said money was no object, and he wanted you to have enough things so you could have a choice of what to wear and not have to do laundry every night. I had to guess at your sizes, but I got some stuff with elastic waists just in case I was wrong in my assumptions." Then the other woman began dumping the bags and showing off what she'd bought.

A shy smile formed as Allye's words sank in. The thought that Ro wasn't thinking about money, only her comfort, made Chloe feel good. Really good.

Allye smiled back as she said, "Ro doesn't have to let you stay here, Chloe."

"What do you mean?"

"Rex has a ton of contacts. And I mean a *ton*. This is what the Mountain Mercenaries do. They help get women out of bad situations. Ro could've asked Rex to set you up with one of the underground resources he has. You know, a safe house? You'd be just as safe there as you are here. But for some reason, Ro refused to even consider it. I know for a fact Gray suggested it. But you're still here. He gave me his own money to get you stuff to wear. And he insisted that I find this for you." Allye pulled out a bottle from a small bag she'd been holding.

Chloe recognized the brand of lotion she used.

"I'm going to say this only once, then I'll never bring it up again . . . but I feel like I kind of have to."

Chloe tensed.

"Don't hurt him," Allye said. "These guys . . . they're total badasses. Professional soldiers. They can kick ass like you'd never believe. They go into situations no one else would dare. They take chances, and they'll do whatever it takes to rescue women. I don't know the other guys all *that* well yet, but I know Gray, and I have a feeling that deep down, they're all scarred in one way or another. They're all committed to saving women and children from the evils in the world, and there must be a deeper reason behind that than just wanting to do the right thing. And if Ro is anything like Gray, once he's committed, he's *committed*. He'll move heaven and earth to make sure you're happy, content, and safe. That's how Gray is with me. I know without a doubt that Gray will never cheat on me, and he goes to great lengths to make sure I'm satisfied . . . in *every* way, if you know what I mean."

Chloe stared at Allye with wide eyes as she continued.

"Ro strikes me as the same kind of man. I'm still getting to know the guys on the team, but I feel they wouldn't be as close as they are if they didn't have the same values and beliefs. Ro acts like the standoffish

Brit more often than not, but he feels as deeply as anyone I've ever met. He likes you, Chloe. I was surprised when he actually left you here alone. He thought you'd bolt. Hell, *I* thought you'd leave. But you didn't. And that means something to Ro.

"All I'm saying is that if you're using his help to get away from your brother, good, I don't blame you . . . but don't lead him on. Ask if you can go into witness protection. Or into the underground program the Mountain Mercenaries have set up. Don't stay here and make him think there's something between you if you don't feel that way."

It was a long speech from the other woman, and Chloe felt the butterflies in her stomach again. She hadn't thought much about how Ro was feeling because she was so uncertain herself and felt so out of control. But the idea of Ro keeping her around for a personal reason was appealing. More than appealing. She thought about how he'd washed her hair, how his hands had felt on her scalp. A man who was simply rescuing yet another woman from a bad situation wouldn't do that, would he?

Allye cleared her throat, and Chloe realized she was waiting for her to say something. "I won't lead him on," Chloe said quickly. She hadn't thought she'd want a boyfriend for a very long time after living under her brother's controlling thumb, but Ro was nothing like Leon. He was bossy and tended to do things without asking her, but Chloe somehow knew if she objected or pushed back, Ro would listen to her and be flexible.

"Cool," Allye said with a relieved sigh. "Now, shall we figure out which of this stuff you like and want to keep?"

Chloe smiled tentatively at the other woman. "Yeah. Thanks."

"You're welcome. I have a feeling we're going to be good friends," Allye said, handing the bottle of lotion to Chloe and turning back to the bed.

Watching her dig through the clothes and start to put them in some sort of order, Chloe gripped the plastic bottle tightly. Allye would never know how much her words meant. It had been a long time since Chloe'd had a friend. A true friend.

"What's taking them so long?" Ro grumbled to Gray later. It had been at least forty-five minutes since Allye had disappeared up the stairs. "How long could it take them to look through clothes, anyway?"

Gray chuckled. "Oh, you have no idea, my friend," he said. "Take my advice: get used to it. And when you have to be somewhere, be sure to tell Chloe the appointment is thirty minutes before the actual time, so you won't be late."

"Seriously?" Ro asked.

"Seriously."

"But you and Allye are never late."

Gray smirked. "Exactly."

Ro shook his head. Then he realized what Gray was insinuating. He echoed Chloe's words from earlier. "She can't stay here forever."

"Why not?" Gray retorted.

"Well, because," Ro said.

"That's no answer," Gray said. "Look, I get it. You're feeling tangled up, and it's hard to reconcile your feelings. I've been there, man. Seriously, I felt the same way with Allye. I let her stay with me because I told myself it was for her own protection. And while it was, there was a fuck of a lot more to it than that. The thought of her leaving was abhorrent. I wanted to be the one to make sure that asshat didn't get his hands on her. But you need to figure out what you want before it's too late. I fucked up and almost lost Allye as a result. Learn from my mistakes, Ro."

"But . . . I . . . it's only been one day. We're not . . . Fuck," Ro swore, frustrated that he couldn't put what he was feeling into words.

Gray put a hand on his friend's shoulder. "One day. One week. Ten fucking years. When you know, you know. I'm not saying you need to propose right here and now. But don't dismiss your feelings for her. The way we live, the things we've done, we deserve to be rewarded. And that's how I choose to look at Allye. She's my reward. We clicked from the very first time we met. The more I got to know her, the more I liked her. I hated leaving her in San Francisco, and when I got my second chance, I took it. Fuck what society says is an acceptable time to date, to fall in love. If it's there, it's there. And for what it's worth . . . it's there, friend. Am I wrong?"

Ro thought about Gray's words for a moment. He was right. He'd never felt this way toward any other woman he'd met over the years, including those he'd rescued. This was something special, and he wanted to see where it might go. Maybe nowhere, but he'd be daft not to pursue it.

"You're not wrong," he told Gray.

Gray nodded. "Of course I'm not."

Both their heads turned at the sound of footsteps on the stairs. Ro stared in anticipation as Allye appeared, then finally Chloe behind her.

He couldn't take his eyes from her. It didn't make any sense how excited he was to see her when he'd just been in her presence not too long ago, but from the moment she'd disappeared up the stairs, he'd looked forward to seeing her again.

Ro had loved seeing her in his sweats and T-shirt; something about her wearing things that had been next to his own body was a turn-on. But seeing her in clothes that fit her was even better. She had on a pair of navy-blue leggings that clung to every curve of her legs. Her calves looked impossibly tiny, but her thighs were thick and curvy. The thought of having those legs wrapped around his hips as he thrust between them was almost more than he could take.

Forcing himself to look at the rest of her, he inhaled sharply at the shirt she was wearing. It covered much more than the corset she'd worn at the club, but that was what made it so much sexier. The white shirt was sheer, and she had some sort of camisole under it. He could see the lace through the shirt. She was well endowed, and his T-shirt had somewhat hidden the curves of her breasts, but the camisole was formfitting and showcased her assets in a way that was sexy even as it was innocent.

Allye went straight to Gray, and he put an arm around her shoulders. Chloe stood nervously at the bottom of the stairs, her hands wringing together in front of her.

Wanting to reassure her, Ro moved to stand in front of her. "You look great," he said softly.

Chloe's eyes went to the floor. Then he saw her take a deep breath and look back up at him. "Thanks. Allye wouldn't tell me how much everything cost so I could pay you back."

Ro shook his head. "You don't owe me a penny," he said easily.

"But—"

"No buts," he interrupted. Then, not able to help himself, he reached for one of her hands and brought it up toward his face. He brushed his lips against the back of it, then turned it over and smelled her inner wrist. Smiling, he looked back into her eyes. "I see you got your lotion," he said with satisfaction.

Chloe nodded. "Thank you."

"You're welcome."

"So . . . what's the plan for tomorrow?" Gray asked.

Reluctant to let go, Ro forced himself to drop Chloe's wrist. He wanted to haul her into his arms and bury his nose into the space between her shoulder and neck but refrained.

"That depends on Chloe," he said.

"Me?" she asked.

Ro nodded. "It seems to me that you've had way too many people making decisions for you and not enough opportunity to make your own, at least publicly. I told you that we needed to talk. That we need to know all about your brother and what you know of his businesses and what his motivation might be, but in return, you should also be informed of everything *we* know. Between all of us, we might be able to connect some dots."

"Okay. And?" Chloe asked.

"I had thought to give you some more time."

"Time for what?"

"To trust me. To trust that I wasn't just pumping you for information to do something to make things worse for you."

Chloe bit her lip, and Ro had a feeling she'd thought that exact thing at some point. He pushed through the disappointment. "But with Harris going to the cops and the media and saying you were kidnapped, our options are limited, and we're going to have to do something sooner rather than later."

"I'm okay with meeting with your team," Chloe said softly. "As long as you're there," she added hastily.

Ro couldn't stop himself from reaching out and taking her hand in his once more. "Why wouldn't I be there?"

She shrugged. "I don't know. I mean . . . I'm just nervous to meet those guys who stole me yesterday."

"Kidnapped, you mean," Allye said with a trace of humor.

"Hush, Allye," Gray scolded.

"Why? Might as well say it like it is," she retorted.

Chloe's lips quirked up.

Ro sighed. "I'm never going to hear the end of that, am I?"

"That you had to kidnap Chloe to get her away from her brother? Nope," Allye confirmed. "I mean, you guys are the ones who usually *save* women who've been snatched. For you to have resorted to kidnapping a chick yourself is really kinda hilarious."

Gray turned serious eyes to Chloe. "Black, Ball, and Meat would never hurt you."

She nodded, but Ro could still see the uncertainty in her expression.

"They remind me of some of my brother's bodyguards," Chloe admitted. "There was one time—before I knew I wasn't free to go where I wanted, when I wanted—that I went to have lunch with some friends. I hadn't been at the restaurant for twenty minutes when two came in and hauled me out of there. It was embarrassing and humiliating. They didn't hurt me when we were around others, but as soon as they got me in the car, the one who wasn't driving held my arm so tightly, I had a hand-shaped bruise on my arm for a week. When I complained to Leon, he blew me off and said the guy probably just hadn't realized his own strength, and if I weren't such a wuss and if I hadn't left without telling him where I was going, it wouldn't have happened."

"Listen to me," Ro said sternly. "My friends and I are *not* like them. We would sooner kick our own arses than hurt you. And him making you think that was your fault is rubbish. *Nothing* that happened was your fault." His voice gentled. "If you're not comfortable meeting with the team, you can stay here, and we'll figure something else out."

"Maybe she could call in, or use Skype," Allye said. "I could stay here with her while you guys meet."

"Or we could all come here," Gray said. "Instead of meeting at The Pit."

"I don't want to leave her alone," Ro said, not breaking eye contact with Chloe. "And not because I don't trust you," he told her. "Now that Harris has gone public with your disappearance, I'm not willing to gamble that he hasn't figured out who I am yet. Or where I live."

"Is me being here putting you in danger?" Chloe asked suddenly.

"No. And nothing that happens from here on out is your fault either," Ro said succinctly. "Nothing. Got it?"

When she didn't agree, Ro sighed. He turned to Gray. "I'll call you later and let you know what we decide."

Gray nodded. "Come on, Allye. Let's go."

Allye nodded but stepped over to where Ro and Chloe were standing. Without warning, she put her arms around Chloe and hugged her hard.

Ro saw Chloe tense, but then relax and return the hug. Allye pulled back and looked at Ro. "Take care of her," she ordered bossily. "And she needs to do a load of laundry. No one wants to wear underwear straight from the store."

Ro turned to stare at Chloe. Did that mean she wasn't wearing anything under her clothes? Without thought, his eyes dropped to her chest, and he swore he could see her nipples under her shirt, now that he knew she wasn't wearing a bra. Just as quickly, he imagined dropping to his knees in front of her, pulling her leggings down, and burying his head between her thighs.

Swallowing hard, he turned from the temptation that was Chloe and nodded at Allye. "Of course."

"Ro, I'll talk to you later. And Chloe, you've got nothing to fear from the rest of our team. We'll do whatever it takes to protect you. Believe that," Gray said, before he turned and left the house with Allye.

And before he could blink, Ro was alone with Chloe. He couldn't get the thought of her being bare under her clothes out of his mind. It was silly, really. He'd removed her corset the night before, so he knew she hadn't worn anything under his T-shirt, but he'd left the minuscule thong in place when he'd stripped her.

It wasn't as if that small piece of cotton did much to shield her from view, but somehow, knowing she was naked under her new clothes made him struggle to control himself.

They stood there, staring awkwardly at anything but each other, before Ro chuckled and broke the silence. "Come on, I'll show you where the washer and dryer are and leave you to it."

"Thanks," she said quietly.

Thirty minutes later, Ro had forced himself to think of anything but underwear, camisoles, and boobs. He and Chloe were sitting in his living room.

"Want to play a game?" he asked after she'd told him she wasn't interested in watching the telly.

"What kind of game?" she asked suspiciously.

"War."

"What?"

"War. You know, the card game?"

Her brows furrowed, but eventually she agreed.

Ro got up from the couch and grabbed a deck of cards. He came back over to where she was sitting and pulled the coffee table away from the couch. He sat down across from her, on the other side of the table on the floor, and shuffled the cards.

Grinning, she slid to the floor and sat with her legs crossed, the table between them, her back against the couch.

"Rules are, the highest card wins. If there's a tie, we put three cards facedown and one faceup. Again, highest card wins."

"Are aces high or low?" she asked.

Ro smiled at her. "High." It wasn't so much that he wanted to play a game, but he did want her to stop thinking so hard about everything that had happened to her recently. After she relaxed, he'd feel her out and see what she really thought about the meeting with the team. He wasn't going to leave her home by herself—not because he didn't trust her not to run, but because he didn't trust that bloody tosser, Harris. Ro would never forgive himself if her brother found out where she was hiding and dragged her back to BJ's, or worse, got rid of her altogether.

He patiently dealt the cards and laid down the first one to get the game going.

Her eight beat his two. And the game was on.

Chapter Ten

Chloe had never thought she'd be sitting on the floor playing War with someone like Ro. He wasn't the kind of man who she'd thought would have the patience to sit for hours and play the monotonous and somewhat boring game. But somehow it wasn't boring playing with Ro.

She'd laughed more than she had in the last three years. Ro was a poor loser, and when he got down to having only seven cards, he'd scowled at them, and at her, and pouted. But then they'd had a tie, and he'd won an ace back from her, and he'd quickly won back most of the cards he'd recently lost.

In the past, if someone had scowled at her like Ro had, she would've been more than a little leery, but instead she'd mocked and teased him for being a poor loser. And remarkably, he'd taken her teasing without complaint, and then crowed when he began winning once more.

Chloe knew what he was doing, and she didn't mind. She knew he was trying to relax her, to make her stop thinking so much about her brother and what had happened. She actually appreciated his efforts. Lord knew she'd just about reached the end of her rope. She'd gone from being completely sure she'd landed in another awful situation that morning to being entirely relaxed by the time the sun had set.

Some might say she wasn't being smart, but Chloe knew better. Ro wasn't like her brother or his friends. She'd been around him long enough to be able to tell the difference. She might've been freaked out that morning, but she felt as if she'd had good reason. Leaving her alone, and giving her the tools to take off if she wanted to, had done exactly what Ro had hoped it would. It had made her trust him.

Chloe laughed when he lost another tiebreaker, and she won back one of the two aces he had in his pile.

"Bloody hell," he swore under his breath as she collected the cards gleefully.

She heard the dryer buzz in the background and blushed anew. She really needed to stop being embarrassed about doing laundry, but it was obvious that Ro hadn't thought about the fact she wasn't wearing anything under her new clothes until Ally had mentioned using the washer and dryer. She'd seen his eyes drop to her chest and hips before he'd looked away.

Instead of feeling embarrassed or creeped out by him looking at her, it had aroused her. Which shocked the shit out of Chloe. How had she gone from feeling totally disassociated from her body and not wanting any man near her, to wanting Ro to touch her? All over?

Standing, Chloe said, "I'll go and get that." She motioned to the laundry room with her head.

"Are you seriously going to take your cards with you?" Ro asked.

She mock-glared down at him. "Uh, yeah. The last time I got up, you stole an ace from my stack," she scolded.

"I did no such thing," Ro said with wide, innocent eyes.

Chloe's lips twitched. He was the worst liar. At least, he was *pretending* to be the worst liar. "Whatever," she told him as she headed for the dryer.

"Want something to eat?" Ro called out behind her.

Chloe turned. It was late. They'd stopped and had sandwiches for dinner, but she was hungry again. It was dark outside, and she was used to staying up way past midnight at the strip club. She wasn't ready to go to bed yet; besides, she was winning the game again. "Do you have any junk food?" she asked a little shyly. Yes, she knew she shouldn't eat snack foods, but it had been so long since she'd indulged.

"I think I can rustle something up," Ro said dryly. "Go on. Get your clothes. But don't dally. I've got a lucky streak coming. I can feel it."

Chloe couldn't help but laugh, as she expected he wanted her to.

As she folded the warm, dry undergarments and other miscellaneous items of clothes Allye had bought for her, tears suddenly pricked her eyes. Standing in front of the machine, holding a pair of lacy black panties, Chloe tried to remember the last time she'd felt so normal. And failed.

She hadn't been allowed to do her own laundry at Leon's house. They had staff for that. She wasn't allowed to eat what she wanted. No one had asked her if she was hungry—they simply cooked what Leon or Abbie told them to and had it ready on a set schedule. The clothes she was expected to wear were chosen each morning by Abbie. She'd done her best to rebel, but she'd had to be sneaky. Anything more could mean another beating. While she'd tried not to be intimidated by her brother, she'd still done what he wanted most of the time to keep up the pretense that he completely controlled her.

It felt so good to no longer have to hide. To be able to do what she wanted, when she wanted. To eat what she wanted. To do her own laundry. She knew most people wouldn't understand her joy over such simple pleasures, but she'd been playing a role for so long, it felt amazing to be able to let down her guard and just be herself.

Looking at the watch Allye had gotten her, Chloe realized that she and Ro had been playing the same game of War for five hours. *Five* hours. And she'd never been happier.

"Are you all right?"

Ro's husky question surprised her, and Chloe dropped the pair of panties she'd been holding and immediately threw herself to the side, putting her back against the wall, prepared to protect herself.

"Bloody hell," Ro swore, taking a step away from her, holding his hands up, showing her he was unarmed. "I'm sorry, love. *Again.* I know better than to surprise you."

Chloe shook her head and put a hand on her chest, right over her racing heart. "No, I'm sorry. I shouldn't be so jumpy."

"Rubbish," he said immediately. "You have every right to be wary. I should've made more noise walking back here. I'll work on that. You need any help?"

Chloe dropped her hand and shook her head. "I'm almost done."

Ro stepped toward her and picked up the pair of panties she'd dropped. He stared at them for a long moment before holding them up so he could get a better look. She saw him swallow hard, then he met her gaze.

The heat she saw there almost singed her. She couldn't have moved if her life had depended on it. Licking her lips, she didn't know what to say.

"For the record, these are way sexier than the thong you were wearing last night," Ro said calmly. His eyes went from her face to her chest, and she saw his lips part erotically. "As is that," he said, dipping his head to indicate her chest. Then he cleared his throat, carefully folded the panties in his hand, and laid them on top of the dryer. "Take your time. I'll be waiting to kick your butt in War when you're done." Then he turned and left the small laundry room.

Chloe stood stock-still for the longest time. Then she slowly looked down, inhaling when she saw herself.

She'd been unsure about wearing the sheer white top with the lacy camisole underneath, but Allye had reassured her that she was perfectly decent, and that it looked cute with the navy-blue leggings. But seeing herself now, Chloe realized that while she might've been perfectly decent before, having been turned on by Ro's presence, her nipples had gotten hard.

And they were doing their damnedest to poke through both the cotton material of the camisole and the silky blouse.

She got Ro's point, loud and clear, and agreed. She'd seen naked men before, of course she had, but somehow seeing the passionate look in Ro's eyes was more of a turn-on than naked flesh. And right before he'd turned to leave the laundry room, she'd seen the erection in his pants.

He was attracted to her. The *real* her. And that felt incredible.

Ro's erection was a tease that was more exciting than if he'd dropped his pants. They were definitely on the same page as far as what was erotic and sexy, that was for sure.

The question was, where did they go from there?

He'd reassured her that when she went back into the other room, they'd pick up their game of cards where they'd left off, but would things be awkward between them? Would he expect more from her than she was willing to give him?

And just like that, her nervousness and distrustfulness came back full force. What was she doing? She was alone in Ro's house and had nowhere to go. He could do anything he wanted with her, and she wouldn't be able to stop him. He was bigger and stronger.

It took her another ten minutes of slowly folding the rest of her stuff to stop herself from freaking out. As she left the laundry room with a basket of freshly washed and folded clothes, she was much more cautious than she'd been when she'd entered.

Placing the basket on the floor next to the stairs, she entered the living room—and stared.

Ro was sitting back in the same spot he'd been in for the last few hours. The coffee table was overflowing with bowls of snacks: pretzels, chocolate candy, popcorn, tortilla chips, melted cheese, salsa, nuts— and there were even several meat sticks still in their wrappers.

Chloe came forward cautiously. "What the heck?" she asked as she got closer and saw how much food Ro had brought to their card-playing area.

"You said you wanted snacks," Ro said, shrugging. "So I got you snacks."

Chloe took her spot and simply stared. "Ro, there's enough food here for an army," she protested. But her mouth watered at all the junk food. It had been so long since she'd had any of this stuff. And she wanted it. Bad.

"Yeah, well, we're playing War. We need the fuel," he countered. "I believe it's your turn," he said, nodding toward the cards she clutched in her hand.

Chloe relaxed. She tried to tell herself that she'd misunderstood the look in Ro's eyes, but she knew she was lying to herself. There was some serious chemistry between them, but he was being as gentlemanly as he could be with her, and she appreciated it.

But a small part of her wondered how he'd react if she made the first move. What would he do if she walked over to him and lowered herself onto his lap, like she had last night? Would he shove her away, would he keep his eyes on her face as he had before, or would he grip her hips tightly and grind her down on his lap?

Remembering the bulge behind his zipper as he'd stood in the laundry room, looking at her erect nipples, she wondered how it would feel between her legs.

"Snap out of it, Chloe," Ro ordered. "It's your turn."

She would've been offended if she hadn't glanced up right then and caught him staring at her boobs.

Smiling to herself, Chloe decided right then and there to just go with the flow. Reaching out and grabbing a handful of chocolate, she used her other hand to turn over a card. The game was back on. Everything else would happen as it happened.

Ro struggled to keep his mind out of the gutter and on the game. But it was hard. *He* was hard. He'd been that way since he'd seen the sexy-as-fuck panties Chloe had dropped when he'd scared her.

Then he'd looked at her and seen her nipples poking through the material of her camisole and shirt. He'd wanted to push her up against the wall, lift her so his head was even with those beauties, and take them into his mouth. Feel her writhe against him as he sucked and bit her tits.

Even watching the pleasure she took in eating the snacks he'd set out was turning him on.

They'd been playing for another thirty minutes when he carefully brought up the subject of the next day. He needed to figure out what to do, and now that she was relaxed once more, it was time.

"I'd like you to come with me tomorrow," he said as he placed a card on the table. "The Pit is a local pool hall that me and my friends use as our home base, so to speak. You'll be safe there."

Chloe put one of her cards down and smiled as she won, jack over ten. "Okay," she said as she placed another card faceup, reached for a tortilla chip, and dipped it into the *queso*.

"Okay?" he asked as he laid down another card. He won with his three over her two.

"Yeah. Okay."

"Chloe," he said patiently, "you don't have to."

She looked up then. "Yes, I do. You don't want me here alone in case Leon comes, trying to find me. I don't *want* him to find me. So I need to go where you go. And if you're going to meet with your team, I am too. I need to tell them what I know about my brother."

Ro swallowed hard. He was surprised at how much her trust meant to him. "As Allye said, the two of us could stay here and call in to the other guys. Or we could have all of them meet here."

She stared at him, her eyes full of understanding about the situation. She was smart, very smart, and even that turned Ro on. "The best thing would be for you and your friends to continue doing what you always do. And if that means going to the bar or whatever you want to call it where you usually meet, then that's what you should do. The last thing you need is my brother getting suspicious."

"You're amazing," Ro said softly.

She shrugged. "I'm desperate," she countered just as quietly. "And I'm out of guesses, Ro. I don't know *where* the brother I used to know went. I've thought about it over and over and over again, until it makes my head hurt. I don't know why he changed into the awful person he is today. Why he hates me so much. Ever since my dad died, he's gotten worse and worse. I want to know why, and I want to be free of him once and for all. I'll do whatever it takes to make that happen. I want to meet with your friends. I want to tell you everything I know because, like you said, maybe it'll help you guys connect the dots with what *you* know. If I don't pull up my big-girl panties and do this, it'll just make things worse in the long run."

Without thought, Ro got up on his knees and leaned across the table. Chloe had a chip in one hand and a card in the other. He put his hand behind her neck and pulled her closer. She rose to her knees, mimicking him, and gasped in surprise, but he didn't see any fear in her eyes.

"We're going to figure this out. Together," he said softly.

She nodded.

"So you'll come with me to The Pit tomorrow?"

She nodded again.

"And you won't be afraid of Black, Ball, and Meat?"

"You'll be there?" she asked.

"Of course."

"Then I won't be afraid of your friends," she said matter-of-factly.

"Bloody hell," Ro whispered. "I'm sorry," he told her.

"For what?"

"For this."

Then he kissed her. It wasn't a short peck on the lips either. He took her mouth as if he were a man starving and she were a feast. Ro ran his tongue over her lips and growled in contentment when she immediately opened for him. When her tongue came out to shyly meet his, he pushed it back into her mouth and took control of the kiss. The hand behind her neck tightened, and he held her still as he took what he'd dreamed about since he'd first seen her in his driveway.

Throughout it all, Chloe didn't protest. She didn't try to pull away and, in fact, opened her mouth wider and tilted her head, giving him access to take what he wanted.

Reluctantly, Ro eventually pulled back, scared of what she would say, what she would do.

Watching her carefully, Ro was relieved when she licked her lips sensually, but didn't berate him or jerk out of his hold.

He held on to her nape for a beat longer, then forced himself to let go and sit back. She stayed hovered over the coffee table for a second before sinking back to the floor herself. Then she smiled. "Well, then," she said slowly. She brought the chip in her hand to her mouth and placed the card faceup on the table. "Your turn."

Ro returned her smile, adjusted his cock in his pants so it wasn't pressing on his zipper, and flipped over a card from his pile. He wasn't sure where they'd go from here, but for now, he was content to sit with her, play cards, and watch her eat whatever her heart desired. It was a start.

Chapter Eleven

Chloe was nervous, but she did her best to keep that fact from Ro. She didn't think she'd fooled him that morning, but he was being nice and not mentioning it.

She was nervous, but not scared.

And the difference was huge. For the last few years, she'd been angry, but frequently scared. Scared to be around Leon and Abbie. Scared when he left one of his bodyguards to watch over her. Scared her brother would find out she was siphoning funds. Scared he'd find out she was plotting to disappear. Scared the Mafia would show up one day and drag her off to torture her. Scared when she was working at the club.

But Ro didn't scare her. He merely made her nervous. Probably because she felt something for him . . . in a way she hadn't felt in a very long time. Last night had been eye-opening for her. Seeing his gaze on her and the desire in his eyes had made her feel pretty and feminine. Not like an object to be had or controlled, which was how she'd felt around the men Leon had set her up with.

And that kiss.

Chloe wanted to fan herself just remembering it.

The hand at her nape had felt like a brand, but instead of causing panic, it had made her want to lean in closer. He'd kissed her like she'd never been kissed before. He was in control, which wasn't surprising, but he was gentle about it. One of the last men she'd gone out with at Leon's insistence had kissed her at the end of the night, but his kiss had been way different. His had been about control and *force*.

Chloe knew if she'd protested, tried to pull back, or otherwise given him the smallest sense that she didn't want him to kiss her, Ro would have let go.

But she hadn't wanted him to let her go. The way he'd dominated her had been hot. Because he'd been concentrating on *her* pleasure, not his own. How she knew that, Chloe had no idea, but she did. Ever since, all she could think about was how it would feel for him to kiss her all over. To touch her with his hands as he took her mouth.

They'd played the stupid card game well into the night. Around twelve thirty, he'd finally called it quits. She'd been winning, and he said he'd put their cards aside so they could take it up again at a later time.

He'd told her to go on upstairs and get to sleep, as they would most likely be headed out early the next morning. She hadn't thought about the fact she was sleeping in his room until she was snuggled under the covers in the new pajama set Allye had bought her.

His earthy, masculine scent permeated everything. The pillow smelled like him. The sheets smelled like him. Chloe had clutched a pillow to her chest and turned on her side, inhaling his comforting scent.

Then she'd sat up. She couldn't take his bed. He had to have a guest room in the house. It was big. If nothing else, she could sleep on the couch downstairs as she'd done that afternoon as she'd napped.

She'd gone downstairs to tell Ro that under no circumstances was she going to take his bed, but he'd squashed all her arguments with one sentence.

If I can't be by your side, I can protect you better if I'm down here.

He'd proceeded to tell her all about the alarms he had on the windows, so no one could sneak into any room without setting them off. About the alarms he had on his driveway, so no one could drive down it without him knowing. And even about the perimeter alarms he had set up around the house itself, so no one could sneak around his property on foot.

But it all faded in light of his first words: he could protect her better if he was downstairs and she was in his bed.

She hadn't known what to say. How did she tell a man who protected and saved women for a living that no one in a very, very long time had cared enough about her to keep her safe?

This morning, she'd woken and sat up, only to find Ro standing in the doorway. He was leaning against the doorjamb, arms crossed, muscles bulging in the black T-shirt he was wearing, jeans outlining his thick legs and impressive crotch, his feet bare, watching her.

"Uh, good morning," she'd said quietly. "Am I late?"

He'd shaken his head. "No, love. You're perfect."

They'd stared at each other for a heartbeat before she'd asked, "Is everything all right?"

He'd pushed off the jamb and stood straight. He'd slowly walked toward her until he was standing by the side of the mattress. Then he'd leaned down and kissed the top of her head. He'd stayed there for a heartbeat before audibly inhaling.

"Ro?"

"I love lilacs. At least on you," he'd said, then stood straight. "I've got breakfast downstairs when you're ready. If you can manage one more day of not getting that wound wet, it would be best. Tomorrow, I think it'll be set enough for you to shower normally. If you need anything, let me know."

And with that, he'd nodded at her and left her alone in his room.

He'd made a big breakfast, complete with eggs, bacon, biscuits, and fresh fruit, and she'd eaten a bit of everything. He'd called Black, and they'd made arrangements to meet at the bar in an hour. Black had apparently volunteered to call the others and let them know.

And now here she was.

They were sitting in his McLaren outside the run-down-looking building called The Pit.

"You okay?" Ro asked.

Chloe nodded.

He put his hand on her knee. "It's going to be fine," he said.

"Are you sure?" she couldn't help but ask. "You don't know Leon. He isn't going to just go away. It's why I planned to get as far away from him as possible."

"I never thought he was," Ro returned.

"Then what are we going to do?" she asked.

"We're going to go inside. I'll introduce you to my friends, and we'll talk. We'll come up with a plan. If it doesn't work, we'll go with plan B. If that doesn't work, we'll go with plan C. We'll do whatever we can to make sure you're safe, and to free you from being under your brother's thumb. My goal is to ensure you can do whatever you want and go wherever you want. If you want to move to London to get away from everything, I'll make that happen for you with the contacts I still have there. If you want to move to New York City, or bumfuck middle-of-nowhere Idaho, I'll help make that happen too. But if you decide that you like living here in Colorado Springs, and you want to stay, you better believe I'm all for that, and I'll bend arse over end to make that happen."

"Ro," Chloe choked out, understanding what he was saying without coming right out and saying it. He wanted her here. With him. But like usual, he wasn't pressuring her. Was giving her a choice.

"Come on, love. Let's get you inside before someone sees you and the cops show up."

That got her moving. Chloe nodded, and before she knew it, they were walking hand in hand at a brisk clip toward the front door.

"Is this place even open at this hour?" she asked as they approached.

Ro chuckled. "This place is open almost twenty-four seven. The regulars start coming in around ten, and the diehards don't leave until about three in the morning."

"Wow. And I thought the men at BJ's were bad," Chloe dead-panned as Ro held open the thick wooden door.

"The men who come here are generally good. They like to play pool, drink beer, and listen to either rock 'n' roll or country music. I'm not saying shit doesn't happen here, but for the most part, the men keep to themselves and aren't out to cause trouble. Many are veterans who need a place to belong, or to get away from their lives for a while."

Chloe nodded and looked around the dimly lit bar as Ro closed the door behind them. It didn't look a lot different than she imagined it would. A large bar was to her right, with a couple of patrons nursing beers. There was a jukebox in a corner to her left and tables set up around the room. A hallway led to what she assumed were the restrooms. A door in the back center of the room led to another space, which held pool tables.

Ro didn't give her time to look around further, instead putting a hand on the small of her back and leading her straight to the bar. A tall man stood behind it, drying a glass with a hand towel. He was tall—of course he was; it seemed as if all Ro's friends were tall, except for Black—but more than that, he was big. His arms were huge, as if he was a bodybuilder or something. He had a wide chest, and even his hands were big. He had a bushy, brown beard with streaks of gray, and Chloe could see a scar running down the side of his neck and disappearing into the collar of his shirt because the hair from his beard didn't grow on the scar tissue. He was tan, and both arms were covered in black tattoos.

Chloe would've turned and walked as far away from the man as she could get if Ro wasn't standing right next to her and if his hand wasn't urging her forward. This man reminded her way too much of the bodyguards Leon employed. She knew if he hit her with one of his mammoth hands, she'd be knocked unconscious immediately.

"Hey, Dave," Ro said easily as they stopped in front of the scarred wooden bar.

Dave scowled, which freaked Chloe out even more. "She the reason you boys are here so early?" His southern accent was thick, and his voice was low.

"Unfortunately, yes," Ro answered.

Dave turned his piercing brown eyes on her, and Chloe wanted to cringe, but she forced herself to meet his gaze. She stood straighter and told herself that with Ro next to her, she was safe.

He looked at her for a long moment, then smiled as he turned back to Ro. "She don't look kidnapped to me."

Without waiting for Ro to respond, she said, "I wasn't kidnapped. My brother's an asshole and has a tendency to pout when he doesn't get what he wants."

Dave's smiled widened, and Chloe was amazed at how it softened his entire countenance. "Guess she told me," the bartender said, nodding at Ro. "Glad to hear it, darlin'," he told Chloe. "Now before you head back and start talking shop . . . what can I get you to drink? Water? Juice? Mimosa? Shot of Jack Daniel's? One of those fancy English beers Ro likes so much? Tell me what you want, and you'll have it."

Chloe blinked and looked up at Ro. "Is he for real?"

"Uh . . . yeah?" Ro answered, clearly confused.

"He's obviously seen my picture all over the news and thinks I'm kidnapped. He knows that my brother is looking for me. He's just going to ignore all that and ask me what I want to drink?"

It wasn't Ro who answered, but Dave. He leaned over the bar, getting closer to her, and said in a low, serious tone, "Those guys in the back are good men. They take protectin' women seriously. If you say you aren't kidnapped, then I believe you aren't kidnapped. I'm not gonna call no damn cops and rat you out just because your face is on the TV. I trust Ro and the others to figure out your situation and do what's right. Now what do you want to drink?"

"Water's fine," Chloe said immediately, not sure if she was still scared of the large bartender or not.

Dave stood up straight and nodded. He grabbed a bottle of water from a fridge behind him and asked, "You want me to twist the top off?"

Chloe nodded.

With a flick of his wrist, she heard the seal on the water break, and he handed it to her without completely removing the cap. Automatically, Chloe reached for it and held it tightly as Ro lightly gripped her arm and steered her away from the bar.

"Thanks, Dave," he said before they walked away. "I'll let you know if we need anything."

"You do that," Dave replied, then turned away to do something behind the bar.

Ro led her to a doorway in the middle of the back wall. Chloe could see pool tables beyond the entrance.

"He's intense," she whispered up at Ro.

He smiled. "Nah, he's harmless."

"Harmless, my arse," Chloe said, mimicking Ro's British accent.

Just as they stepped through the doorway, Ro threw his head back and laughed at her response. He turned her to the right—and Chloe swallowed hard.

Ro's laughter had drawn the attention of the five men sitting at a table. They were all staring at them as they approached, as if they'd never seen a man laugh before.

"Morning, guys," Ro said as he steered Chloe to a seat with her back to the room.

"What's funny?" Arrow asked.

"Yeah, what the fuck do *you* have to laugh about?" the man Chloe recognized as Black asked.

"I don't think I've ever *seen* you laugh," Meat mused.

Chloe knew her face was red, but she tried to ignore it and took a sip of the water she still held in her death grip.

Ro sat down and scooted his chair toward hers until their thighs were almost touching. It seemed awkward, considering how much space there was between each of the other men at the table, but she wasn't about to say anything because having him close made her feel better.

"Chloe's British accent is spot-on," he told his friends. "She was mimicking me, and doing a bang-up job of it, if I do say so myself."

The tall blond man at the table ignored the conversation and leaned over, holding his hand out. "I'm Ball," he said seriously. "I'm sorry for what happened the other night."

"How's your arm?" she asked. Sitting with the men now, she could tell they were genuinely worried about her. There was no doubt they were strong and domineering, but the compassion and concern shining in their eyes was easy to read.

"I'm fine," Ball told her. "And even though I'm not particularly happy it was *my* arm your teeth ran into, I'm proud of you for fighting back. Not many women in your situation can find the strength to do so."

"I was scared," Chloe demurred. "And desperate."

"I know. And you still did everything you could to get away from us. A lot of women simply give up. Give in to whatever's happening to them. You fought us and pleaded with us till the very end."

Chloe looked down at the bottle resting on the table in front of her. "I don't remember a lot of what happened there at the end."

"It's because of the drug," Black told her matter-of-factly. "We took you to Ro's place; he fixed up that gash in your head and put you to bed. That's it."

Chloe appreciated the short and succinct information, though she had a feeling that wasn't exactly all that happened. But she let it go. They had bigger things to worry about. "So . . . now what?" she asked.

"So, your brother has escalated his kidnapping story for the national-media outlets," Meat informed them. "CNN, the *TODAY* show, even Fox News has picked it up. He's insisting that you're mentally ill, and that your situation is dire because you don't have your medications."

Chloe blanched. "He's threatened to have me committed in the past if I don't do what he wants," she admitted. "It's just one of his more sinister threats. I know if he could get away with it, he'd dope me to within an inch of my life and leave me to rot in some mental facility somewhere," she admitted to the men. "He's probably trying to plant the seed so when he gets me back, he can do just that, and no one will question it."

"*If* he gets you back," Gray said quietly, speaking up for the first time.

"What?" Chloe asked.

"You said *when*. You mean, *if* he gets you back."

"Oh. Yeah. That's what I meant," Chloe said lamely, knowing she hadn't misspoken.

"Why don't you start from the beginning," Ro suggested. "You said you hadn't always lived with your brother, right? Tell us everything you can about your family."

Chloe took another sip of her water and looked around the table. The men all looked solemn and serious. Meat had his laptop out, and she could see his messy brown hair over the top. Arrow's hair was dark, but she couldn't tell exactly what color because it was shorn so close to his head in a buzz cut. The others all stared at her with a mixture of curiosity and patience. Not one of them looked put out. Chloe didn't know if it was because of their backgrounds as soldiers, or if it was just the way they were.

She felt a hand on her leg and looked over at Ro. "Start wherever feels comfortable," he said. "Don't think about what you're saying. Just talk. Let us decide what might be pertinent and what isn't."

"This is hard," she told him, trying to ignore the others.

"I know it is. But you're doing amazingly well. I wish you could understand how unbelievably strong you are. If you could have seen some of the other women we've gotten out of situations like yours, and how terrified they were to talk to anyone, you'd understand. If it makes you feel better, talk to me. Ignore the others, and just tell *me*."

"Maybe if we had a deck of cards and could play War, this would be easier," Chloe joked.

Ro didn't even crack a smile. "I can make that happen, love," he reassured her.

Sighing, Chloe shook her head. "I was kidding."

"I'm not," he returned.

Chloe took a deep breath. Ro said she was strong, but she didn't feel anything of the sort. But he told her to start anywhere, so she supposed she should start from the beginning.

Chapter Twelve

Ro wanted to pick Chloe up and take her out of there but knew he couldn't. They needed more information, and Chloe was the only one who could give it to them. She held on to the water bottle in front of her as if it was the only thing keeping her sane, and he could see the pulse in her throat beating wildly. Laying a hand on her knee, he squeezed it lightly, trying to let her know she was safe. That it was okay.

He wasn't sure what he'd expected her to do, but when she moved a hand from the bottle and gripped his tightly, he melted. Her hand was cold and wet from the condensation. She'd reached out for him. *She* reached out to *him*. It was a huge step, and one he wouldn't take for granted.

Turning his hand over, grasping hers palm to palm, and intertwining their fingers together, he held on, trying to ground her and give her support as she began to speak.

Her voice shook, but the more she talked, the more it evened out.

"I always thought we were a typical family. I'm five years older than Leon, and I loved having a little brother. I would play with him after school, and we would run around like crazy in our yard under the watchful eye of our nanny. My dad worked long hours, but he always tried to come home and have dinner with us. My mom was great. She didn't have a full-time job, but volunteered a lot—hence the nanny.

"When I was in high school, I stopped spending so much time with Leon because, well . . . I was a teenager. My friends were more important to me than an annoying little brother who got into my stuff and bothered me. I guess that's when we really started growing apart. I went off to college and got my degree in accounting. I worked for a tax place for a year or two but didn't really enjoy it. It was boring, and the only thing clients were worried about was paying less money on their taxes than they should. I met a man one year who worked for Springs Financial Group, and I guess he saw something in me and was impressed. He invited me to interview there. I got the job, did a bunch of training, took some classes, and eventually became a financial adviser. My mom died around the time I got the job," Chloe said. "She was shot on the way to one of her volunteer things one morning."

Ro jerked at the information. He'd known Chloe's parents were both deceased, but not that her mom had been murdered.

"What was her name?" Meat asked.

"Louise."

"Did they find out who shot her?" It was Ball who asked that time.

Chloe shrugged. "Unfortunately, no. It was ten years ago, and I guess gangs were a pretty big problem at the time. She was going to a bad part of town to help build a Habitat for Humanity house. She was at a stoplight. Someone walked up to her car, shot her through the window, then stole her purse."

"Not her car?" Arrow asked.

"No. The detectives think it was all about the quick money for drugs or something. They interviewed a ton of people, and there were fewer surveillance cameras back then, so they had no real evidence other than the bullet casing being traced back to a stolen gun, which they never found."

"That sucks," Ro said, squeezing her hand.

"Yeah," Chloe agreed. "It did."

She took a deep breath, then continued. "Anyway, so I started my new job and didn't see much of my dad or brother. I was busy. They were busy. I tried to make it a point to see my dad at least once a week, but he seemed to be trying to distance himself from me. I'm not sure if seeing me reminded him of my mom or what."

"That's tough," Ro said. His family issues were a bit different from hers, but he definitely understood complicated family dynamics. He hadn't told her about his family, but he would. He had a feeling she'd understand better than most.

"What were your brother and father doing during this time?" Gray interjected.

Chloe shrugged. "The same stuff they did while I was in college, I guess," she said. "My dad continued working long hours, and Leon started college himself."

"Where did he go?" Meat asked, taking a break from typing on his computer to ask.

"He started off at the University of Southern California, but after his freshman year, he came home and went to the University of Denver."

"Why?" Black asked.

"Why what?"

"Why did he switch schools?"

Chloe shrugged. "I'm not sure. I never asked. I just assumed it was because he wanted to be closer to home."

"Hmmm," Black murmured. "Okay. Sorry to interrupt. Go on."

"Right, so I was working for Springs Financial Group, and things were going well. I had a few big clients, and I was helping build their portfolios. I'd figure out where they should invest and give them advice on long-term investments, life insurance, and things like that. I was there around five years or so. I had my own condo downtown and a lot of friends."

She paused to take a sip of her water.

"Then what happened?" Ro asked.

"Everything fell apart," Chloe said sadly. "Leon called me one day and told me Dad had been killed in a home invasion. He said he'd been out with friends, but someone had broken in and taken Dad by surprise. He'd been working in his office, and someone came in and shot him. They didn't take anything either. Just shot him and ran. I was so upset. Leon had just gotten his master's degree months before, and he seemed absolutely inconsolable. He swore that he'd find out who did it and make them pay, but as far as I know, Dad's murder is also unsolved as of today."

"Hmm. Knew Ray Harris had been killed, but I'm going to have to get my hands on that police report," Meat muttered under his breath.

Ro saw Chloe looking at Meat, and he gently reached out a finger and brought her eyes back to his. "Go on, love. What happened after your dad died?"

Sighing, she said, "Everything went to shit."

"Tell me," Ro cajoled.

"Things started going wrong at work. Clients that I'd worked with for years were suddenly requesting another adviser. I missed work because of legal stuff me and Leon had to deal with. It seemed to be one thing on top of another, and before long I was called into my boss's office and told that things weren't working out. I was fired. I was devastated and didn't know what to do. I tried to find another job, but the financial community in Colorado Springs isn't that big. I got a few interviews, and some of them looked really promising, but none panned out.

"It got so bad that I knew I'd have to dig into my savings, and I really didn't want to. Then Leon offered to let me move back home. He'd inherited the house when Dad died. I jumped at the chance, not only to live rent-free, but to get to know my brother again. I regretted growing apart from him." She snorted. "But I should've thought things through a bit more. Leon wasn't just being generous; he wanted something from me."

"What'd he want?" Arrow asked.

"He wanted me to take over the financial aspects of running the house. At first, I was happy to do it. It kept me busy and my mind off the fact I couldn't find another job. I started out paying the household bills and the staff, but soon I started giving Leon advice on investments, taxes, and deductions. I remember when he came to me and told me he wanted to buy the building that is now BJ's. He was so excited and told me all about how he was going to make it a gentleman's club, and it would be the premier place for men to go in Colorado Springs who wanted a little fun.

"I told him it was a bad idea, but of course he ignored me. I helped him set up the business because I still thought, since he was my brother, I should support him. He put me in charge of all the accounting and paperwork for the club. It wasn't what I envisioned myself doing, but I did it anyway. For my brother.

"Around that time, he also asked me to take a look at the investments of a couple friends of his. I did it, happy to be helpful. I didn't realize who his friends were then, because they were using pseudonyms . . . otherwise, I would've said no.

"Anyway, after several months, I wanted to do something else with my life. Find my own place, get another job. But every time I brought it up to Leon, he had a reason why I should wait. He was very convincing, and I honestly thought he needed me. But when he found out I'd made a few appointments to actually look at apartments, he lost his mind."

Chloe paused in the telling of her story and gripped Ro's hand so hard, he knew he'd bear the marks of her fingernails on the back of his hand. He didn't say a word, simply held on, letting her know he was there. And that he wasn't judging her.

"He forbade me to move out, and when I ignored him and left anyway, he dragged me home—and hit me for the first time. And he explained about his criminal connections, said if I left, the Mafia would most certainly kill me. When I tried a second time to leave, deciding

I'd take my chances with the Mafia, he dragged me into a room and watched as his henchmen beat the shit out of me. I'll never forget him just standing there . . . smiling as they did it. They broke a couple ribs, and something was wrong with my knee as well.

"I couldn't get out of bed for quite a while, and Leon would come visit me in my room. He told me the 'friends' whose investments I had worked on were actually Joseph Carlino and Peter Smaldone. Those huge Mafia guys up in Denver. Leon told me they would kill me, slowly, if I tried to back out of doing their books. Said that he was trying to protect me. I knew he was lying about wanting to protect me, but I absolutely believed him about the Mafia. Leon scared me, but the Mafia terrified me."

"Can't say I blame you," Arrow said gently.

"Even if I wanted out, I was stuck," Chloe said dejectedly. "Leon brought me into this world of corruption and deceit and didn't care when I called him on it. He belittled me; told me that I was a Harris, and it was time to start acting like one. He claimed that Dad had been working with the Carlino and Smaldone families for years. That *they'd* been the ones who'd taught Dad how to extort and blackmail people and businesses for money. Leon said Dad had passed the family secrets on to him, and it was about time I joined the business in more than name only. He said that he'd done what he had to do in order to keep me in the fold. And now I had to stay with him for my own safety.

"I'd never seen Leon so out of control. He was enraged that I wanted out, saying that if I left, he couldn't protect me from the Mafia. I actually believed that—up to a point. So I agreed to keep working with him, but secretly started planning to do what I could to get away." Chloe let out a bitter laugh. "I planned to use my savings, but he and Abbie had drained it dry without my knowledge. I was penniless, and because of the way he kept me busy and close to home, I'd lost touch with the friends I'd had before I'd moved in with him. I had no car,

Leon took my driver's license, and I was completely dependent on him for everything.

"So I decided that it was safer for me to play along. The last thing I wanted was another beatdown like the one he and his henchmen had given me. I pretended to go along with everything he wanted. I needed time. Time to make a plan to get away. Time to figure out what to do to stay off the Mafia's radar. Time to build up enough money to escape."

"How?" Gray asked.

"Very slowly. Too slowly. I was in charge of both Leon's money, and Carlino and Smaldone's. I opened a new account and began to transfer funds into it. Only a little at a time, so no one would get suspicious. And only from Leon's accounts. A dollar here. Five dollars there. I was extremely cautious about it and never risked moving anything that would be missed, mostly siphoning money from the interest the accounts were earning. It's why I stayed with him so long—because it took forever to build that account up. I still hadn't gotten quite enough in there that I felt comfortable disappearing—but then things got *really* intense."

"What happened that day I first met you?" Ro asked. He'd wondered about that day ever since he'd seen the taillights from Abbie's Mercedes disappear.

Chloe sighed. "Leon had set me up with one of his friends. A man he'd said was perfect for me. He'd been doing this for a couple of years. In fact, he seemed desperate to marry me off, for some reason. I didn't want to go, but he wasn't taking no for an answer, and I knew if I continued to push, he might get suspicious of the meek persona I'd been portraying for so long. And there was always a chance of another beating. So I went. Let's just say it didn't go well."

"What happened?" Ball asked.

"The man was fifty-eight and had been divorced twice already. He couldn't take his eyes off my boobs the entire lunch. We were sitting in a booth in the back of a restaurant, and he tried to feel me up. I took offense to that and told him off. He called Leon. Told him to come get me, and that he wouldn't marry a cold bitch like me no matter how much money was involved."

"What does that mean?" Black asked. "Your brother was going to pay him to marry you?"

"I have no idea," Chloe said. "Leon was furious, though. But I was just as mad. Instead of doing what he wanted me to, as I'd been doing for years, I made the mistake of telling him the guy was a jerk, and I didn't want to be set up with any more of his friends. He got so mad that he *literally* kicked me out of the car. He'd punched me a few days earlier, and he got me in the exact same spot when he booted me out the car door. I started walking . . . and you know the rest," she concluded, looking at Ro.

"Why'd you call Abbie to come and get you?" Ro asked, shaking his head. "You could've told me what was going on then, and I would've helped you."

Chloe smiled sadly. "I didn't know what else to do," she said. "I should've. But I didn't have my passport. I couldn't access the money I'd been squirreling away without it. I thought if I could just get my passport and the few other things I'd hidden in my closet, I'd be good to go. It was a terrible decision on my part," she finished darkly. "He started training me to work the private rooms at BJ's that night."

There was silence around the table for a long moment. Ro held Chloe's hand and did his best to keep his cool. He wanted to head out right that second and teach Leon a lesson, but he had to stay calm. For her.

"Something doesn't make sense," Meat said after a while.

"What?" Arrow asked.

"If Leon inherited the house, and presumably his father's money, why bring Chloe in at all? If he hates her as much as it seems he does, why not just take it all and be done with her?"

"What did the will say?" Ball asked Chloe.

She shrugged. "That everything went to Dad's firstborn son?"

"Are you asking or telling?" Black asked.

"I never saw the will," Chloe admitted. "A lawyer came to the house and explained it to us. He said that Leon inherited the house and everything else. He said that Dad hoped Leon would help take care of me if I needed it. At the time, I *didn't* need it. I had a job, a place to live—I was comfortable. When Leon invited me to move in, he said that Dad would've wanted it that way. I didn't think much more about it."

"You didn't contest the will?" Arrow asked.

Chloe shook her head. "No. I didn't need Dad's money. I know he was rich. I mean, it was hard to miss with our house and all, but it never crossed my mind to sue my own brother. I had my savings, a job, friends . . . I didn't need it."

"Meat, can you—"

"On it," Meat said before Gray could finish his thought.

"What?" Chloe asked.

"What if Harris *didn't* inherit everything?" Ro asked quietly. "What if the money was to be split evenly?"

"But the lawyer said—"

"Did you know the lawyer?" Ro interrupted.

Chloe slowly shook her head. "I'd never seen him before. The guy Dad had used almost my whole life died not too long after Dad did. Heart attack."

"Fuck me," Meat muttered, his fingers flying over the keyboard.

Chloe looked from Meat to Ro, then around the table at the other men, before her gaze went back to Ro. "Do you really think all this is because of *money?*"

"Love, people will kill others for a measly five grand. Your father was loaded. Like, *really* loaded. Money does crazy things to people. If your brother wanted to keep all the money your parents had, there's no telling what he'd do to get it."

"Holy shit," Chloe whispered. "Leon has regular lunch meetings with a bunch of cops," she added.

Meat's fingers stalled, and he looked up at her. "Damn."

"Who else?" Ro asked.

"Politicians, heads of companies, university leaders . . . lots of people," Chloe said.

"Shit, shit, shit," Meat said, looking back down at his keyboard. "Okay, might have to bring in reinforcements on this one. I got this . . . although it might take me longer than planned. I'll have to go into the dark web and work behind the scenes to get info."

Meat continued to mumble under his breath as Arrow asked, "What are we going to do about the kidnapping thing? If Harris has friends in high places, it's only a matter of time before he figures out who we are and has the cops breathing down our necks . . . and probably Rex's too."

"We could use our contacts and send Chloe out of town via the underground," Ball suggested.

"We could say she's an abused spouse needing to lie low for a while, and Ro is her bodyguard," Black added.

"That wouldn't work because she's been all over the news. Besides . . . she's not married, and everyone knows that too," Gray said.

"We could just stay in my house until it blows over," Ro suggested.

"Press conference," Chloe blurted—and everyone stared at her in disbelief. Even Meat stopped typing to gape at her.

"Leon's not going to give up. He'll continue to put himself on every news show he can. He'll stir everyone up, get them to believe I'm mentally deficient, and when he does get his hands on me again, he'll lock me away forever, claiming that I have PTSD or something, and I need to be hospitalized for my own good."

Ro swallowed hard. She was right. Absolutely right—and it sucked. But he didn't know exactly where she was going with her idea. "So you want someone to go public and say that you're safe and sound and not kidnapped?"

"No," she said, and Ro relaxed. The last thing he, or Rex, wanted was publicity.

"Not someone. *I* want to call a press conference and tell the world that I wasn't kidnapped, and that I'm perfectly fine."

"No," Ro protested immediately. "No bloody way."

"It's the only way," Chloe said calmly. "You know it is."

"No," Ro said again, but this time it was Arrow who butted in.

"She's right. It's brilliant."

"It's rubbish!" Ro exclaimed, letting go of her hand for the first time, shoving his chair back, and standing to pace near the table. "The press'll eat her alive! They'll want to know where she was, why she didn't contact her brother, what happened when the car crashed . . . it'll go on and on. They won't let up with the questions."

"That's why we'll figure out what she should say before she talks to the press," Arrow argued.

"Abso-bloody-lutely not," Ro declared. "And that's final."

Three hours later, Ro watched as Chloe stood on the stairs of the county courthouse in downtown Colorado Springs and spoke to the press. She looked absolutely beautiful and poised. Only he could tell she was scared out of her wits.

Allye stood next to her, holding her hand, lending her support. They decided it was better if Chloe stood with a woman so as not to give the press any more fodder for gossip. If he'd stood up there with her, it would put the spotlight on him as well as her, and that was the last thing the Mountain Mercenaries needed.

The chief of police was speaking to the small crowd of mostly news reporters before saying, "I know we're all glad to see Ms. Harris safe and sound, and she has some things to say before we'll take questions."

Ro was sweating bullets. They'd prepared a short-and-sweet statement for Chloe to read, vague in detail, but they all knew it was the questions that would make or break their cover story. She'd already spoken with a detective from the police department. They couldn't know if he was one of the men Leon had in his pocket or not, but after a tense hour while she was behind closed doors, she'd exited the room and had given Ro a surreptitious nod, letting him know that as far as she could tell, their story had stood up to the initial scrutiny of the police.

She'd gone straight from the police station to the courthouse, and now Ro and the other mercenaries were surrounding the crowd. They'd been extra watchful for anyone suspicious, and so far, they'd been lucky to have seen no one but the reporters.

"Thank you all for coming today and for being concerned about me," Chloe said in a steady and strong voice. "It's comforting to know that when someone disappears, there are good people like all of you who care and want to bring them home. As you can see, I'm fine. I was never kidnapped, and I'm sorry my brother ever thought that for a second. I hit my head in the accident, and apparently, I wandered away from the scene looking for help. I collapsed and was found by my friend, Allye Martin. When I woke up and realized what was going on, it was too late, and my brother had already panicked and informed everyone that I was kidnapped. But again, I'm fine. Safe and sound."

The second she finished her little speech, the reporters went crazy, calling out questions.

"Why did your brother think you were kidnapped?"

"Where were you this entire time?"

"Why didn't you call him?"

"Is anyone coercing you to talk today?"

"Are you back on your meds?"

All the things they'd talked about and guessed would be asked, were asked. And Chloe handled each and every question like a pro. She didn't waver in her responses and reassured everyone over and over again that she was happy and healthy, and it had all been a big misunderstanding.

She laughed off the question about her mental health by saying the only meds she was on were vitamins and birth control, and that her brother had clearly misinterpreted her monthly mood swings for something more. She'd even blushed as she'd said it, giving credence to her performance.

Just when Ro was relaxing, thinking they'd pulled it off and she'd be able to show her face around town without having to worry about anyone thinking she'd been kidnapped, a limo came speeding up and slammed on its brakes at the edge of the crowd of reporters.

Immediately on alert, Ro began to make his way toward it.

His gut rolled, as he knew exactly who would be getting out. And he was right. They'd discussed the possibility that her brother might show up. They'd just hoped they could get the press conference done and get Chloe out of there before he did.

Leon Harris burst out of the car, and the reporters parted like the Red Sea as he made his way up the stairs toward his sister.

Ro's fists clenched, and every muscle in his body was on alert. If Leon did anything to hurt Chloe, he'd pay. Even if it hurt the Mountain Mercenaries' reputation. The only thing that kept Ro from going to Chloe's side was the fact that Allye was with her. And also, for some reason, Leon wanted his sister alive.

They hadn't figured out why yet, but he'd had plenty of opportunities to kill her over the years and hadn't. He didn't think Leon would blow his "nice guy" cover in front of all the news cameras.

The second Harris got to Chloe, he wrapped his arms around her and hugged her tightly. He'd stepped away from the microphone, forcing her backward a couple of steps. Ro watched carefully, and saw Chloe bring one arm up and wrap it around her brother's back. To all the cameras watching, it looked like a tender reunion scene, but Ro knew Chloe, even after just a couple of days together. He could tell she was freaking out.

She hadn't let go of Allye's hand, and to give the other woman credit, she didn't step away from the sibling as they embraced. Leon hugged Chloe for a beat longer than was appropriate for a brother and sister, and when he pulled back, Ro saw the sneer on his face for a split second before he turned to their audience.

"Thank you all for your concern and help in locating Chloe. I'm so glad she's okay and back where she belongs. I couldn't have done it without you. Thank you." And with that, he tried to step down the stairs, still holding on to his sister's hand.

But Chloe didn't budge.

Leon stood there with his arm outstretched awkwardly for a moment, then finally dropped his hand. He had a short conversation with Chloe there on the steps, and Ro saw her shake her head several times. She clasped Allye's hand tighter and pasted a fake smile on her face.

Obviously not wanting to do anything in front of the cameras that could be taken the wrong way, Leon slowly turned his back on his sister and made his way through the group of reporters, answering questions as he went.

At the last second, before Leon got back into the car he'd arrived in, Ro took a step away from where he'd been concealed behind a tree on the courthouse lawn, making sure Leon saw him clearly.

The two men stared at each other. Ro narrowed his eyes in warning at Leon, but the other man either ignored the warning or didn't catch it, because he just turned and climbed into the back seat.

The limo drove away much slower than it had arrived, and the reporters started dispersing, wanting to get the raw footage back to their news stations to be edited as soon as possible so it could be shared on the evening news.

As they'd planned, after Chloe shook hands with the chief of police and anyone else still loitering around, she and Allye made their way to Gray's Audi. Ro didn't move until both women were safely inside the vehicle, then he ran toward Meat's Hummer. Ball was driving, since Meat was ensconced back at his own house in the basement, on his computers.

Arrow and Black pulled out in front of Gray's Audi in Arrow's pickup, and they made their way toward Ro's house, taking the long way, making sure they weren't being followed by any of Leon's goons or nosey reporters.

The second Ball stopped the Hummer, Ro was out and striding up to Gray's car. He had the door open and Chloe in his arms before he'd even thought about it. He hadn't bothered to look around to check for danger or to check out the property. His only concern was getting to Chloe and making sure she was all right.

The second his arms closed around her and he smelled her lilac lotion, he relaxed. Ro didn't realize how stressed he'd been the last couple of hours until he was holding Chloe.

"Are you okay?" he asked.

She nodded but didn't lift her head.

It was enough. For now.

Chapter Thirteen

Two days later, Ro'd had enough. After the press conference, Chloe had shut down. She'd been polite and gracious, but anytime he brought up her brother and what he'd said to her on the courthouse steps, she'd changed the subject and made up an excuse to leave the room.

Ro was done dancing around the topic.

He didn't like the fact that Chloe was on edge, and he really didn't like the fact that she was obviously scared and hiding it from him. She jumped at every little noise, and when his phone rang, she stared at him with such trepidation as he spoke to whichever one of his friends was on the other end of the line, it made his heart hurt.

She went to bed way too early, especially for someone who was used to staying up into the wee hours of the morning. The one time he'd tried to check on her, he'd found she'd locked the bedroom door.

She was pulling away from him, physically and mentally, and Ro was done.

After dinner that night, as usual, Chloe helped him with the dishes, then said a quiet good night and told him she was going to head up to bed. She'd even changed into her pajamas—sleep shorts and a short-sleeve shirt that matched—before dinner.

Stopping her with a hand on her arm, Ro shook his head. "It's time we finished that game of War," he told her.

"Oh, I'm too tired for that tonight," Chloe told him, trying to pull away.

"Tough," Ro said with no emotion. Ignoring her protests, he walked with her into the living room and plopped her arse on the sofa. "Sit. I'll get the cards."

"But—"

"No, love."

Ro knew she was glaring at him as he walked over to the bookcase and the two stacks of cards they'd put there after finally quitting the other night. He also knew he was pushing his luck, but when she didn't get up, he decided to count that as a win.

Instead of sitting on the other side of the coffee table this time, he sat next to Chloe, leaving a foot of space between them. He handed her the stack of cards, then flipped over one of his own on the cushion between them.

For a moment, he didn't think she was going to give in. But after letting out a resigned sigh, she flipped over one of her cards without a word.

They played in silence for a while. She won a few rounds, as did he. After a time, Ro began to talk about nothing in particular.

He talked about the weather, about the last two cars he had worked on in his garage, even about the stray cat she'd found out he was feeding. He didn't bring up her brother, or her situation, keeping the conversation light.

Eventually, he was rewarded when Chloe began to respond to his conversational gambits. She rolled her eyes when he asked about the clothes that were delivered the day before. "Allye is crazy," she mumbled. "She went way overboard ordering clothes online. I can't pay her back until I get access to the account I set up, but I'm pretty sure trying to do that right now isn't the best thing."

Ro chuckled.

Chloe glared at him. "What?"

"Nothing."

She paused, refusing to put down another card. "Seriously, what?"

Ro looked into her eyes and internally sighed in relief at the irritation there. She'd been suppressing any and all emotion, except fear, ever since they'd arrived back at the house after the press conference, so seeing any other kind of reaction now was a step up from the way she'd been acting. "First of all, when the time is right, Meat'll handle getting that money for you. That's the least of your worries."

"But I don't have my passport or any other ID."

"He'll take care of that too."

Chloe huffed out a noncommittal breath. "What's the second thing?"

"What second thing?"

"You said *first of all*, which means that there has to be a *second of all*," Chloe told him.

"Oh, right. Second of all, Allye didn't pay for the things she ordered online for you."

"What? She didn't?"

Ro stared at her with a blank expression on his face.

"Oh, for God's sake. You did? You can't buy me clothes for the rest of my life, Ro."

"Why not?"

"Because!"

He chuckled again. "That's not a reason."

"Because," she tried again, "you've done too much already. I don't like owing people anything. And they were expensive, and there were too many of them. I'm going to send most of that stuff back. It's—"

"I feel like I haven't done enough," Ro interrupted her. "As you've told me several times, I had you kidnapped. You were hurt, then drugged. Now you feel trapped in the house because Harris is still out there. You won't tell me what he said to you, and it's killing me because I want to fix this for you. From where I'm sitting, I haven't done *nearly* enough."

"Ro, you've done—"

"And you don't owe me a bloody thing. This isn't a tit-for-tat situation. As far as expensive goes, you've seen the McLaren, right? I have money, love. Too much of it. I don't flaunt it, and no one knows exactly how much I'm worth because that's the way I want to keep it. Suffice it to say, getting clothes for you hasn't even made a dent. You aren't going to send anything back, because if you do, I'll turn around and get you twice as many things, and they'll probably be the wrong sizes and horribly outdated because I won't have Allye to help me this time."

They stared at each other for a beat. Ro was pissed she was even thinking about sending back any of the things he'd gotten for her, and he could tell she was just as irritated at him.

Between one blink and another, something changed in her gaze, however. She went from being upset with him to giving in.

"You've got money?" she asked.

Clenching his teeth, Ro nodded.

"I wasn't aware Rex paid you guys all that much."

Ro wanted to regret bringing it up in the first place—because talking about his finances meant talking about his past and how he'd acquired that money—but he couldn't. He wanted to share more about his life with Chloe. But it had been so long since he'd talked about what had happened to him, he wasn't sure where to start or if he could even do it.

Looking down at the cards in his hand, he placed one faceup on the cushion between them. He could tell she was staring at him, but eventually she continued the game.

"I was a member of the SAS. British special forces," Ro said as he collected the eight she'd lost to his queen. "All I'd ever wanted to do was be a soldier, from the time I was a little boy. Pop was perplexed because he'd always been a businessman. He didn't really have an aggressive bone in his body. But he supported me. When I'd go home on leave, we'd talk for hours about my job, the missions I'd been on, and the latest and greatest technologies we were using."

"What about your mom?" Chloe asked quietly.

Ro didn't like to think about his mother, but fair was fair. "My mum married my dad for his money. I think Pop thought he could make her love him as much as he loved her, but after several years of marriage, he realized it wasn't ever going to happen."

"Did they get a divorce?"

Ro chuckled, but it wasn't a humorous sound. "No. Pop wouldn't go against his vows. He took them seriously. She'd given him a son, me, and he'd committed himself to taking care of her for as long as they both shall live."

"I'm sorry."

Ro shrugged. "As I said, Pop wasn't exactly all that assertive. Mum walked all over him, and he did whatever she wanted. He ignored the affairs she had and tried to pretend everything was fine."

They both put down ten cards, and he laid out the three cards by rote, then flipped over the tiebreaker card. Chloe had a king showing to his five. Sighing, he watched as she collected the cards, including his last ace. It was only a matter of time before she won the game. He should've felt something about that, but he couldn't at the moment.

"I was on a joint mission with a group of Marines. We were using a brand-new weapon. It was supposed to have been tested extensively and deemed safe. My unit was chosen to sit inside the tank and fire the weapon. It was an honor to have been chosen." Ro shuddered, and it took a moment for Chloe's hand on his forearm to register.

"You don't have to tell me," she said quietly.

"Long story short, something went wrong, and the explosive malfunctioned inside the barrel. It exploded, and flames shot out the wrong end, engulfing the inside of the tank with deadly gases. I tackled one of my mates and took the brunt of the flames on my back. The Marines realized what happened immediately and were doing their best to get the hatch open and get us out. It took too long."

Ro looked up at Chloe. "Two of my mates were killed. Their lungs were seared by the initial blast of gases. It took three months for my back to heal up enough for me to go home from the hospital."

"And the teammate you shielded with your body?" Chloe asked quietly.

"He was fine."

"Thank God. I'm glad you're okay."

"Pop visited me as much as he could. As soon as I was discharged, he brought me home to continue healing. He was great."

"And your mom?" Chloe asked, obviously homing in on where he was going with his story.

"She wasn't happy I was there—until she found out the government was going to be paying out a tidy sum for the pain and suffering me and my teammates went through. But it wasn't enough for her. She hired a pricey lawyer, at Pop's expense, of course, and they went behind my back and sued the government for an obscene amount of money on my behalf."

"Can they do that?" Chloe asked. "I mean, you weren't a minor, so wouldn't *you* have to sue?"

Ro shrugged. "That's what I thought. Turns out, the government was eager to be done with the entire incident. It was quite the blight on their reputation. They paid. Twenty million pounds was deposited into my account. Hush money. It was tainted from the get-go, and I didn't want anything to do with it."

"But your mom did."

Ro nodded. "My life was hell living with them, and I moved out the second I was able. But Mum made Pop start to badger me about the money. She thought she deserved at least half since she did all the work in getting the lawsuit set up. I knew Pop wasn't speaking for himself, was only doing what his wife was ordering him to, but he didn't have the balls to tell her to sod off. The last time he came to my flat, I was awful to him. Said things I regret to this day. Told him Mum was a scheming bitch, and he needed to step up and divorce her already. I told him I didn't want to see him again until he'd washed his hands of her. He didn't raise his voice to me, didn't argue. Simply told me he was chuffed that I was his son, and then left."

"Chuffed?" Chloe asked.

"Pleased. He told me he was proud of me. It was the last time I ever saw him. He went home and hung himself."

"Ronan!" Chloe exclaimed. She leaned forward and put her cards on the coffee table, wrenched the cards out of Ro's hand, then scooted over until she was practically sitting in his lap. "I'm so sorry."

"Me too," Ro said. "Mum didn't even care. She told me it was my fault, and if I'd only given them some of the money from the settlement, Pop wouldn't have done it."

"You know that's bullshit, right?" Chloe asked, putting her hands on his cheeks and forcing him to look at her.

Ro looked into her brown eyes and told her something he'd never admitted out loud before. "It's not rubbish. I didn't want the money. If I'd given it to them, then Pop would still be alive today."

"Fuck that," Chloe said fiercely. Then she shifted so she was straddling him.

Ro's hands moved automatically to steady her and to make sure she didn't tumble off his lap. She leaned into him, her nose touching his, and said in a low, urgent tone, "I'm sorry, but your mom is a money-grubbing bitch. Your dad was proud of you for all that you did in the military, but also because of the man you are. You didn't give in to the pressure from her, and I know if he were alive, he'd say the same thing."

"He killed himself because of me. The last thing I told him was that I never wanted to see him again."

"It sounds to me like your dad had a lot more issues than you probably knew about. You said it yourself, he wasn't assertive. He probably kept a lot bottled up inside him . . . the English way and all, you know." She gave him a small, sad smile. "He loved you, Ro. You can't take this on your shoulders. Unfortunately, people kill themselves every day, and most of the time they aren't thinking about anything other than the amount of pain *they* are in. They aren't thinking about the people who love them. They aren't thinking about what their actions will do to others. All they can concentrate on are their own feelings and how desperate they are to make the pain stop. I'm guessing this wasn't a spur-of-the-moment thing for him."

Ro swallowed. "Credit card records proved he'd purchased the rope three weeks before he did it."

"Exactly." Chloe moved her hands until they were between the couch and his back. She squirmed a bit until they were chest to chest. Her legs were open, and her core was pressed against his crotch. She buried her face into his neck and said softly, "Your pop loved you, Ro. I'm sorry that happened to you. I'm sorry your money feels tainted. That sucks."

It *did* suck, but having a soft and compliant Chloe in his arms didn't.

"You'll keep the clothes?" he asked.

He felt more than heard the chuckle that came up from her chest. "Yeah, Ro. I'll keep them. Thank you."

"Arrow was one of the Marines who helped get me out of that tank," he told her.

She lifted her head to stare at him in surprise. "He was?"

"Yup. He kept in touch throughout my recovery and rehabilitation. When I was officially discharged from the British Army, he contacted me and said someone had a job offer for me."

"Rex," Chloe surmised.

"Rex," Ro agreed. "I came over to the States and to this run-down old pool hall. When Rex didn't show, I thought it had all been a bloody joke. Me and the others bitched about the fake job offer for a while, then decided we might as well stay and play some pool. We got pissed . . . er . . . drunk, and a few hours later, Rex called each of us, one after the other, and offered us jobs with Mountain Mercenaries."

"I'm glad," Chloe said, resting her head back on his shoulder.

Ro could feel her warm breath against his neck. He wasn't turned on; he felt comfortable and mellow with her in his arms. He also felt lighter for having told her his story. He hadn't told many people. Rex knew, and Arrow, of course, but he didn't think anyone else knew about the amount of money in his bank account. He didn't parade his money, except for the McLaren. He worked as a mechanic; his house was nice but nowhere near a mansion. He lived a low-key life.

"Have you seen her since?" Chloe asked.

Knowing she meant his mum, Ro nodded. "Once. I went back to England to confront her. To get information. To find out if she knew Pop was that unhappy. She answered the door of her flat wearing a Louis Vuitton dress, Manolo Blahnik shoes, and she'd obviously had cosmetic surgery. A man twenty years younger came up behind her and asked who I was. I turned and walked away without saying a word. As far as I'm concerned, I'm an orphan."

"I'll adopt you," Chloe teased.

"Done," Ro replied immediately.

"I was kidding," she said.

"I wasn't."

They sat together like that for a long time. Ro thought Chloe had fallen asleep. Their chests rose and fell together, breathing in tandem. Her warm breath feathered against his neck, and he played with the ends of her long black hair with the hand at her back. He'd never been so comfortable in all his life.

"He told me I'd be back," Chloe whispered in a tone so soft, Ro wouldn't have heard if her mouth weren't next to his ear. "When he hugged me, he told me I'd been naughty, and he'd kill anyone and everyone who helped me if I didn't come back to the house by this weekend. I think because of the way I'd been acting around him, he honestly thinks I'll go running back just so I don't anger him."

Ro's muscles immediately tightened, and the relaxed feeling he'd had was replaced by one of utter rage. He managed to keep his touch on her back and waist light and calm. "What else?" he asked. "Give it all to me."

"He said he had a special evening planned for my first night back at BJ's, and then he'd be moving me to his whorehouse, where he'd lined up enough men for a month to teach me a lesson. Then after, he was going to hand me over to Smaldone and Carlino so they could do what they wanted with me."

"What'd he say as he was leaving? When he tried to get you to go with him?" Ro asked.

"See you soon," Chloe whispered.

Ro brought his hands up to either side of her neck, his thumbs at her jaw, and lifted her head from his shoulder. He felt her fingernails dig into his back in her agitation. He met her worried gaze with his steady one.

"I wouldn't be able to stand it if something happened to you, or Allye, or any of the others," Chloe admitted. "When I was planning on leaving on my own, it wasn't as scary. It was just me. But now . . . if he finds out you've been helping me, he won't rest until he's hurt you all too. It's not just me anymore."

Ro smiled. He knew it wasn't a happy-go-lucky smile either. It was determined and evil. "That bastard isn't going to win, love. I won't allow him to."

For the first time since the press conference—that he knew of—tears filled her eyes. "You can't guarantee that."

"I can and I will," Ro insisted. "We've been tiptoeing around your brother, but it's time to stop fucking around."

"What are you going to do?"

"Honestly? I don't know. A lot of it depends on what Meat finds in his research. He's good, but he's having some issues. He's asked a friend of his to help him."

"A friend?"

"Yeah, a guy who seems to know everyone and is able to somehow find the impossible."

"Sounds like someone who might be handy to have around," Chloe joked, obviously trying to force her tears back.

Ro slowly moved his hands up to her face and brushed the stray tears away. Then he leaned up and kissed each cheek, the slight tang of salt exploding on his tongue. He gently kissed her mouth, lingering when she sighed and parted her lips for him. Ro ran the tip of his tongue over her bottom lip, then took it between his teeth. He bit her lightly, and when she moaned and shifted on his lap, he let go.

"Don't leave," he begged. "I know things seem impossible and scary right now, but don't go."

She didn't say anything, simply stared at him.

"If you go, I'll move heaven and earth to get you back. There's nowhere Harris can hide you that I won't find you. I won't give up. I'll spend every pound in my account to find you, love. You know I will."

"I'm not worth it."

"Bollocks," Ro said immediately. "You're worth a fuck of a lot more than you'll ever know. There's something between us, Chloe. Tell me you feel it. Tell me I'm not the only one," he ordered.

He didn't think she was going to admit it. She sat on his lap and stared at him for several minutes. Ro refused to break the silence. She was stubborn, but he was more so.

"You're not the only one," she finally whispered shyly.

"Damn straight."

She giggled.

"What?"

"Shouldn't you have said *bloody straight*? *Bloody* is English for *damn*, right?"

He smirked. "Yeah, but *bloody straight* sounds weird."

She laughed again, and the sound went straight to his cock. He pulled her harder into him, letting her feel how much she affected him.

The second she realized what she was feeling between her legs, she stilled. "You're hard," she said breathlessly.

"I am," Ro agreed, and pulled her closer when she tried to squirm backward.

"But . . . when we were at BJ's just like this, you didn't . . ."

"You weren't there of your own free will," Ro told her. Then he let go of her waist and put his arms on the back of the couch. "But here, you're free to do what you want. And hearing you laugh, and knowing I've done that—made you forget your worries for half a second and genuinely laugh—yeah, it's a turn-on."

He thought she might scoot backward. That she might be awkward about his obvious arousal, but she surprised him by moving her hips closer, even leaning back a bit to fit her core closer to his.

"I like it."

"It?" he asked cheekily.

Blushing, she said, "Yeah. It. Making you hard. Feeling you under me. Knowing I can arouse you. *It.*"

"I like it too," Ro said. Then he put his hands under her arse and stood in one fluid motion.

Chloe squealed, but wrapped her arms around his neck as he walked toward the stairs. She didn't ask where they were going, simply held on. That turned Ro on more.

He walked them up the stairs and straight to his bedroom. The second he opened the door, he groaned.

"What?" she asked, lifting her head.

"It smells like you in here," he told her. "Lilacs. Fuck, I'll never be able to smell them again without getting a woody."

She giggled, and once again Ro felt his cock jump in his pants. What it was about her laugh that made him hard, he didn't know. No, that was a lie. He *did* know. He loved making her feel happy. It was way too obvious there hadn't been much happiness in her life over the last few years.

He strode up to the bed and dropped her without ceremony. Chloe shrieked as she bounced on the mattress. Then she laughed some more and scooted backward. She didn't look scared of him in the least, thank God.

Ro followed her down and physically turned her onto her side, then snuggled up behind her. He didn't say a word, simply buried his nose in her hair and held on.

"Um . . . are you okay?" Chloe asked tentatively.

"For the last two nights, I've thought about you sleeping up here alone, in my bed, and it killed me. I knew you were upset and that you weren't talking to me about Harris. I wanted to force my way past that locked door and take you in my arms, just like this. Can you humor me for tonight? I know it's early, but maybe for a while? Then I'll go back downstairs, and you can get some sleep."

"It's not too early," Chloe said. "And you have no idea how badly I wanted to go downstairs and climb into your arms just like this on the couch, and have you hold me and tell me everything would be all right."

"Everything *is* going to be all right," Ro said immediately.

He felt Chloe sigh, and, if possible, she melted even farther back into him.

"I hope so."

"Know so," Ro ordered.

After a minute or so, Chloe said, "I think the best thing that ever happened to me was being kidnapped."

Ro chuckled. "Well, let's not make a habit of it, shall we?"

"I won't if you won't," she responded cheekily.

"Deal." He closed his eyes and pulled Chloe closer. He'd never had a woman in this bed. And now it smelled like her. The sheets, the pillow, even the quilt, held the faint scent of lilacs. He wanted it to permeate his skin as well, wanted to carry her with him everywhere he went. Ro had never felt like this. Ever.

He was more satisfied holding her in his arms doing nothing but sleeping than he'd ever been with anyone else before.

Chapter Fourteen

Chloe woke up slowly after the best sleep of her life. She was still wearing her pajamas, and it didn't look like she and Ro had even moved an inch overnight after he'd gotten up a little bit after they'd settled and put on a pair of sweats. She was on her side, in the same position she'd fallen asleep in, and he still had his arm around her.

The second she stirred, he moved too. She shifted to her back, and he hovered over her with a small smile on his face.

"What?"

"You're beautiful."

She rolled her eyes at him. "My hair is probably a rat's nest. I haven't worn makeup for days, my clothes are wrinkled, and I know I'm about thirty pounds heavier than I should be."

Ro immediately countered with, "Your hair is mussed, and I love seeing it this way as a result of sleeping in my bed all night. You don't need makeup—you're beautiful just the way you are. I don't give a shit about your clothes, and you are the *perfect* size." His hand had moved from her upper arm, where it had been resting, over her belly to her waist, and then down to her thigh. He shifted onto his back, then pulled Chloe until she was straddling him. He adjusted her a bit until her core was pressed against his cock. A very hard, impressive cock.

"I love your shape," he said, his eyes roaming her body freely and greedily. The lust she saw there made her dampen between her thighs.

Men at BJ's had looked at her body, but somehow, with Ro, it was different. His gaze was almost reverent.

With one hand on her waist, holding her to him, he used the fingers of his other hand to drive her crazy. As he spoke, they flitted up and down her body with feather-light touches. "Your tits are gorgeous. Full and heavy. Your nipples are begging for my touch. Your arms are toned and strong, so you can hold yourself up as I take you from behind. Your belly is soft, exactly how it should be. I can take you hard and won't hurt you. Your thighs will feel so sweet and warm around me as I make love to you."

Chloe knew she was blushing furiously, but she didn't stop his words or his soft touches. He slowly spread his legs under her, forcing her legs farther apart as he did. She was spread wide over him, most of her weight resting on his crotch.

She braced herself on his chest and panted hard as she stared down at Ro. She wanted him. She'd only known him for a few days, but she felt closer to him than any man she'd ever met. And not just because of her current situation with her brother. If they'd met five years ago, before everything started, she had a feeling she'd feel exactly the same way she did right now. That he was somehow meant to be hers, and she was meant to be his.

"Are you wet, love?"

Chloe licked her lips and nodded, trying not to be embarrassed. This was Ro. She shouldn't be embarrassed about anything with him.

"May I feel?"

Hesitating, wondering if they were moving too fast, despite how she felt about him, Chloe didn't answer right away.

Ro's fingertips brushed up and down her arms, leaving goose bumps in their wake. "That's all I want to do, for now. I know this is fast, but I can't seem to help myself."

She saw the uncertainty in his eyes and wanted to reassure him that she was right there with him. "Please," she said.

The slight arrogance returned to his eyes immediately. The passion returned as well. One hand went to her ass and palmed her cheek, and the other pressed against her core.

She jolted in surprise. For some reason, she thought he'd go slow. Tease her with his touch. But he didn't tease. His hand slipped down and covered her pussy. He growled possessively in his throat. Her pajamas had seemed perfectly respectable the night before. She hadn't thought twice about wearing them around him because she felt comfortable with Ro, but now she felt almost naked sprawled on top of him.

Chloe tried to shift in his grasp, but his hands kept her immobile.

Ro's fingers inched slightly down her thigh to dip under the cotton shorts and began making their way back up.

"Ro," she protested.

He stopped. "Please, love. Let me give this to you. Let me make you feel good."

How could she say no to that? She couldn't. And didn't want to.

Nodding, Chloe kept her eyes on his face, not quite ready to look down her body at where his hand was.

He didn't have any such insecurities; his eyes were glued between her legs.

At the first brush of his fingers against her wet panties, Chloe jerked. He grinned, and she saw him lick his lips.

"Soaked," he declared. And without hesitation, he pulled the crotch of her panties to one side, and then he was touching her.

"Oh my God," Chloe breathed as his thumb immediately went to her clit and began to stroke, even as two fingers sank deep inside her body.

He didn't say anything as he concentrated on finding out what she liked. When he pressed hard against her clit, she backed away from his touch, but when he ran the digit lightly and rhythmically over her sensitive button of nerves, she arched toward him.

"Mmmm," he murmured.

"Ro," she said, not sure what she was asking for.

"Yeah?"

"More," she begged.

His thumb immediately moved faster, flicking her clit over and over with increasing pressure. Before she knew what she was doing, Chloe began humping his hand. The feel of his large, calloused fingers inside her felt better than anything she'd done to herself in the past.

He stopped moving his fingers altogether, and she moaned in protest.

"Take what you need, love," Ro told her. "Fuck my hand."

If she'd been thinking clearer, Chloe might've been embarrassed, but he'd brought her so close to the edge, she didn't hesitate. Her hips undulated over him, moving up and down and back and forth, reaching desperately for the orgasm that seemed just out of reach.

Whimpering, she grabbed hold of his biceps and begged, "Please, help me."

Without making her ask twice, Ro used his hand at her hip to hold her still, and the other, the hand deep inside her body, began to move. His fingers pushed in and out of her soaking-wet channel, and every time he pressed in, his thumb flicked against her clit.

"That's it, love. Fuck, you're beautiful. Relax. Let go and trust me to take you there."

Chloe barely heard his words; she was lost in sensation.

Then he turned his hand slightly so his fingers were facing forward, and he curled them on the next press inside her.

"Ro!" she exclaimed and tightened around him.

"That's the spot," he purred, more to himself than her. "Hang on, love. Here we go."

She had no time to question him as he began to piston his fingers in and out of her faster and faster, each time hitting a spot that made her want to press down harder against him, yet pull away at the same time. Then with one last thrust, he left his fingers there and brushed back and forth over the highly sensitive spot inside her while his thumb flicked her clit harshly.

That was it. She flew over the edge with a shriek, not knowing or caring where she was or about anything else that was going on around her. Ro kept his fingers in place, prolonging her orgasm for several beats before he gently removed them. He straightened her panties but kept his hand on her.

Eventually, Chloe went boneless and fell on top of Ro's chest, panting hard as if she'd just run a marathon. She didn't stir until she felt him move his hand from between her legs. Out of the corner of her eye, she saw him bring it up to his mouth and place two fingers in his mouth.

"Oh my God," she said, squeezing her eyes shut.

"Delicious," he said reverently.

Chloe squirmed with renewed desire and realized she was still straddling his waist, and he was still as hard as ever.

"Do you want me to—"

"Yes," Ro said, interrupting her. "Absolutely. But not right now. Just rest."

"But it's not fair."

"I've got you in my arms, sated and relaxed, Chloe. My fingers smell and taste like you. I've got your lilac scent all over me and on my sheets. I'm harder than I've ever been in my life, but I don't have the motivation or energy to move. Later, love. We've got all the time in the world."

"'Kay," she mumbled.

They lay like that for thirty or so more minutes, relaxing and dozing. His erection eventually softened somewhat, though it never went flaccid. Eventually, he sighed and said, "We should probably get up. I've heard my phone vibrating a couple of times, and I know you probably want to clean up."

Now that he mentioned it, she did feel wet and uncomfortable between her thighs. Pushing up, Chloe forced herself to meet his gaze. "Thank you."

"You're welcome," Ro said immediately. "No more degrading comments about yourself now, hear me?"

She smiled down at him. "If it gets me more of that, it might be worth it."

"Brat," Ro said, then sat up effortlessly with her on his lap. "Come on. Up. You can use the loo first while I check my phone."

"Did you know your mom was a multimillionaire?"

The question was so ridiculous, Chloe almost laughed. But when she saw Meat wasn't kidding, she asked, "What?"

When Ro had finally checked his phone that morning, he saw he'd received several calls from Meat. The other man wanted to come over and "chat."

He'd arrived with Arrow after she and Ro had breakfast, and they were now sitting at the dining room table having that chat.

"She had four hundred and sixty-seven million dollars in her accounts when she died," Meat informed her and Ro.

Chloe shook her head. "No. That's not right. My dad was the one with money. Not my mom."

"Not true," Meat disagreed as he clicked some buttons on his laptop. "Oh, don't get me wrong, your dad had money, but it was more like ten million dollars in investments when he passed away, not the almost half billion that was in your mom's name."

Chloe stared at Meat in disbelief.

"You didn't know," Arrow commented unnecessarily.

Chloe shook her head anyway. "No. I had no idea. But my dad got that when she died, right?"

"Not exactly," Meat said.

"I don't get it," Chloe said.

Meat looked up from his laptop. His dark-gray eyes met hers. "As far as I can tell, when your mom passed, the money didn't go into your dad's account. I'm not sure why. It's just sitting in the same investment accounts, earning interest. There's one account I haven't been able to get into yet to check out, but my friend is working on that one to see if there's anything interesting there. But when your dad died, *his* money definitely was taken over by your brother. For the last five years, money has been bled out of his accounts little by little—or not so little by little—and now there's only about a million and a half left."

Chloe shook her head ruefully. The way Meat said "only" a million and a half was almost laughable. She'd made a healthy salary as a financial adviser, but nothing close to that. It would have taken her at least fifteen years to save that much money with her former salary, and that was if she hadn't spent any of it. "I told Leon over and over that he was spending more money than he was making in interest, but he didn't want to listen to me. Kept saying that a big payout was just around the corner."

"And was it?" Arrow asked.

Chloe shrugged. "I have no idea. I mean, he had large payments made into his accounts at least once a month, sometimes twice, coming from someplace other than his businesses. Once I found out about the Mafia, I assumed those were extortion payments." Her lip curled. "I feel so badly for whoever he was blackmailing. I mean, I simply can't imagine doing something like that."

"Any luck on getting a copy of her father's will?" Ro asked Meat.

Chloe felt his fingers brush against her nape. He'd put his arm on the back of the chair when they'd sat down, and he'd been playing with her hair for a while, but this was the first time he'd touched her skin. Shivering at the light touch, she forced herself to pay attention.

"That's the weird thing. I got a copy of the will, but it looks funny."

"Funny how?" Chloe asked.

"I don't know. Just funny."

"Can I see it?" Chloe was frustrated with herself as soon as the question left her lips. She'd been acting timid for so long, she'd fallen back on that behavior too easily for her peace of mind. "I want to see it," she said firmly, phrasing it as a statement rather than a question this time.

"Of course," Meat said. "Let me pull it up." He clicked on a few more things, then turned his laptop toward her. Chloe pulled it closer and leaned forward, feeling Ro's hand move to her back. The little circles he was tracing made her remember how his hand had felt between her legs that morning, and she shot him a small smile before turning back to the document in front of her.

The men were quiet as she read it over. It was much shorter than she'd expected it to be, especially for someone like her father, who'd always been working and seemed to have his hand in a lot of pies, so to speak.

Looking up, she asked, "Is this it?"

Meat nodded. "See what I mean? Funny."

"May I?" Ro asked, and Chloe's stomach tightened. She'd thought he was reading over her shoulder the entire time. But he'd respected her enough to wait. And to ask. She nodded and pushed the laptop toward him.

She read it again, over *his* shoulder, at the same time he did.

When he was done, Ro grunted. "On the surface, it looks legit. Ray left all his investments and business assets to his firstborn son. There's no mention of Chloe or his wife at all."

"He obviously updated it after his wife died," Arrow said.

"I guess . . . ," Ro said, his voice trailing off as he thought.

"Anyone heard of the witnesses?" Meat asked.

Chloe leaned in and concentrated on the signatures and printed names.

Jackson Smythe and Theodore Clarke.

She shook her head. "I haven't."

"They aren't anyone your father worked with?" Meat pressed.

Chloe shook her head again. "Honestly, I have no idea. I mean, Leon told me that Dad had started working with Joseph Carlino and Peter Smaldone—that those two taught Dad how to extort money from people, and he in turn taught Leon. There's obviously a lot I didn't know about my dad."

"Was your dad the kind of person to leave you out of his will because you're female?" Arrow asked.

"If you'd asked me five years ago, I would've said absolutely not. My dad loved me. He was proud when I got my degree and when I was hired by Springs Financial Group. That doesn't mean that he wasn't a tough businessman or that he told me everything he was doing, but the man I knew wouldn't have left me out altogether. But after Leon told me what he was doing with the Mafia, and how he was making money, I'm not sure I ever really knew him all that well."

"Think, Chloe," Arrow requested. "Is there anything you can remember, knowing what you know now, that seemed off? Anything he said that you thought was weird back then or anything that he did? Was he more security conscious before he died, or did he talk about hiring bodyguards or anything?"

Chloe blinked at the questions that seemed to come out of left field. She pressed her lips together and thought back. Of course, now that she was *trying* to think about things, the harder anything was to remember. "I wasn't living at home," she protested. "I was on my own, doing my thing. I told you guys that I didn't spend a lot of time with my dad and brother."

"We know," Ro soothed, rubbing her back once more. "Close your eyes and think. Even if it's something small, it might mean a lot."

Chloe did as he suggested and closed her eyes. She could smell him next to her. He might like the way she smelled, but whatever soap he used was masculine as hell on him, and she loved it.

She thought about the times she *had* gotten together with her dad back then. She remembered the lunch they had to celebrate her getting the job with Springs Financial. She remembered calling and telling him about the first big account she'd been put in charge of. She remembered going over to the house on Leon's twenty-fifth birthday and celebrating.

Her eyes popped open as that awkward dinner replayed itself in her mind.

"What, love? What did you remember?" Ro asked, obviously having been watching her carefully.

"I went to the house when Leon turned twenty-five. He'd gotten his master's degree in accounting a couple months before that. He was working for my dad, but things seemed tense between the two of them."

"How long was this before your dad was killed?"

Chloe shook her head. "I'm not exactly sure. Several months. We were eating dinner, and Dad asked me how work was going. I told him well and that I'd gotten a raise. He congratulated me, but then turned to Leon and said, 'Looks like *one* of my kids can turn a dime into a quarter.' I didn't understand what he meant, but Leon scowled at him and excused himself not too long after that."

"Was that all?" Arrow asked with uncanny insight.

"No. After my brother had left the table, Dad turned to me and said he was proud of me, and that everything I had learned in school and everything I was doing for Springs Financial would serve me well when I turned thirty-five."

"Thirty-five?" Meat asked. "How old are you now?"

"Thirty-four. My birthday is in two months," Chloe told him. "I asked him what he meant, and he blew it off, saying that he was positive I was going to make my first million before that time."

"Would you have?" Arrow asked.

"Maybe. I mean, I had tried to put away as much money as possible. Anything I didn't need to live on, I saved."

"Hmmm," Arrow murmured, but didn't comment further.

Chloe looked from one man to the next in confusion. Arrow looked contemplative. Meat looked hyped up on sugar and caffeine, but he always looked that way.

When she looked at Ro, she had to turn her head away quickly and try not to blush, because he'd been looking at her with a mixture of admiration and lust. Ever since that morning, he hadn't been able to keep his hands off her. She realized that he'd been subtly touching her all day. He'd brushed up against her back as they worked in the kitchen making breakfast. His foot had twined with hers as they ate.

It was safe to say that Ronan Cross seemed to like her. And the feeling was definitely mutual.

Suddenly, she was tired of thinking and talking about her family. She wanted to forget everything but the man sitting next to her. She hadn't forgotten how unselfish he was by putting his own pleasure on the back burner.

She thought they were on the same wavelength, until he announced, "Harris told Chloe at the press conference that she'd be back at his house by this weekend, and that he'd kill anyone who helped keep her away from him."

The words sounded harsh just put out there like that, and Chloe inhaled sharply. She jerked away from Ro but didn't get far. His hand snaked out and landed on her opposite hip, preventing her from standing up or scooting her chair away from his.

"I have no idea what he's got planned, but that's only three days from now. We need to figure this shit out and shut him down before he can execute whatever plan he's got."

"You want to go underground?" Arrow asked.

Chloe could feel Ro's eyes on her, but she couldn't look back. She figured he wanted to ask her what she wanted, but she didn't *know* what she wanted. A part of her wanted to hide as far away as possible from her brother, but another part wanted to stand up to him. To spit in his face and tell him he wouldn't get away with whatever he was trying to do.

Instead of answering Arrow's question, Ro asked quietly, "You think Carlino and Smaldone know the details of Harris's side businesses?"

There was silence as Meat and Arrow digested the question.

"Fucking brilliant," Meat said. "I'll call Rex and get him on it."

"What?" Chloe asked, thoroughly confused.

"You'll call me later and let me know?" Ro asked, standing at the same time Meat and Arrow did.

"Let you know what?" Chloe asked again, standing up herself and staring at the three men.

"I'm sure Rex will want to talk to Chloe himself," Arrow put in. "You know, to get all the facts."

"The facts about *what?*" Chloe asked, close to stomping her foot in frustration.

"Thanks, guys. We'll lie low here until we hear from Rex or someone else from the team."

"Sounds good."

"Hey," Chloe complained as the men headed for the front door, "what's going on?"

"Bye, Chloe," Arrow said. "Hang tight—this'll be over before you know it."

Typical as ever, Meat didn't say anything, just exited the house and headed for Arrow's truck.

Chloe stood with her hands on her hips as Ro closed and locked the door. He stepped to the alarm system and armed it. When he turned back to her, she tapped her foot impatiently. "Ronan Cross. What the hell was that?"

Without a word, he came toward her, bent down, and threw her over his shoulder. With her head hanging down his back, her hands holding herself up on his hard ass, Chloe gasped in surprise. "Ro!"

"It's later," he told her, striding up the stairs as if she weighed nothing at all.

With those two words, all thoughts of her brother, the situation, and what the Mountain Mercenaries were keeping from her leaked out of her head, and all she could think about was the virile, impatient man under her, and what was about to happen.

Chapter Fifteen

Ro knew Chloe had questions, but he had no answers, only suspicions. Meat and Arrow would get with Rex, and their handler would take things from there. For now, though, he couldn't resist Chloe anymore. Sitting next to her for the last couple of hours had been torturous. Her fresh lilac smell reminded him of how she'd tasted on his fingers after he'd made her come.

As someone who took relationships very slowly, he was acting extremely out of character, but Ro knew beyond a shadow of a doubt that Chloe Harris was meant to be his. Everything about her appealed to him. Her strength. Her body. The fact that even though she was scared and unsure about everything going on, she still didn't back down from sharing as much information as possible.

Her brother should've broken her. She should be scared of her own shadow. Worried about everyone and everything around her. Cowering in the face of meeting new men. But she wasn't, and that seemed like a miracle. *His* miracle.

He especially liked the look in her eyes when she met his gaze. As if she felt the same way about him as he felt about her. They'd connected. On a level he'd never connected with anyone before, and there was no way he was going to let her slip through his fingers.

He knew the clock was ticking down for Harris, but it also somehow felt as if their time together was going to come to an end sooner rather than later. He'd do whatever it took to keep her safe, but he knew better than anyone that sometimes the best-laid plans meant nothing in the face of fate.

Shit happened.

But it wasn't going to happen to his Chloe before she understood to the depths of her being how much she meant to him. He didn't fall into bed with women. Typically, he dated them for several weeks before even thinking about making love. But with Chloe, he not only wanted her physically, he wanted to get to know everything about her. Let her into his life.

Ro hadn't told anyone the entire story about his pop and mum. It was common enough knowledge that his pop had killed himself, but the events leading up to and after his death? Not so much. Chloe knew he was worth a lot of money, but she hadn't asked questions about it. The last woman he'd opened up to about the fact that he had money in the bank had immediately wanted to know how much, why he didn't live in a fancier house, and why he was still working as a mechanic.

Not his Chloe. She didn't seem to give a rat's arse.

He wanted her. Every way he could get her. Wanted her to open up to him and be vulnerable, just as he wanted to give her everything he had and be vulnerable to her. He didn't know where the feeling was coming from, but he wasn't hiding from it.

The smell, taste, and sight of her from that morning had had him half-hard ever since. The meeting with Meat and Arrow was important, literally a matter of Chloe's life or death, but he couldn't get his dick to behave. Every time he'd brushed her hair off her shoulder, the fresh scent of lilacs wafted up into his nose. She'd applied her lotion after climbing off his lap and getting ready for the day. He'd almost jacked off in the bathroom after she'd left because the smell of lilacs was still so strong from her morning routine.

He'd never get enough of it.

Never get enough of her.

It was time she realized that he was in this for the long haul. He wouldn't insist she move in with him after they figured out things with her brother, though. She'd been stifled for too long for him to do that to her, but she'd know that he wanted to be a part of her life. He'd help her find a job, a flat, a car, but ultimately, he wanted every second of her spare time. However much that was.

It was insane. This insatiable need to have her with him happened too soon. But he couldn't deny he'd been obsessed with her from the second he'd seen her in his driveway. So, technically, it hadn't been days, it'd been weeks. That seemed more acceptable.

Ro knew he was splitting hairs, but he didn't care.

He strode into his bedroom and bent down once more, dumping Chloe on her back on his bed, as he had the night before. There was something so caveman about the action. He loved it, but more important, he thought she did too. She stared up at him with wide eyes, pupils dilated with desire.

He simply stared at her for a long moment.

"Ro?" she asked uncertainly.

He leaned over her, caging her in with his hands on the mattress on either side of her shoulders. "I want you," he said huskily. "I want you under me, over me, on your knees in front of me, and any other way I can get you. I want your scent all over me, and I want to mark you as my own. This is crazy fast, but I don't give a fuck. I need you, Chloe. More than I've ever needed anything in my entire life. But this is your choice. Say yes, and we'll spend the rest of the afternoon in this bed. But if you're not ready, just say the word, and I'll go find something to distract me. I'll never force you, love. Ever. It doesn't matter if you say yes today or a year from now—I'm not going to change my mind about how I feel for you."

Her eyes were wide, and she stared up at him with her mouth partially open. She was breathing hard, and her fingernails dug into his biceps, the cotton of his T-shirt dulling the bite.

Ro didn't move as he waited for her decision. He kept his eyes glued to hers, willing her to see to the heart of him. That he'd never hurt her. That he'd treat her right, both in and out of the bedroom.

She licked her lips and took a deep breath.

Ro's muscles tensed as he prepared to back off and somehow make himself leave the room. He ran through the mechanics of the foreign car he had in his garage at the moment. If she wasn't ready, he could spend the rest of the day out there, controlling himself and keeping himself busy. He might even—

"Yes."

His attention snapped back to Chloe. She looked a bit unsure, but she was also calm.

"Yes?" Ro asked, wanting confirmation before he touched her.

She nodded. "Yes. I want you too. I've thought about nothing else since this morning. I want you so deep inside me, I don't know where you stop and I start. Make love to me, Ro."

For a second, Ro was paralyzed with lust. But when Chloe's hands moved from his arms to his hips and pulled his shirt out of his jeans, he moved.

Leaping off the bed, Ro grabbed the collar behind his head and stripped away his shirt. "Clothes. Off," he ordered harshly, as he toed off his shoes and his hands went to the button of his jeans.

Chloe immediately sat up and began to disrobe just as quickly and urgently. By the time he was naked and climbing back on the bed, she'd removed everything but her underwear.

The vision of her lying on his bed wearing only a tiny pair of white cotton panties was sexier than anything he'd ever seen in his life. Her skin was pale, a stark contrast to her long black hair. Seeing that hair against his white bedding was life changing, and he made a vow then and there to always have white sheets.

Her tits were large, and as she shifted on the bed impatiently, he wanted nothing more than to lean down and take a nipple into his mouth and suck. But he waited. This was the first time he'd seen Chloe willingly naked, and he wanted to savor every single second.

Her fingers went to the elastic of her panties, but he stopped her. "Wait. Let me look at you."

She looked him in the eye and nodded. Then, like a siren of old, she brought her arms up over her head and stretched.

"Fuck," Ro groaned, taking in every nuance of the delectable feast below him. "You are so bloody beautiful," he said reverently.

"You aren't so bad yourself," Chloe whispered back, her eyes glued to his raging hard-on. He was already dripping precome, and her stomach sucked in when a bead slid down the mushroom head of his cock and landed there.

Leaning over so he was on all fours, Ro nuzzled between her breasts, inhaling deeply. She took a breath herself, and he felt his cock brush against the soft skin of her belly as he dipped down closer, eager to smell more of her. "For the love of God, don't ever change your lotion," he murmured, feeling drunk on her scent.

"I won't," she said quietly.

He felt one of her hands land on the back of his head to hold her to him, and he closed his eyes in ecstasy. He was frozen in indecision. He wanted to do so many things. Kiss her mouth, suck her tits, yank her panties down and bury his face between her thighs and eat her to multiple orgasms. But the only thing he could really think about was getting inside her.

He could feel the precome leaking out of his body in a steady stream now. He was so close to orgasming, it was embarrassing. He should have more control than this. But he didn't. He had none. The sight of her naked on his sheets had pushed him past what he could handle.

"Take off your underwear," he got out between clenched teeth.

She didn't protest and immediately began to wiggle under him. Her hips came up off the bed and pressed against his cock, and Ro groaned in sexual agony.

He heard her giggle, but he couldn't smile. Couldn't do anything but pray he didn't spray all over her stomach like an untried lad of thirteen.

When he felt her hands return to his sides, he shuddered, goose bumps breaking out on his arms at her touch. "Ro?" she asked, sounding unsure.

He couldn't have that.

"I need you," he said after a moment. "So bad I'm hanging on by a thread. I thought I could go slow. Taste every inch of your skin, make you come several times before taking you. But I can't. I need inside of you so badly I'm shaking."

And he was. His arms holding himself over her were trembling.

Ro felt Chloe's legs rise up, and the warm skin of her inner thighs squeezed his hips. "Take what you need, Ro," she said softly. "Take me."

Ro clenched his teeth. "I need to make sure you're ready for me," he said.

"I'm ready," she reassured him.

"Need to get a condom," Ro said, desperately trying to hang on.

"I'm safe," she told him. "Abbie forced me to get an IUD inserted; she didn't want to have to deal with any accidental babies after she and Leon started making me have sex with the customers at the bar."

Her admission made Ro furious. He wanted to kill her brother and his girlfriend more than he'd ever wanted to kill anyone. The rage made his lust diminish a bit, but her next words notched it right back up to where it had been, and even higher.

Chloe leaned up so her lips were near his ear and whispered, "I want to feel you bare. I've never had anyone without a condom before. Never felt anyone fill me with their come. I want it to be you, Ro. Fuck me. Please."

And he was gone. Ro walked closer on his knees and forced her legs farther apart under him. He grabbed his weeping cock with one hand

and grasped one of her tits with the other. Running the bright-purple head of his dick over her slick folds, he used his own juices to further lubricate her.

"I can't be gentle," he warned her. "I need you too much."

"I don't want gentle," she countered. "I just want you."

And with that, Ro was done trying to engage in any kind of foreplay. He lined the head of his cock up with her soaking-wet hole and pushed in until his balls touched her arse and he couldn't go any farther.

Her inner muscles were clenching so tightly, he almost shot off right then and there, but he managed to stave off his orgasm. Looking into her eyes, he saw the way she was pressing her lips together tightly.

"Fuck," he said. "I'm sorry. Shit, shit, shit." Ro started to pull back, but Chloe's hands slapped down on his arse and held him in place.

"It's been a really long time," she said calmly. "And you're not exactly small. Just give me a second."

Ro leaned down, and even that small movement made a burst of precome ooze from the tip of his cock, buried deep inside her. Trying to ignore the way she felt around him, Ro kissed her lightly. But soon the light and easy kiss turned into much more. Chloe ate at his mouth, trying to inhale him. He allowed her to take control of the kiss, as it was taking all his concentration not to come.

He felt her relax bit by bit, and after a moment, she spread her legs wider, and Ro felt himself press inside her even deeper. He pulled back, panting. "Bloody hell," he murmured. "You're killing me, love."

"But what a way to go," she said, her warm breath wafting over his lips. "Fuck me, Ro," she ordered.

"Don't want to hurt you."

"You won't."

"This isn't going to take long," he warned.

"Okay."

"This means something," Ro told her, holding her gaze.

The tears that sprang into her eyes would've worried him, but she gripped his arse with her fingers and tried to pull him even closer. Then she said, "To me too."

And he was lost.

Despite the grip she had on him, Ro pulled almost all the way out of her hot, wet body, until only the very tip of his cock remained inside of her. Then he slammed forward until his balls swung against her arse. He did it again. And again.

On the fourth thrust, he exploded. There was no way he could've held back the monster orgasm that had been hovering on the brink all day. He jerked inside of her and felt his come coat her inner channel with heat. His cock pulsed with every spurt of his release.

Ro remotely felt Chloe's fingers move from his arse to his chest. She pinched his nipples as he came, which made his orgasm all the more intense.

When he'd given her everything he had in him, Ro looked down at her, not sure what to say. He hadn't come that fast . . . well, ever.

"Feel better?" she asked with a little smirk.

"Fuck," Ro swore, loving the satisfied look on Chloe's face. He sat back on his heels and grabbed hold of her hips, holding her to him. His cock was softening, but he was still half-hard inside her. Making sure not to lose their connection, he pulled her farther up his lap until she was resting on her shoulder blades.

"Ro?" she asked, uncertain.

"You didn't come," Ro told her, even though it was obvious. "There's no way we're done yet. Put your hands above your head."

She did as he ordered, smiling at him.

Ro took his time looking at the beautiful, lush woman under him. Her breasts listed slightly to the sides of her chest, and her nipples were hard little buds on the tops of them. Her hair was mussed, and her skin was blotchy with desire.

He looked down at her pussy for the first time and felt his dick twitch deep inside her as he got a good look. Her folds were spread wide around his cock, and their excitement was smeared at the base of it. She didn't wax or even shave, but her hair was trimmed, giving him an excellent view of her inner folds and her clit. She was absolutely beautiful—and she'd be even more amazing coming all over his cock.

Using one finger, he pushed back the protective hood of her clit until he could see the small bit of sensitive flesh there. Then he began to lightly stroke it. She squirmed in his lap and moaned.

"Like that?" he asked.

"As if you have to ask," she breathed.

Smirking, Ro kept up his sensual assault, loving how her inner muscles clenched around his cock every time he brushed her clit. Her hips began to undulate, and he thought back to how she'd fucked his fingers earlier that morning as he made her come. The feeling was so much better around his dick.

"That's it," he murmured. With every squeeze of her arse, he felt his come leaking out around his dick and onto his thighs under her. She may not have had anyone bare inside her before, but this was a new experience for him too. Sex without a condom was messy . . . and he loved it. Loved having their scent all over him.

Her chest shone with perspiration, making the lotion she'd put on earlier smell all the more potent. Ro felt as if he was drunk on the combined smell of sex and lilacs.

Chloe was beautiful in her passion. She didn't shy away from what he was doing to her and, in fact, seemed to revel in it.

"I'm close," she told him breathlessly.

Reaching for one of her hands, he moved it down until her fingers were touching herself. "Show me what you like," he ordered. "Get yourself off."

She didn't hesitate. Using two fingers on her clit, Chloe fingered herself hard and fast, using a lot more force than Ro would've. Since his hands were free, he used them to grab her hips and hold her on his lap more securely. She was jerking and humping against him so hard now that it was a challenge to keep her on his cock.

Her nipples were as hard as rocks on her chest, and she brought her other hand down from over her head and grabbed her tit, pinching her own nipple.

"Ro. Oh my God . . . Ro!" she exclaimed.

Then he watched as she flew over the edge. Her hips shot upward, her arse cheeks clenched, her inner muscles tightened around his dick, her head flew backward, and she shuddered through her release.

Ro moved even as she was still in the throes of her orgasm. He shifted his knees out from under her so her arse was back on the bed, and he began to fuck her. Thrusting through her fluttering inner muscles, he gritted his teeth as her body tried to suck him in, then keep him there as he pulled back.

Chloe was moaning nonstop now, clutching at his arms as he fucked her hard and fast. The squelching noises coming from between their legs should've been embarrassing, but they only made the moment hotter. Between his first release and her orgasm, she was soaked. Ro could feel their combined juices coating his balls and his thighs, and it felt amazing, lending a whole new dimension to sex he'd never experienced before.

He lasted longer this time than he had the first, but he felt his impending orgasm way faster than he would've liked. He enjoyed being inside Chloe. Loved the way she felt around him. Before he was ready, Ro was coming again. He shot off inside her, then forced himself to pull out and spill the rest of his orgasm on her belly and tits. Rope after rope of his come shot through the air and landed on her body, marking her.

When Ro forced his eyes up to Chloe's face, he was relieved to see a satisfied smile curving her lips. He looked down once again and was suddenly embarrassed at what he'd done. He hadn't planned it, but at the last second, he'd wanted to see her covered with his seed.

"I'll just go and—"

She cut off his words by reaching up and tugging on his arms. Ro acquiesced and came down over her, his elbows taking his weight so he didn't crush her. His soft cock was nestled against her belly. The smell of sex, sweat, and lilacs was strong between them.

"That. Was. Amazing," Chloe said softly. Her eyes were closed into slits, and Ro let out the breath he didn't realize he was holding. Knowing he needed to get up and clean them both off, he literally wouldn't have been able to move right then even if Leon Harris himself had strode into the room with a gun pointed at them.

"Thank you," Ro told her.

"No, thank *you*," she countered.

"I came too fast," he admitted.

"No, you didn't. You have no idea how good it makes me feel to know you wanted me so badly, you couldn't hold back."

Ro grimaced. "I have a feeling I'll always want you that badly. I'm going to have to work on my control if I want to make it good for you."

Her eyes popped open, and she stared at him in disbelief. "Make it good for me? Ro, if it was any better, I'd be a puddle of goo at your feet right now."

He couldn't help the sense of pride that moved through him at her words. "We're kinda messy."

She chuckled. "Yup."

"We should shower."

"Yup."

But neither of them moved.

Finally, deciding maybe a nap was in order before they got up, he shifted to the side, keeping Chloe tucked into him. They moved as one until he was on his back and Chloe was lying on top of him. Chest to chest, they lay there, breathing together until they both fell into a light, sated sleep.

Chapter Sixteen

Chloe felt deliciously relaxed the next morning. Ro had kissed her awake and told her to take her time getting ready. He was already showered and dressed and looked like he'd been awake for hours. She'd simply moaned as he'd chuckled and kissed her once more on the forehead before leaving her in bed.

She'd gotten up thirty minutes later, sore in the most delicious places. Ro might've come quickly that first time, but he more than made up for it throughout the rest of the previous day and night. She woke up at one point with his head between her legs and halfway to an orgasm before she realized what was going on. Ro had made love to her in several different positions, always making sure she was comfortable and okay with what he was doing.

And oh, was she okay with what he was doing.

She'd lost count of the number of orgasms he'd given her. She was sticky and sore—and she couldn't wait to do it again. The entire bedroom smelled like sex, which only made her smile wider. There were pillows strewn all over the floor, and the comforter was hanging off the end of the bed like a drunken sailor.

All in all, it had been exhausting and amazing.

Chloe felt better after a long, hot shower. She'd lathered herself up with lotion, smiling at the memory of Ro ordering her to use the lilac scent for the rest of her life.

She stared at herself in the mirror for a long time. She wasn't sure what Ro saw in her that made him so sure he wanted to be with her for the long haul. He'd made it clear last night that was what he wanted. As they'd been cuddling between bouts of sleeping and sex, he'd talked to her about his job with the Mountain Mercenaries. How it was sometimes dangerous, but that he and his friends were very careful. He told her how he hoped she and Allye would hang out when they were gone, keeping each other company. He even admitted that he'd bought his house because there was the possibility of adding on to it if he met someone and wanted children.

Yes, he'd made it more than clear that he wanted her around for the long haul.

If Chloe was honest with herself, she wanted that too. After losing both her parents, she'd thought that moving in with Leon would ease some of the loneliness she'd felt over missing so much of her family. But that obviously hadn't turned out the way she'd planned.

Staring at her dark eyes in the mirror, Chloe made a promise to herself. *No matter what happens with Leon, I'm going to fight for Ro. I deserve to be happy, and Ro makes me happy.*

"Chloe!"

She jerked her head toward the bathroom door upon hearing Ro call her name from downstairs. She rushed to the top of the stairs.

"Ro?"

"Are you ready? Can you come down here?"

"Coming!" she called out, wondering what was wrong. She could tell that something was up. She didn't think Ro was the kind of man to holler often. He was more the silent-and-deadly type.

Hurrying down the stairs, she saw she was right—something *was* up. Instead of smiling at her and giving her another good-morning kiss, he was pacing next to his kitchen counter, his hand going through the dark locks of his hair in agitation every now and then.

He held out his hand, making Chloe feel a little better. She rushed to his side, sighing in relief when he closed his arm around her. "What's wrong?"

"Not sure. Rex is on the phone."

Chloe blinked. "Rex?"

"Yeah, love. My handler."

She knew who Rex was. She'd heard the guys talk about him with respect, deferring decisions to the mysterious man. "What does he want?"

"I want to talk to you," a deep, obviously digitally altered voice said from the phone sitting on the counter.

"Oh . . . um . . . okay," Chloe stammered. She hadn't realized he'd been on speaker this whole time.

"Tell me about Smaldone and Carlino," Rex ordered gruffly.

Chloe started, and was glad for Ro's arm around her waist. "I don't know anything about them," she said.

"Yes, you do," Rex countered. "And I need to know everything *you* know before I call to have a little chat with them this morning."

"Can you do that? I mean, just call them up?"

Rex chuckled, and Chloe suddenly realized that she was smiling right along with him. His laugh was deep and low, just like his voice, and she relaxed a bit. He sounded gruff and mean, but that small little laugh made her feel better. Leon rarely laughed. And when he did, it made the skin on the back of her neck crawl.

"Not exactly. They don't really take calls from every Tom, Dick, and Harry. But they know me. They'll take my call."

"Oh. Okay," Chloe said.

"You told my team that you were advising them. That you'd done their taxes. I need to know everything about that, Chloe," Rex said, his tone not quite as fearsome as it had been moments ago.

Ro steered her to a chair at the counter and helped her to sit. He then grabbed a cup of coffee that was sitting on the counter and slid it over to her. She took a sip gratefully. It was hard to think clearly before her daily dose of caffeine.

"Chloe?" Rex asked with a hint of impatience in his tone.

"Sorry. I'm here. I'm just . . . I'm trying to put my thoughts in order and figure out what's important and what's not."

"Tell me everything," Rex said immediately.

"But . . . it's just that . . . Well, as their accountant and adviser, I'm not legally allowed to talk to you about their financial situation."

Her words hung in the air, and there was silence from the other end of the phone.

Then Rex asked, "Are you shitting me?"

Chloe swallowed hard and tried not to cringe. "No. I mean, these kinds of things are regulated, and I could lose my license. It's bad enough I lost my job, but I do still have my credentials. I don't want to lose them."

"Chloe—" Ro said, but Rex beat him to whatever it was he was going to say.

"You're in deep shit," the handler for the Mountain Mercenaries said bluntly. "As you've told my team, at this point, if your ass of a brother gets busted, you'll be held just as accountable as he is in regard to his business dealings. You knew what was happening, and in fact, you actively managed the investments. If anyone goes down with Leon, or with Carlino or Smaldone, it'll be you, simply because your name is all over their accounts. Losing your license is the least of your worries.

"You want to end up being smuggled over the border and being forced to work in a brothel in Mexico City or Guatemala? Because if your brother gets his hands on you, that's where you'll end up. He doesn't want to kill you, for reasons we're still trying to figure out, so he'll move you somewhere out of the way where we can't get to you. Cosa Nostra isn't a group to fuck around with. I need to know everything you know, so I can see if I can bargain with them. Period. Got it?"

Chloe swallowed hard, doing her best to keep the coffee she'd just ingested from coming up all over Ro's beautiful granite countertop. She got it. She'd been naive. And Rex was trying to help her.

"Yes, sir," she said meekly.

"Good. Now talk to me," Rex ordered.

So she did. For the next half hour, she told Rex and Ro everything she could remember about the Mafia family's taxes and investments. Where they were funneling money, how much they were underpaying, their pseudonyms, even down to the write-offs they were claiming. She even told them everything Leon said they'd do to her if she said anything about their financial information and if she left town. She hadn't thought she knew as much as she did, but after talking for thirty minutes without stopping, leaving her throat dry and scratchy, she realized how deep her brother had buried her.

Rex had been silent on the other end of the phone, and it wasn't until she looked up at Ro and asked, "They're going to kill me, aren't they?" that Rex spoke again.

"No one's gonna touch you, Chloe," he said. "Leon Harris is the one in the wrong here. Not you."

"But I filed those taxes. I filled out the paperwork and signed the forms for the overseas investments."

"You did," Rex agreed. "But Peter and Joseph aren't idiots. They also aren't the type of men to kidnap and torture women for no reason."

"But they're Mafia," Chloe whispered.

"They are. And while they're certainly dangerous men who have no problem using whatever methods necessary to extract information, I haven't ever heard of them torturing women."

Chloe wrinkled her brow in confusion.

Studying her expression, Ro asked, "What?"

"Peter Smaldone came to the house and beat the crap out of me."

There was silence in the room for a tense moment before Rex said, "That's impossible."

"But he did. He introduced himself to me. Said that he'd gone light on me, and if I didn't stay and do their books, that next time he'd do worse. *Really* hurt me."

"What'd he look like?" Rex barked.

Chloe winced. She didn't like the other man's tone. Even digitally altered, she could easily hear the disbelief. And the thought that he didn't believe her hurt. "He was about my height. Dark-brown hair. Had a scar going through one of his eyebrows."

"That wasn't Smaldone," Rex said succinctly.

"But—"

"Chloe," Rex interrupted, his voice gentling, "I don't know *who* that was, but it wasn't Peter Smaldone. He's got blond hair and is about six feet. And he definitely doesn't have any scars on his face."

Chloe closed her eyes, awash in embarrassment and self-recrimination. Despite everything else Leon had done, she still almost couldn't believe it. But of course . . . he'd lied to her.

She felt Ro's hand curl tighter around her waist. Felt his body heat as he stood close.

"One more question before I let you go," Rex said.

Chloe nodded, then realized that Rex couldn't see her. Even though she'd been talking to a phone, for some reason it seemed as if the man were right there in front of her. "Okay," she said softly as she opened her eyes and stared at the phone.

"Are you all right?"

Chloe blinked. She'd expected to hear something about her brother. Or the Mafia. Or investments and taxes. Anything but that.

Ro nudged her and nodded to the phone with his head. She opened her mouth to respond when Rex spoke again. "Is Ronan treating you all right? Because if he's not, I can get you moved to a safe house."

"No!" Chloe exclaimed immediately. "I don't want to go. I want to stay with Ro."

"She's not going anywhere, Rex," Ro said, speaking directly for the first time in quite a while.

Rex chuckled again. "Just making sure. Welcome to the family, Chloe."

Ro growled under his breath and picked up the phone. "He hung up," he said, then pocketed the cell phone.

Her brows furrowed, and she looked up at Ro in confusion. "What did he mean?"

"You're one of us now," Ro told her calmly. "You have nothing to worry about in regard to Carlino and Smaldone. Once Rex talks to them, they'll know you've had nothing to do with whatever shit Leon has been pulling. Rex will make it clear that you're off-limits, and that he won't tolerate any blowback on you, no matter what you know about their finances. He'll also make sure they know you'll keep your mouth shut, and that you have no intention of ratting them out to the authorities about anything."

"I don't get it. I mean, you're right, I'm not going to say anything to anyone. I just want all this to go away, but what family Rex was welcoming me to?"

"*His* family, love. Mine," Ro said, pulling her up to stand next to him. "Rex was making sure you wanted to be here, and that I had claimed you, with his asinine suggestion to put you in protective custody."

"Oh," Chloe said, understanding dawning. "But he hasn't ever met me."

"Love, he hasn't met *me* either," Ro countered.

"Seriously?"

"Yup. Rex doesn't mess around with his privacy. I know you noticed that he alters his voice on the phone. He's extremely paranoid. Neither myself nor any of the other guys have met him face-to-face. Ever."

"That's weird," Chloe told him.

Ro shrugged. "Maybe. But we figure he has his reasons. Now, are you really okay with being here? I'm not sure it's safe for you to go out.

Not with Leon planning something and things with the Mafia up in the air."

Chloe laid her head on Ro's chest and wrapped her arms around him. "For now, yes. I'm not saying I want to spend the rest of my life locked up in your house, but if I have to be locked up somewhere, I want it to be wherever you are."

She felt his arms tighten around her. "It won't be the rest of your life. Trust me. Trust Rex. Leon won't be a threat for much longer."

"Ro?"

"Yeah, love?"

"What will happen to the women at the club? Or at that whore-house he told me he ran? I know many of them aren't there because they want to be."

Ro stiffened for just a second. "We'll help them. If they have families they want to go to, we'll get them there. If not, Rex will help them get somewhere safe where they can start over. Live the way they want to."

"Thank you."

"No, thank *you*," Ro countered. "Thank you for hanging on for so long. Thank you for trusting me."

"You're welcome," Chloe murmured softly.

Ro pulled away and put his finger under her chin. "Hungry?"

Chloe nodded, then grinned. "I worked up quite an appetite last night."

And just like that, the mood changed. She felt Ro's cock grow hard against her belly at the same time as he inhaled deeply. Then he smiled and shook his head. "Lord, you've got me by the bollocks, woman. I don't think I'll ever have enough of you. Come on. Let me feed you before you drain me dry again."

Chloe pushed her hips against him, loving the feel of his arousal. "Hey, you were the one who said I had to stay here for a while. I don't want us to be bored. Although I suppose we could watch TV or something."

"We're not watching the telly," Ro growled, letting go of her and backing away toward the refrigerator. "We're gonna eat breakfast, and then I'm going to take you back upstairs and show you exactly how not boring things around here can be."

Chloe nodded and climbed back up onto the chair. Her panties were damp, and she could feel her nipples tightening under her bra. It felt too small and constricting, but she knew she wouldn't be wearing it much longer.

"Sounds good. Will you let me make lunch?"

He cocked his head. "Lunch . . . ?"

"Yeah. You've been doing all the cooking. It's time I earned my keep around here."

He leaned over the counter and held her gaze. "You don't have to do a bloody thing, love. All you have to do is stay strong for me, and alive. That's it."

His words shouldn't've have made her thighs clench together, but they did. She'd spent the last five years being belittled and called lazy. She hadn't been allowed to cook or do anything for herself. She knew Ro wasn't cooking for her to be controlling. He was doing it because he wanted to take care of her. But she wanted to do the same for him.

"It's been about three and a half years since I've been allowed to work in a kitchen," she told him. "I might be a bit rusty, but I'd love to see if I can remember how to make you my favorite pasta dish I haven't had in years."

"Done," Ro said immediately. "Anything you want, love, you've got."

Chloe leaned forward until she was nose to nose with Ro. "What I want, is you."

"Fuck breakfast," Ro said under his breath, and stalked around the counter toward her. Before Chloe could utter a word, she was over his shoulder once more, and he was striding up the stairs back to his room.

Chloe giggled and held on.

Chapter Seventeen

The next three days were idyllic for Chloe. She spent her nights in Ro's bed, making love in so many different ways she was delightfully sore, and her days were spent laughing with him as they continued their War card game, watched television, and generally hung out together.

The sex was amazing, but what she loved most of all was getting to know Ro. It had been so long since she'd had even the simplest connection with someone that she found she appreciated it all the more. She *liked* Ro. He was funny, interesting, considerate, kind . . . she could go on and on. And sleeping with him, feeling his warm body next to hers, making her feel not so alone, was a gift. One she'd never take for granted. She had no idea what would happen between them after the threat of her brother was taken care of—*if* it was taken care of—but for now, she was going to live life to its fullest and enjoy every second she spent with Ro.

One day, she even went out to his garage to keep him company while he worked on the engine of a Porsche someone had brought in for service. She'd gotten so aroused watching him bend over the side of the car that she'd come up behind him and copped a feel.

Within seconds, he'd shoved her around to the back of the car, hoisted her up, and fucked her brains out right there against the expensive vehicle. She'd had grease marks from his fingers on her inner thighs, and her ass had hurt from where he'd pounded it against the unforgiving metal, but she couldn't have been happier.

They hadn't heard much from Rex, but each of the other men on his team had come over at some point to talk. Ro complained that they were coming over to check her out and to give him shit about being off the market, but he said it with a smile, so Chloe knew he wasn't exactly complaining.

Ball was still as intimidating as he'd been when he'd held her so tightly the night they'd kidnapped her, something she still gave him shit about, but as she got to know him better, she realized he wasn't nearly as scary as she'd remembered.

Black was her height, but he exuded a dangerous vibe that made her slightly uneasy. Ro told her he used to be a Navy SEAL, and she could've guessed that. He didn't say much, and his black hair matched his nickname. She could totally picture him fading into the night and not being seen by his enemies.

Gray and Allye came over for an afternoon, and Chloe had loved seeing the other woman again. The two of them spent the majority of their visit talking about Allye's dance program for special-needs kids that she'd started, and Chloe had made her promise to email some videos of the recitals. Gray seemed like the most laid-back guy of the bunch, but after hearing Allye's story about how she'd spent hours in the Pacific Ocean with him, and how he'd taken out the horrible man who'd tried to enslave her, Chloe realized sometimes the easygoing men were the most dangerous.

Then there was Arrow. He was the one who intrigued her the most. After hearing that he'd been there when Ro had been hurt, Chloe really wanted to talk to him. She'd touched the scars on Ro's back, seen first-hand how extensive they were. She couldn't imagine being burned as badly as he was and going through the rehab and skin grafts that Ro had to go through.

Luckily, Ro had to deliver the Porsche back to its owner, and he left her and Arrow alone together. He hadn't wanted to go, but Chloe had insisted that she would be fine for an hour or so with Arrow, and that *she* was the one under house arrest, not him. He'd scowled at that, but eventually had left.

The second he'd disappeared down his driveway, she'd turned to Arrow and said, "Tell me everything about the day Ro was hurt."

Arrow had frowned and asked, "He told you about that?"

"Yes."

"Frankly, I'm amazed. He doesn't tell many people, especially the details about what he went through while recovering." He hesitated. "Ro's my friend, Chloe. We've been through a lot of shit together. I feel like I have to say this, even though it makes me really uncomfortable." He paused, and Chloe knew what he was going to say before he said it. "You've basically been held captive a long time and haven't had the opportunity to be in any kind of relationship. Ro really likes you, and it seems as if you like him as well. But if that's not the case . . . I'm asking you to move on as soon as the threat from your brother is over. Please don't lead him on."

Chloe had wanted to be upset with Arrow, but she couldn't. She liked that Ro had people looking out for him. "I'm not leading him on," she'd told his friend. "I like him. A lot. And not just because he's helping me."

Arrow took in her words and finally nodded. "What'd he tell you, exactly?" Arrow asked, resuming their prior conversation. "Because I can't talk about top-secret stuff, and I won't elaborate on anything personal that he hasn't already told you."

Chloe appreciated the fact that Arrow had Ro's back, but she still wanted to know as much as possible. So she recounted what Ro had told her about the accident and his friend dying, and listened as Arrow filled in the blanks as much as he felt comfortable.

When he was done, Chloe's eyes were filled with tears, and she hurt all the more for Ro. He was the strongest man she'd ever met. Arrow told her how he'd gone to see Ro in the hospital and held his hand as the nurses scrubbed the dead skin off his back. It had been excruciating, but throughout it all, Ro had been stoic. Arrow had done his best to keep Ro's mind occupied by telling him stories about his own family, and his unit in the Marines. When he'd been reassigned back to the States, both men had been disappointed.

Chloe had hugged Arrow tightly and thanked him for being there for Ro.

"You don't have to thank me for that, Chloe," he'd responded. "*I* was supposed to be in that tank. It was supposed to be two men from his SAS unit and two Marines. Ro knew I was slightly claustrophobic, but that I wouldn't say anything. He pulled strings to arrange it so the Marines were on the outside of the tank, and him and his friends were on the inside. If I'd been in the tank, it would've been *me* who'd died. I owe him everything."

For the first time, Chloe truly understood the bond Ro and his friends had. It wasn't just that they liked kicking ass and taking names together. No, it went far deeper than that. They had each other's backs, no matter what. No questions asked. She had no doubt if she asked Gray, Ball, Black, or Meat, they'd have stories just like Arrow's. They'd all been there for each other. Saved each other's lives.

She'd never had a friendship like that but appreciated the fact that Ro did. She silently vowed to never come between Ro and his fellow mercenaries. She'd never ask him to quit. Never ask him to stop doing what he did.

He needed it. Just as people like her needed *him*.

By the time Ro returned, dropped off by the ecstatic owner of the Porsche who had gladly driven him home, Chloe and Arrow were fast friends.

It was now two days past the deadline of Leon's threat. Chloe was feeling safer than she had in a very long time. Ro had been talking to Rex, Meat, and the other men on his team on and off over the last three days, but she didn't know what was going on with her brother.

And that was okay.

It felt good to give that burden to Ro.

To let him take care of it.

She supposed that might make her weak, but she didn't care.

They were eating lunch after a vigorous lovemaking session—where Ro had bent her over the side of the couch and taken her hard from behind—when his cell phone rang.

Chloe couldn't hear who was on the other end of the line, but Ro frowned, pushed back from the table, and went into the other room to take the call.

He did that from time to time, and Chloe didn't feel slighted in the least. She'd given her trust to him, and that meant letting him take care of business his way. He'd tell her what was going on when he felt the time was right.

He came back in the room with the frown still on his face.

"Everything okay?" Chloe asked.

Ro shook his head. "I'm not sure. That was Black. He said that Meat and his computer-genius friend had found something, but that he didn't want to talk about it over the phone. Said it was huge, and possibly the key to everything that's been going on."

"That's good, right?" Chloe asked.

"I think so . . . but Black also said that Leon's in the wind. We've had people watching him and Abbie, but the surveillance team went quiet, and when Ball and Arrow went to check it out, they found both men missing."

Chloe sucked in a breath. "Missing?"

Ro nodded. "He called to tell me to keep our heads down and to stay alert."

"What should we do?" Chloe asked breathlessly. "Should we go somewhere? Do something?"

"Calm, love," Ro said, coming to her side immediately. "We're safe here. There's no reason to suspect that Leon has figured out who I am. If he had, he'd have shown up here by now. And if he does, I'm prepared."

Chloe relaxed. This was Ro. He was always prepared. She trusted him. "Okay."

"Okay."

They settled on the couch to watch a movie, and Chloe was just dozing off—when suddenly a loud alarm started blaring, seconds before the glass in the huge floor-to-ceiling windows exploded.

Chloe screamed and found herself on the floor in front of the couch with Ro on top of her, protecting her from flying glass.

"Stay down," he hissed in her ear.

She nodded and stayed flat on the floor.

Ro looked at the watch on his wrist. "Fuck! Somehow they breached the perimeter without setting off my alarms." He sounded extremely pissed off, and Chloe supposed she couldn't blame him.

The noise from the alarm was loud and instantly made her head throb. She was scared and confused and wasn't sure what she should do. Stay put or run like hell.

Ro took the choice out of her hands when he swore again and then hauled her upright without warning, shoving her toward the stairs. She stumbled and would've fallen if Ro hadn't been there holding her up even as he was pushing her forward.

"Stop right there if you don't want her to die," a voice called out above the ringing of the alarm.

Ro stopped and shoved her behind him with one arm as he turned to face whoever had spoken.

Standing in front of them were three men. They were dressed all in black, and two held pistols aimed at their heads. A third was carrying some sort of metal club.

"How'd you get past my alarms?" Ro asked, almost conversationally, as if he were at a meeting of badass, scary, military-type commandos, rather than standing in his own house trying to protect her from strangers.

"We have our ways," one of the men said over the ringing of the alarm. "We don't have a beef with you. We just want the woman."

"Over my dead body," Ro told him, and Chloe felt his muscles tense as if readying for a fight.

One of the men shot at the wall next to them, making both her and Ro lurch away from the bullet and closer to the man standing to their other side.

Everything happened extremely quickly after that. The man with the club swung and caught one of Ro's calves before he could move out of the way. He grunted and went to his knee, but immediately popped up again as if the strike hadn't hurt in the least.

The alarm was still blaring, and it made the fight seem even more surreal. No one was speaking: they simply sized each other up for a heartbeat as if trying to figure out who was going to make the next move.

Then one of the intruders swiftly reached into his pocket and flung something toward her and Ro.

Chloe closed her eyes and ducked at the same time Ro lunged so he was completely blocking her from whatever the man had thrown.

By the time Chloe stood up from the crouch she'd fallen into and opened her eyes, Ro was coughing violently and wavering from side to side in front of her. She had no idea what was in the powder the man had thrown at them, but whatever it was, Ro had taken it full in the face and was having a hard time catching his breath.

The men didn't hesitate to act now that Ro was momentarily stunned.

The man with the club used it on Ro once more, taking him to his knees as he violently coughed and wheezed in his attempt to breathe.

Even though he was clearly in distress, he still hadn't forgotten about her. He did his best to protect her, but the powder was doing its job, incapacitating him quickly.

Another man grabbed Chloe by the arm and leaped out of the way with her when Ro tried to tackle him.

She fought the man as hard as she could, horrified by what was happening to Ro right in front of her, and what the men might do to her if they took her away from the house. She coughed from inhaling some of the powder still hovering in the air. One hand went over her mouth when she began to scream.

"Fmmph uuu," Chloe shouted, but his hand muffled her words.

"Come on, Frank. Hurry up. She's a wildcat," the man yelled impatiently as he struggled to contain her.

Chloe's eyes widened as the man wielding the club came toward her. He had black hair and even blacker eyes. She frantically tried to pry the other man's arm away from her body, with no luck. Tears sprang to her eyes as she realized what was happening.

She was being kidnapped. Again.

But this time it wasn't by Ro's friends.

These men were deadly and ruthless. She could see it in their eyes. Had seen it in the way they'd held the weapons on her and Ro.

The man named Frank came toward her with a syringe in his hand. The sight triggered a sick feeling of déjà vu. "Hold still," he said, a slimy smile on his face. "You wouldn't want me to hurt you with this now, would you?"

Chloe kicked out with her feet and felt good when she managed to make contact with Frank's knee.

"Jesus, Jed, hold her still."

"I am," Jed said, tightening his hold around her torso and moving his hand off her mouth, only to clamp down again—this time covering both her nose and mouth.

Chloe couldn't breathe; almost immediately, black spots began to creep into the sides of her vision.

No. She couldn't die. Not like this. Not here in Ro's house. Not when she'd found a man she could trust and who she wanted to spend her life with.

"Ro!" she tried to scream, but all that came out was a muffled croak.

Frank came toward her again, but she had no fight left in her. The only thing she was focusing on was trying to get air into her lungs. The needle sank into her thigh, but she didn't notice because Jed lifted his hand for a moment. She sucked in air greedily, trying to hoard it before it was taken away again.

The room spun, and Chloe closed her eyes, feeling extremely dizzy. She didn't fight when Jed picked her up and carried her out of the destroyed living room. She heard glass crunching under his feet as he moved through the room but didn't open her eyes. The alarm continued to blare, and she had the momentary hope that one of Ro's neighbors would hear it and come to investigate.

Chloe finally forced her eyes open, and the last thing she saw as Jed carried her out of the house was the third man bashing Ro's head against the floor to keep him from coming after them.

Chapter Eighteen

Chloe frowned. Her head hurt, and yet again, her mouth felt like she'd been sucking on cotton balls. Not that she knew what sucking on cotton balls felt like, but she imagined the feeling in her mouth right now had to be pretty close.

Cautiously, she opened her eyes and looked around. She was lying on a soft bed in a beautiful room. There were heavy red curtains pulled back, letting in the afternoon sun. There was a dresser against the wall across from where she was lying. Turning her head, she saw several pillows next to her, and the gorgeous quilt beneath her looked handmade.

The problem was that she didn't recognize any of it. She didn't seem to be back at Leon's house, but she also wasn't at Ro's.

The thought of Ro had her sitting up suddenly, making her head swim. Refusing to give in to the dizziness, Chloe sat on the edge of the bed and tried to remember what had happened. The last thing she recalled was seeing Ro's head being bashed into the floor.

A whimper escaped her before she could call it back. Throwing a hand up to cover her mouth to prevent anyone from hearing that she was awake, Chloe forced herself to her feet. She stumbled over to the window and looked outside. She seemed to be on the upper floor of a house. She was looking down on an immaculate garden of some sort. The lawn below her was huge. In the distance, she could see several tall buildings. Squinting and tilting her head, Chloe realized the buildings were the Denver skyline. Which made no sense.

Had she been out that long?

Of course she had. She was here, wasn't she? Wherever *here* was.

Dammit! She couldn't believe she'd been fucking kidnapped. Again! She was getting sick and tired of people forcing her to go places she didn't want to go and to do things she didn't want to do. And she'd promised Ro she wouldn't be kidnapped again. She hated breaking her promise, even if it wasn't her fault.

Thoughts of Ro trying to protect her even when he was clearly hurt ran through her brain. As he'd lunged at the man who'd grabbed her, the look on his face had spoken volumes. He'd been enraged that someone had broken into his house, and even more so that they'd dared put their hands on her. But more than that, he'd looked . . . devastated. And she hated that. She wanted to tell him that he'd done everything possible to protect her. That her being kidnapped yet again wasn't on him. It was on the assholes who'd broken in.

Then she recalled the way the man had hit Ro's head on the tile. Ro had to be hurt badly. Had to have been knocked unconscious. There wasn't any way he could've bounced back from that enough to get away . . . was there? The vicious memory—and the other possible outcome to such a beating—threatened to make her knees collapse, but she forced herself to stay standing.

Ro wasn't dead. He couldn't be. No way. Not after everything else he'd been through.

No, Arrow or Meat or someone would go to his house to check on them when Ro didn't answer his phone, and they'd find him and get help.

She wasn't even thinking about her own situation at the moment and what was in store for her. If Ro had been killed because of her, Chloe would never forgive herself.

She spun at the sound of the door opening.

A man she'd never seen before entered the room and met her gaze. He was dressed in a pair of gray slacks with a button-down white shirt. A gray sport coat finished off his ensemble. He looked sleek and polished—and he scared the shit out of her.

Was she in some sort of high-end brothel? Was this her brother's whorehouse? Chloe thought he'd said it was in Colorado Springs, and they definitely weren't there anymore, but maybe he'd branched out? Sold her to someone else?

She wasn't sure, but she knew one thing for certain—she wasn't going to allow this man to take her against her will. No way. She'd fight with everything she had. Now that she'd given herself to Ro, she'd do whatever it took to make sure no one else sullied what was his.

With those thoughts in mind, Chloe's fists clenched, and she readied herself to fight.

"Good evening, Ms. Harris. If you wouldn't mind following me?"

Chloe blinked. She'd expected him to say, *"Get on the bed and spread your legs,"* or something equally crass. But instead, he was polite and sounded downright friendly. And he was waiting for her patiently. He had his hand out as if to show her the way.

She didn't want to go anywhere with him, but she also wanted to get out of there. Going out the window wouldn't work because of how high up they were. She'd fall and break a leg or something, and she'd never get away. She could always make a run for it once she was out of the room.

As cautiously as possible, she walked slowly toward the man in gray. She knew she wasn't walking in a straight line, still slightly dizzy, but she didn't care at the moment. She weaved across the room to where he was standing. The mystery man took hold of her elbow, but he didn't squeeze cruelly, like Leon's bodyguards liked to do. He was simply holding on to her, making sure she didn't topple over. He closed the door behind them and led her down the carpeted hallway toward a staircase.

Chloe's gaze took in everything around her. Later, she might need to describe where she'd been held to the authorities. Expensive-looking pictures on the walls, watercolors of landscapes. Tan carpeting. Lots of natural light. It was a place she would've loved to have had the chance to explore . . . if she wasn't being held hostage, that is.

The man in gray helped her down the stairs. Just when Chloe was going to snatch her arm out of his grip and make a run for what she thought was the front door of the house, she noticed light from an open door down an otherwise dark, long hallway.

"This way, Ms. Harris," the man said, wrapping an arm around her waist and steering her toward the hallway. She struggled for a moment, but she was still too weak from whatever she'd been drugged with.

"Relax," the man ordered. "You wouldn't get five steps before I'd be on you," he said in a perfectly normal, relaxed tone. That made it all the scarier for Chloe. If he'd threatened her in some way, or bruised her arm as he held her, that might've made more sense, but he was acting as if she was a welcome houseguest, except for telling her she couldn't outrun him, of course.

They passed two closed doors before arriving at the one that was open. Without pause, the man at her side led her through the door into what looked like a huge library or office. There were bookshelves along one wall that went from the floor to the ceiling and were stuffed full of books.

A large window ran along the back of the room, the view mirroring the one from the room she'd awakened in, looking out onto the vast grounds.

But it was the man sitting behind a massive desk to her right who held Chloe's attention.

She couldn't look away from him as the man in gray led her to a leather chair and helped her to sit. She barely noticed when he backed away and stood at attention next to the now-closed door.

The man behind the desk didn't look up. Didn't acknowledge her in any way. He was looking down at a spreadsheet of some sort, running his finger up and down rows and rows of numbers. He had dark hair liberally sprinkled with gray. She could see age spots on the backs of his hands. He wore a black sweater with a white collared shirt underneath. A desktop computer sat to his left and an old-fashioned phone to his right.

He exuded power, and as much as Chloe wanted to demand he tell her what the hell she was doing there, she said nothing. Simply waited for him to acknowledge her existence. To tell her what fate awaited her.

After five long minutes of silence, Chloe fidgeted on the soft leather. She was losing her patience and was scared out of her mind. The last thing she wanted was to hear him tell her she was to be sent off to some foreign country to service some sheikh sexually, but at that point, she had no idea what else to think.

After what seemed like an eternity, the man looked up. His brown eyes met hers—and she froze. She hadn't been wrong in thinking this man was powerful. She could tell with just that one glance that he usually got whatever he wanted. That those who worked for him probably bent over backward to do as he ordered.

Chloe almost threw herself on his mercy and begged him not to hurt her, but she held on to her dignity by her fingernails. She didn't think he was working for Leon. No way. This man worked for no one. Others worked for *him*.

"I suppose you're wondering what you're doing here," he said after he'd steepled his fingers under his chin and stared at her for the longest minute of her life.

Chloe simply nodded.

"Do you know who I am?" the man asked, a secret smile on his face indicating that he knew something she didn't. And she supposed he did. He held the cards here. All of them.

Chloe's head shook back and forth.

"Forgive me for not introducing myself sooner. I'm Joseph Carlino. You might not recognize me by sight, but I bet you'd recognize my investment accounts if you saw them, wouldn't you?"

For the second time that day, Chloe saw black dots fill her vision.

This was bad. Very bad. Leon was scary enough. But being in the presence of one of the very men she'd spent the last couple of years doing everything in her power to stay away from was enough to bring her to her knees in absolute terror.

Ro pushed Black's hand away from his head and scowled. "I'm fine."

"I hate to say it, but you're *not* fine," Black said calmly. "You've got a gash on your forehead that matches the one your girlfriend had a week ago. You need stiches, or at the very least, that glue shit you like to use so much."

Ro growled. He actually bared his teeth and growled at his friend and teammate. "I don't give a shit about my head. What I *do* give a shit about is Chloe, and what we're doing to find her and get her away from her wanker of a brother!"

He knew he was being an arse, but he couldn't help it. Black had called him back to update him on their search for Leon, and when Ro didn't answer, he'd called the rest of the team, who'd shown up en masse.

Ro had opened his eyes to four of his teammates standing over him looking pissed off and concerned at the same time. Meat had been sitting at the dining room table, clicking frantically on his laptop and talking on the phone.

The second he saw his teammates, Ro remembered what had happened. Whoever the men were who came for Chloe, they'd been good. *Really* good. They'd been able to circumvent his perimeter alarms so he hadn't any advance warning they were there before it was too late.

Mentally kicking himself, Ro couldn't keep the look of terror on Chloe's face out of his head. Whatever was in the powder that was used to incapacitate him had done its job well. The second he'd inhaled it, Ro had known he was fucked. Now that he could think clearly, and his fucking alarm wasn't blaring in his ears, he figured it was a derivative of pepper spray. At least its main ingredient, capsaicin. He'd taken the brunt of the powder right to his face and immediately couldn't see or breathe all that well.

He remembered Chloe screaming for him, remembered trying to get to her, but everything after that was a blur.

He'd told her over and over that she was safe. They'd made him go back on his word.

"Where the fuck would Harris take her?" Ro seethed. His head was throbbing, but he didn't give a shit. If he lost Chloe, or if her brother forced her to do something sexually, he'd never forgive himself. Never.

"You up for a little B&E?" Ball asked with a dark grin instead of answering his question.

"Fuck yeah," Ro answered, standing.

"You'll need to stop that bleeding first," Black said dryly. "Can't have you leaving your DNA all over Leon's house."

Without another word, Ro headed to the bathroom to get the adhesive glue. It was hard to believe he'd used the exact same stuff on Chloe only a week ago.

Five minutes later, he was back in his living room waiting for his friends to tell him what the plan was.

"Meat's called in some favors to get your windows boarded up," Gray said.

Ro waved off the information. He didn't give a shit about his windows. He needed to *do* something. To find Chloe.

"He's going to head to The Pit to continue doing what he can via computer to find Chloe. His friend is using traffic cameras to see if he can track her from here to wherever she was taken. There aren't many cameras out here in Black Forest, but no matter which way they went, the bastards couldn't have avoided them altogether. He's also going there to give us an alibi, just in case. Dave will vouch that we were all present and accounted for at a meeting. Even said he'd manipulate the security footage, using an old clip to show us all arriving today, if necessary. Give me your phones." Gray was all business, and everyone handed over their personal cell phones.

Ro hesitated. He and Chloe had been together for an entire week. Since they hadn't been apart, they hadn't needed to call each other. But he'd made her memorize his phone number, just in case. If he gave Gray his phone, he wouldn't be able to answer if she called.

"Meat will have them," Gray said, seeing Ro's distress. "If she calls, he'll be able to trace it and reassure her at the same time. You know we need the towers to ping us all at The Pit to cover our asses while we're at Harris's."

Knowing his friend was right, but not liking it all the same, Ro gave his friend his phone without protest.

"We'll find her," Gray said, putting a hand on Ro's shoulder.

Ro nodded. "What's the plan?"

"Harris hasn't been seen at his house all day, but he also hasn't *not* been seen at his house," Black said. "We're just going to go and check it out. We've got one hour."

Ro nodded. He cracked his knuckles in anticipation.

"The two men who were supposed to be watching Harris were found dumped about a mile from BJ's," Meat said from the table, still clicking away at the keys. "They both have nasty head wounds but are alive. They aren't conscious yet, so they can't tell us anything, but as soon as they're able, Rex is on it."

Ro shifted from one foot to the other impatiently. Every second that went by was another second Chloe was in danger. He felt it deep in his bones. They needed to find her. *Now.*

"Let's go," Arrow said. "We can talk about this on the way."

Ro was relieved his friend said exactly what he was thinking.

"One more thing," Gray said.

Everyone looked at him.

"Rex made me promise not to kill Harris. He wants to have a chat with the man."

Ro frowned. He couldn't promise that. No way. Not if Chloe was hurt. Not if Harris had sold her—or worse.

"No promises," Ball said gruffly. "We all know what men like him are capable of."

"And we all know Rex will be the first one in line to cut off his balls if he did something to hurt Chloe," Gray retorted. "All he's asking for is time to talk to the man first. Understand?"

Everyone nodded. They *did* understand. Rex wouldn't protect Harris from retribution if he'd killed Chloe or made her disappear into the underground world of sex trafficking. But he still wanted information first. Information that might save her, or someone like her, from a fate worse than death.

"Let's go," Black said, and he led the way to the door.

Ro followed his friends, teeth clenched, ignoring the pain that thundered through his skull. He blocked it out. The only important thing was finding Harris—and hopefully Chloe as well.

Chloe clenched her hands together in her lap. He hadn't made the slightest move toward her, but she knew he was one of the most powerful men in the Denver Mafia. Leon had told her all about him and what he was capable of. Her brother's overly descriptive narratives of how Carlino liked to torture his enemies was one of the main reasons she hadn't tried to escape. She definitely hadn't wanted this man getting his hands on her . . . and now here she was.

"We need to talk," Joseph said.

Chloe kept her eyes on his, too scared to look away.

"Tell me about your brother."

She blinked. That wasn't what she'd thought he was going to say. She'd thought he was going to bring up something she'd done wrong with his finances. Or tell her that she'd screwed up his investments. Maybe inform her she was now going to have to live in the dungeon in his basement because she knew too much.

Or worse yet, kill her extremely slowly, because of what she knew regarding where he was sheltering millions of dollars.

But tell him about Leon? That was the last thing she figured he'd be worried about. "What do you want to know?" she finally asked in a shaky tone.

"I received an interesting call the other day," Joseph told her, leaning back in his chair like he didn't have a care in the world. "From an acquaintance of mine. After we spoke, I did some research myself, but it seems your brother's not quite as dumb as he looks . . . or actually, his *accountant* isn't. My people couldn't really figure out what we were looking at. So I went straight to the source. Or rather, brought the source to me."

Chloe tried not to hyperventilate. She *had* been creative with Leon's money. She had to be. He was spending it faster than he was making it. Not to mention he was doing some pretty shady stuff. He had a hefty monthly income stream from a source he refused to talk to her about, which she hadn't been able to track down, and several smaller monthly deposits. She'd assumed the larger amounts were from the people he was blackmailing. She hadn't known about the whorehouse he'd started, though, until he'd bragged about it that night in his car. She'd thought all along that it was another strip club.

But regardless, she'd done the best she could to make sure, on the surface, nothing seemed out of the ordinary if someone checked him out or in case of an audit.

"Chloe?" Joseph asked impatiently.

Swallowing, Chloe did the only thing she could. She opened her mouth and told the incredibly scary man everything.

Leon Harris's house was quiet. Ro methodically used his binoculars to scan the windows of the large mansion. He didn't see anyone in the rooms with open curtains, and there were no shadows moving behind the curtains that were closed.

He brought a hand to his throat and pressed against the mic there, opening the connection. "Clear," he said in a toneless whisper.

He heard the others report the same information.

"Stick with the plan," Black said. "Move in three."

Ro stowed the binoculars and prepared to enter the mansion. He was more than ready for this moment. More than ready to confront Leon Harris and make sure the man knew he was out of his league and if he even *looked* at his sister again, he'd regret it.

As one, the team used flashbang grenades to enter the mansion at five different points.

They encountered no resistance whatsoever. In fact, they didn't encounter anyone at all.

The loud explosive devices didn't bring a single person running to see what was going on, and they didn't catch anyone unawares.

When all five men stood in the middle of the foyer at the front of the house, Arrow said what they were all thinking. "Where the fuck is everyone?"

The sick feeling in Ro's belly intensified. It wasn't as if he'd really expected Harris to be here, or Chloe, but he'd seriously hoped. Because if they weren't here, he had absolutely no idea where they could be. And that was bad. Very bad. He knew they'd eventually track them down—it was what the Mountain Mercenaries did—but he couldn't bear to think about what Harris might do to Chloe in the meantime.

"Everyone, fan out. Search every nook and cranny. Under beds, in closets, even in the fucking washer and dryer. Check every single place someone could be stashed. Nothing goes unchecked. If anyone is here, find them," Gray ordered.

Within seconds, Ro was heading up the stairs. He and Arrow went room by room, searching and clearing each. Everything seemed normal, until they reached a room at the end of a hallway. There was a padlock on the outside of the door.

Ro growled low in his throat, instinctively knowing *this* was where Chloe had spent most of her time when she was living here, at least in the last couple of years. Her bastard of a brother had literally locked her in like an animal.

"I got this," Arrow said. "Step back."

Ro gripped the rifle in his hands tighter and did as his friend ordered. He took a step backward and let Arrow take care of the lock. Within seconds, he'd smashed it, and the broken metal fell to the floor with a thunk.

Arrow took a position on one side of the door, and Ro nodded at him. He lifted his foot and kicked the door. It came off its hinges and fell open immediately, and both men surged inside, their weapons at the ready.

They stopped in their tracks at the sight that greeted them.

Two legs were sticking out of the attached bathroom. Definitely female. Definitely not moving.

Ro took a step toward her, but Arrow stopped him with a hand on his arm. "No. I said I got this."

Ro wanted to protest. Wanted to be there for Chloe . . .

But he was a coward. If she was dead, he didn't want to remember her that way. He wanted to remember her eyes sparkling with humor and life. Wanted to remember the way she threw her head back and shuddered when she came around him.

Swallowing hard, Ro nodded at his friend. Turning, he walked over to the closet to check it out.

He eyed the skimpy clothes that didn't fit Chloe's personality at all. They were hanging in neat rows. There were several pairs of high heels lined up perfectly on the floor. Seeing firsthand how she'd been forced to live infuriated Ro. He was supposed to protect her from all this. Keep her safe from her brother. But instead she was—

Ro stopped his line of thought and turned back to the bathroom. Something niggled at the back of his brain after seeing the closet. He strode toward the bathroom and arrived just as Arrow was standing up after examining the woman on the floor.

"It's not Chloe," Arrow said.

Ro nodded. He'd figured that out for himself. The shoes the woman was wearing were way too small. After seeing the high heels in the closet, which had to be Chloe's, it had clicked.

"Is she dead?" Ro asked, not happy about the situation at all.

Arrow nodded. "She's definitely dead." He gestured to the bottles on the counter. Aspirin, Tylenol, cold medicine, antihistamines. Nothing lethal, but taken together, in large quantities, they'd done what the woman had been hoping they'd do.

Ro looked down at the dead woman and saw the foam that had dried around her mouth and the bile on the floor around her. It hadn't been an easy death, but at the moment, Ro couldn't care.

"Any idea who she is?" Arrow asked.

Ro nodded. "Abbie, Harris's girlfriend. But the bigger question is, why is she locked inside this room, dead? From everything Chloe's told us, she's a hard-hearted, nasty bitch. Why would she kill herself? Not only that, would Leon have locked his girlfriend in his sister's room?"

"Maybe without Chloe here to knock around, Leon turned to Abbie?" Arrow suggested.

Ro shrugged. "I don't know, but at the moment, I'm more concerned about finding Chloe."

The two men left the woman on the floor and finished their inspection of the room. In the drawers were more skimpy clothes. There weren't any pictures, books, or anything else that proved a woman as caring, enthusiastic, and interesting as Chloe lived there.

"Fucking arsehole," Ro said under his breath.

Then he remembered something Chloe had told him one night.

He went back into the closet and knelt, examining the floor. Finding what he was looking for, he pried up one of the boards and inhaled deeply. Under the floor were Chloe's passport, a couple of changes of clothing, and a few knickknacks that obviously had sentimental value. Stuff she'd squirreled away for when the time came for her to escape.

He grabbed the passport and stuffed it into a pocket, trying to concentrate on the task at hand, not how scared his Chloe must've been while she'd been living in this house, hoping her stash wasn't discovered.

"Come on, we need to keep looking."

Hearing Arrow's words, Ro nodded and took a deep breath. Chloe was never coming back here. Ever. Not if he had anything to say about it.

After another twenty minutes, all five men met back downstairs to report.

"It looks like there were people here not too long ago," Black said. "I'm guessing servants. There's food on the stove, and the kitchen door was ajar. They probably heard the flashbangs and ran. We didn't see any vehicles leaving, so it's likely they fled on foot."

Arrow looked at Ro, then said, "We found the girlfriend. Dead of an overdose in a locked room upstairs. We had to break the padlock to get inside the bedroom."

"Hmmm," Ball said. "Any chance she locked herself in?"

"None," Ro answered.

"So someone locked her in, and she killed herself. Interesting," Ball mused.

Ro ground his teeth in frustration. Nothing. They had nothing more now than when they'd arrived. Abbie was dead—that was one person Chloe didn't have to worry about again—but they had no more clues as to where her brother had fled to.

He followed his friends out of the house and back to their vehicles. As soon as they were on their way to The Pit, Gray called Rex to report in.

Ro was only half listening to his friend when the words *fire* and *arson* penetrated. He waited impatiently for Gray to hang up and talk to them.

The second he clicked off the phone, Gray said, "BJ's burned to the ground late this morning. Officials are still investigating, but early thoughts are that it was arson. There's no information about injuries or deaths yet."

Ro had been about to suggest they storm the strip club to see if Harris was keeping his sister there, but with the news that the club had burned down, he was at a loss.

"What now?" he asked, frustrated and angry.

"We go to The Pit and hope like hell Meat's got something for us," Gray said grimly.

Ro wanted to hit something. Or someone. Wanted to be out doing something, not sitting around waiting for information. The longer they waited, the farther and farther away Chloe could be. Every rescue they'd been on to help kidnapped women ran through his mind. Every brothel they'd raided in foreign towns. Every broken and humiliated woman they'd brought back to her desperate family.

That couldn't be Chloe. It couldn't. The thought of her beautiful smile and strong spirit being snuffed out was almost painful.

The rest of the ride back to The Pit was done in silence. No one wanted to bring up the awful possibility that Harris had gotten to his sister and disappeared.

Chapter Nineteen

Joseph Carlino hadn't said a word throughout Chloe's nervous babbling. She'd told the man *everything*. How much she'd loved her job at Springs Financial Group. About her dad's death. How her brother had invited her to move in with him until she was back on her feet. About how she couldn't find a job and how she'd started helping Leon. How she'd done Carlino's taxes for two years before she'd known who he was. How she'd helped Leon buy the club. Even all the details of how he and Abbie had kept her a prisoner in her own house, locking her in her room at night and making her work at BJ's. She described, in detail, her plan to escape her brother and how she'd hidden her passport under the floor in her closet and had been slowly stealing money from Leon for years so she could get away. She even blabbed about how Leon had threatened to send her to his whorehouse to work.

Then, when Joseph simply stared at her and calmly asked if that was all, she'd blurted out everything that had happened in the last week. How Ro had saved her from other clients that night at the club—including the embarrassing details of pretending to give him a blow job even though he hadn't gotten hard. She told the taciturn man about being "kidnapped" by Ro and his friends—but, even though she was petrified of being found out, she was careful not to mention the Mountain Mercenaries or Rex. She told Carlino about spending the last week with Ro. Told him what Meat had discovered about her mom being rich, though she admitted she didn't fully believe it. She explained why her father's will seemed funny.

And at the very end of her nervous outburst, Chloe told the head of the Denver Mafia that she loved Ronan Cross after being with him just one week, and that she knew it was too soon but she couldn't help it.

By the time she finished talking, Chloe was exhausted. She was sweating and felt as if she'd run a marathon. She glanced at her watch to see how much time had gone by. It seemed like hours. She was shocked to see she'd been talking for only twenty minutes.

She'd blabbed her entire life story in twenty freaking minutes.

Chloe glanced up at Joseph and waited for him to say something. Anything. He kept his intense gaze on her and still had his hands steepled at his chin.

Finally, he dropped his hands and said, "Thank you for being honest, Chloe. I appreciate it. You look tired. I'll have a tray brought up, and you can nap. I'll see you again at dinner."

And with that, he used his head to motion toward the man in gray, still standing at the doorway. Before she could process what was happening, the man was at her side and was helping her stand with his hand at her elbow once again.

"Oh, but—"

"Dinner, Chloe," Joseph said firmly. "I have work that needs to be done."

He looked back down at the spreadsheet in front of him. It was an obvious dismissal, and Chloe had no choice but to go with the other man.

Confused, worried, and feeling sick to her stomach, Chloe didn't fight the return trip up the stairs and back to the room she'd woken up in. The man bowed as he left her standing next to her bed. "Is there anything you'd like me to tell Cook you'd like to eat?"

Chloe mutely shook her head. She felt like she was in the twilight zone. She'd been kidnapped from Ro's house, and she still had no idea if he was all right or not. Yet, here she was, being treated like she was an honored guest. It was disorienting and frightening at the same time.

She waited until the man had been gone for a few minutes before tiptoeing to the door of the bedroom and cautiously turning the knob. Surprisingly, it opened easily. They hadn't locked her in.

She blinked at another man standing in the hallway. He was dressed just as nicely as the man in gray, but he looked both bigger and stronger.

"Can I help you, miss?" he asked.

Chloe hurriedly shook her head and shut the door, shivering. So she wasn't a guest, after all. She had no doubt that the man in the hall would prevent her from leaving. She wasn't physically locked in the room, but she may as well have been. She *still* couldn't believe she'd been kidnapped again.

Instead of crying, Chloe got mad. Enough was freaking enough. She was getting out of there and back to Ro if it was the last thing she did.

"I talked to Joseph Carlino three days ago," Rex said.

The Mountain Mercenaries were at The Pit and were huddled around their usual table in the back, talking with Rex on the phone.

"And?" Ro asked impatiently.

"And he had no idea that Harris had purchased a strip club, *or* that he'd started his own prostitution ring. Needless to say, he wasn't happy."

Rex recounted their conversation, but the news wasn't exactly a surprise. The Carlinos and Smaldones had stuck to other money streams, partly because of Rex. The leaders of the Cosa Nostra knew if they wanted to keep the man out of their business, they had to avoid exploiting women. And they had. Until Leon Harris had branched out. Since they'd invited Ray Harris to join their group, expectations were that when he passed away, his son would also stick to extortion and blackmail and other crimes that would keep the Mountain Mercenaries off their backs. To learn the younger Harris had deliberately misled them and used his Cosa Nostra connections to operate both the strip club and brothel had infuriated them.

"What does this have to do with Chloe?" Ro asked gruffly, not giving a shit about strippers or prostitutes at the moment.

"Patience, Ro," Rex scolded.

"Piss off, Rex!" Ro snapped, scooting his chair back and flexing his fists. "This isn't *your* woman who's missing. It's *mine*. She's scared to death of her brother, and we're sitting around with our thumbs up our arses. We need to find her before she breaks."

"Sit down," Rex barked, and Ro did.

How the man knew he'd stood, Ro had no idea, but he wouldn't be surprised if there were surveillance cameras in The Pit that they, or even Dave, didn't know about. "I have a theory. Meat, want to share what you and your friend found?"

"Gladly," Meat said. "First of all, Louise Harris was indeed killed as a result of a random carjacking. She was on her way to help build a house for the homeless when a crackhead shot her in the head and stole her purse. We found out earlier that she was loaded. Like, super loaded; we told you guys that. But what we didn't know was that there were stipulations attached to her money. It could only be passed to her daughters. Not her husband. Not her sons. Not her brothers or other distant relatives. The money was *specifically* to be split among and inherited by any female offspring—when they turned thirty-five."

Ro sucked in a breath, but he didn't have a chance to comment before Meat continued.

"But until her thirty-fifth birthday, a stipend was to be deposited every month into Chloe's account. It looks like her father had that money funneled to his own account."

"How much?" Gray asked.

"Fifty g's."

Gray whistled.

"Right. So, fifty thousand a month was going to her father, but when he died, Leon was in charge of the stipend," Meat shared.

Ro shifted in his seat as everything started to become clear. "The bastard knew about the rest of the inheritance, didn't he?"

Meat nodded. "Absolutely. And that lawyer who read his dad's will wasn't a lawyer at all. Leon hired him to forge the documents and put on a good show when Chloe was there for the reading. He claimed all his dad's investments and took over the family businesses as well."

"Why did he want Chloe alive, then?" Gray asked. "If she was dead, her fortune would probably go to the next of kin, right?"

Meat shook his head. "No. That's the craziest part. All the money, *including* the monthly stipends, would go to the charity of Chloe's choice. And if she died before claiming her inheritance and hadn't named one, it would be dispersed to the charities her mom had picked before her."

"*All* of it?" Arrow asked.

"Every penny," Meat confirmed.

"So her ass of a brother *couldn't* kill her. He's just been stealing her money all these years, and she's had no clue," Ball summarized. "But where is she now?"

Ro realized he was clenching his teeth so hard it was making the vein in his head throb. Which in turn was making his headache worse. He wanted the answer to Ball's question more than he wanted his next breath.

"And why is Harris's girlfriend lying dead in his house?" Black added.

"And who burned BJ's to the ground?" Arrow put in.

"And where's Ray Harris's real will?" Gray asked.

"As I said, I called Joseph Carlino," Rex said again, picking up the story. "He wasn't pleased to hear about Harris's side ventures. Even less that it was *me* calling to tell him about them, especially after he and his associates have gone out of their way to keep me out of their business."

"Bloody hell," Ro said, pushing back his chair once more. He didn't need Rex to draw him a fucking picture.

He also didn't hesitate, just turned his back on the table and headed for the door.

Gray caught his arm. "Ro. Wait. Where are you going?"

"To get my woman back," he said with conviction.

"I'm driving," Ball stated. "Meat, give me your keys."

Without hesitation, Meat threw the keys to his Hummer across the table. Everyone knew Ball was the best driver out of all of them. If anyone could get them to Chloe fast, it was him.

"Don't worry about me. I'll just hang out here," Meat called out as Gray, Arrow, Ro, Ball, and Black ran out of the room.

Chloe hadn't slept. The man in gray had brought up a tray, as he'd promised. It held some cheese, cold cuts, and delicious-looking pastries, but Chloe's stomach was rolling, and she knew if she tried to eat anything, it would just come up again.

So she paced the room, bit her fingernails, and tried to come up with a plan. She had no idea why she was here and what Joseph Carlino was going to do with her. She was still terrified that he'd think she was hiding something and torture her to find out what he wanted to know, despite Rex's assurances, but she'd told him everything—except any mention of the Mountain Mercenaries. She didn't care what he was doing with his money. All she wanted was to go home to Ro and pretend she'd never heard of the Carlino or Smaldone families.

Refusing to give in to despair, she'd searched the room for anything she could use as a weapon. The closest thing she'd found was a hairbrush. Fat lot of good that was going to do. There was no phone, no knives or forks included with the food tray, not even a loose spring or anything else she could make into a shank of some sort.

She was going to have to use her head. She couldn't overpower any of the men, and they'd drug her again in a heartbeat if they thought she was trying to escape.

Two excruciating hours later, a tap sounded on her door. Expecting someone to enter, she waited.

When the tap came again, Chloe wrinkled her brows and said, "Come in."

It was the same man in the gray suit from earlier.

"Ms. Harris. If you would be so kind as to allow me to escort you to dinner?" He held out his arm as if they were at a fancy party or something.

"And if I'm not hungry?"

"You don't have to eat, although I know for a fact that Cook has outdone herself tonight. Your presence *is* required, however."

"I figured," she said under her breath. Then, straightening her spine and trying not to be intimidated, she marched toward the door and past the man, refusing to take his arm. He didn't seem put out in the least. Simply shut the door behind him and walked slightly behind her down the hall and the stairs, then gestured to her right to enter the large dining room.

She stopped short at seeing the group of people assembled in the room.

Joseph Carlino was there, of course, but there were also three other men as well. She hadn't seen any women since she'd woken up, and that worried Chloe, but she tried not to let anything show on her face.

The man in gray led her to a seat next to Joseph, and Chloe reluctantly took it. She looked around the table, memorizing the faces of the others who were there. She didn't remember seeing any of them before.

The man on her other side was younger than Joseph, but he had the same hard look in his eyes as the head of the Carlino family. He was wearing a pair of khakis and a long-sleeve shirt with a black tie. He had blond hair and was fairly slender.

The two men on the other side of the table both had light hair too, and were well built. They were obviously younger than either of the men to her right and left. They were wearing polo shirts and staring at her intently. Even though at first glance they seemed to be scarier than Joseph and whoever was sitting on her other side—at least stronger and more muscular—she had a feeling they weren't the ones she needed to worry about.

Swallowing hard and trying not to puke, she sat and waited for whatever was going to happen to play out.

Joseph picked up a hand and gestured to someone standing off to the side, and immediately a door opened and servants entered with plates. They placed the appetizers in front of everyone, and Chloe glanced down to see a delicious-looking crab cake and two fried shrimps.

Joseph picked up a fork and began to eat, as did everyone else.

Chloe was so stressed, she didn't think she could eat anything, but rather than just sit there, she did her best.

"Good girl," Joseph said under his breath as he continued to eat.

Relieved that he didn't seem to be upset at the moment, Chloe decided that, at the very least, she needed to keep up her strength. And if this was her last meal, her stressed mind decided she should just try to enjoy it.

And so the evening went. They would finish one course. Then servants would enter to clear their plates. Then they'd put something else down in front of them. Salad. Palate cleanser. Soup. The main course was filet mignon—cooked exactly how she liked it—mashed potatoes, green beans, and scallops. She wasn't much of a seafood lover, except for shrimp, so she left those untouched on her plate.

Dessert was an amazing piece of key lime pie, complete with a huge stack of meringue on top of the limey goodness.

Chloe hadn't thought she could eat anything, but once she started, she realized how hungry she was and cleaned each of her plates, except for the scallops, of course.

The men kept up a steady stream of chatter. Mostly they talked about sports and the latest in the local news and political arenas. She wasn't asked for her opinion, and she didn't volunteer it.

Once the dessert plates were taken away and coffee was brought out, Joseph turned to her. Chloe knew her reprieve was at an end. Tensing, she waited to see what her fate would be.

"Ms. Harris. As I mentioned earlier, the other day, I heard some distressing news. I didn't want to believe it, but when my associates here"—he nodded to the men across the table from her—"investigated, they found the accusations to be true."

Chloe didn't respond. He hadn't actually asked her anything, and she had no idea what he was talking about.

But apparently he didn't need her to say anything, because he continued. "I had that little issue taken care of, but since, I've learned of more and more upsetting news. You confirmed most of it today."

Chloe shivered but couldn't take her eyes from Joseph's.

"You have a choice to make, little one."

She frowned at the term of endearment. At least it sounded like a term of endearment. "Me?" she whispered.

"In my world, women are to be respected. Always. And not only because I don't want the Mountain Mercenaries breathing down my neck."

She gasped at hearing the name of Ro's team. She suddenly realized if the head of the Denver Mafia knew about the Mountain Mercenaries, they were maybe a much bigger deal than she'd thought they were. Not to mention, if *this* man didn't want to be on their radar, Ro and his team were definitely a powerful group.

Strangely enough, that comforted her. Made her feel as if she had a shot at getting out of this, since she was with one of the Mountain Mercenaries.

"Your brother has taken it upon himself to slander the Cosa Nostra reputation. He has defiled what we do and what we stand for. No matter what decision you make tonight, he will be punished as a result."

"He will?"

The man on her other side spoke to her for the first time. "Yes. He's your brother, and I realize that blood ties are strong. But he is not *our* brother . . . and restitutions must be made."

Chloe swallowed and turned her head to look at him. He smiled at her and nodded. "My name is Peter Smaldone. The men sitting across from you are my sons."

She stared at the man. Rex had told her earlier that Smaldone hadn't been the one to beat her up, but she only now realized it hadn't truly sunk in until this moment. She was face-to-face with the truth.

For years, she'd done what Leon had ordered her to do because she was scared the Mafia would come back and torture her. But it had all been a ruse. A lie to control her. And she'd fallen for it hook, line, and sinker. She'd hated her brother for a long time, but every new act of treachery was yet another hard pill to swallow.

She took a deep breath to try to control her emotions, then nodded at Peter. She did the same to the two men across the table. Then she turned back to Joseph. "I don't understand. Restitutions?"

"You were led to believe that your father was killed in a home invasion, is that correct?"

Chloe nodded. "Yes. Someone broke in and shot him when he was working in his office."

"That was a lie."

She inhaled sharply and stared at Joseph in distress as the older man continued.

"Your brother had him killed. Hired a drug addict from the streets to do it. He let him into the house and led him right to your father's office. He was shot in the head, and Leon paid the druggie two grand. The moment the man was back on the streets, he arranged for *him* to be killed as well. No witnesses, you understand."

Chloe felt dizzy with shock. *Leon* had their father killed? "Why?" she croaked.

"Why? For your money, of course."

"My money?" Chloe asked.

"Ah yes . . . you don't know about that either. You, little one, are worth a half billion dollars."

Chloe blinked and stared at Joseph, shaking her head.

"Your mother was a rich woman," Peter said. "But the money could only pass to a daughter. Your father was getting fifty thousand a month as a stipend to manage the funds. When Leon graduated from college, he was given a year to triple that money, or he was out of the family business. He decided to kill your father and get all the money instead."

Joseph continued the story. "But unfortunately, Leon was informed by your father's lawyer that the monthly allowance would immediately be transferred to *you*, and he wouldn't get any of it. He was further informed that if you were killed, all your money would go to charity, and not to your closest living relative—him—as he'd assumed. Given your brother's immense greed, I imagine this wasn't what he wanted to hear, and it enraged him."

Chloe's head swung between Peter and Joseph in disbelief. She could barely believe anything they were saying.

Peter continued. "So instead of killing you and losing the money forever, he decided to try to marry you off to one of his friends, so they could work out together how to divide your money. If that didn't work, he figured he would cow you enough to do whatever he wanted. He was planning on eventually blackmailing you and then forging documents for you to sign, giving him access to the money."

"But he had to get rid of the family attorney first," Joseph continued. "He had him killed, as well—made it look like a heart attack. And your dad's will was forged so it appeared Leon got everything. He managed to get you fired from your job, spread rumors that you were dishonest and incompetent so no one else would hire you."

"How in the world do you *know* all this?" Chloe asked, her head spinning.

Joseph then nodded at a man standing next to a door before he looked back at her. "So you have a decision to make," he said, repeating what he'd said before he and his friend Peter had rocked her world. "Leon Harris has brought way too much attention to us. He's since learned the error of his ways and has kindly told us everything we wanted to know. Namely, what he's been up to the last five years."

A commotion at the door made Chloe turn to look. She gasped in horror.

Two of the men who had kidnapped her from Ro's house stood there—holding Leon between them.

His head drooped, and he barely looked conscious. He had blood all over his clothes, and if she wasn't mistaken, there were a few fingers missing from both hands.

Leon had been right all along. Joseph Carlino *was* known for having people tortured. But she knew her brother had never thought he'd be the one at the older man's mercy.

Leon had terrorized her for years, telling her what would happen if she left, if she stopped doing the Mafia's books. And now she had visual proof of those threats.

Chloe swallowed hard and did her best to keep the delicious dinner she'd just eaten from coming back up. She turned away from the sight of her brother and looked back at Joseph as he continued to speak.

"He was stubborn, but in the end, he told us everything. He will be dying tonight, little one," Joseph told her gently, but with steel in his eyes. "*Your* choice is how merciful we will be."

Chloe stared at the man in shock. For a short time, before Leon's arrival, she'd almost begun to think maybe he and Peter had gotten a bad rap when it came to their reputations. The fancy dinner, the good manners, the normal conversation.

But she understood that everything he'd told her he'd learned because her brother had been tortured.

"He's your brother, and you have the right to spare him more pain, but remember what he had planned for you. You would've essentially become another of his sex workers. You wouldn't have had a choice. He was going to film your . . . liaisons . . . and sell them on the internet. Online porn is big business, and he was making quite a bit of money from the little videos he made at his strip club and at the brothel. He made a profit from downloads, but also from making those who didn't want their faces all over the internet pay to keep their activities anonymous. His web domain has been compromised and all the videos erased. The strip club he built is no more. We had it burned to the ground this morning. And the brothel also no longer exists."

"The women?" Chloe asked fearfully.

"Such a tender heart," Peter said behind her, but Chloe didn't turn to look at him. She only had eyes for Joseph. She knew he was in charge here.

"Safe. Those who wished to go home to their families were given a generous stipend and will be escorted to either the airport or the bus station. Those who prefer the lifestyle will be given money and an invitation to join reputable establishments, where they can continue their chosen profession legally and safely."

Chloe sighed in relief.

"I'm sure you understand, however, that we can't have others in La Cosa Nostra thinking they can do their own thing. We have rules. Strict ones. And Leon thought he was immune to them. That is not the case. I'm sorry, but this will be the last time you see your brother. The police will announce that they found his remains in the strip club he so dearly loved."

Chloe knew she paled, but she couldn't look away from the man next to her as she asked, "And me?"

"And you *what*, little one?"

"I know about you. I know where your money comes from, where it's invested and sheltered, and what you're planning on doing with my brother."

He stared at her for a long time before answering. There was no sound in the large dining room except for the occasional moan from her brother.

Joseph's jaw tightened several times, but he finally spoke. "I trust that after tonight, our paths will not cross again. You will deny any knowledge of what happened with your brother, and you will forget everything you know about me and my business partner."

Peter's hand fell onto her shoulder, and Chloe swallowed the bile that crept up her throat. "In fact, I suggest that you find another profession. Financial advising isn't something that you want to do for the rest of your life. It might cause too many questions from the authorities, don't you think?" Peter asked.

"Yes, sir," she answered immediately.

The hand left her shoulder, and Joseph put his finger under her chin and tipped it up so she had no choice but to look at him. "I'm sorry about Frank and Jed. They do tend to get a little . . . enthusiastic in their duties. I hope you weren't hurt when they collected you?"

She almost snorted at his use of words but refrained. Collected, her ass. They'd kidnapped her, plain and simple. "No. But I'm worried about Ro."

"He's fine," Joseph reassured her. "He probably has a headache, but he's okay."

She sighed in relief. "Are you sure?"

"I'm sure. So . . . your brother?"

Chloe turned to look at the men in the doorway once more. She didn't see the boy she used to play with. She saw the man who was going to force her to have sex with strangers and film it to sell on the internet. Who had stolen money from her. Threatened her. Held her captive.

Who'd had their father, and who knew how many others, murdered.

Feeling sick, she closed her eyes, looked down at her hands, and said, "I don't have a brother."

She heard movement near the door but didn't look up again until the room was silent. She didn't know what Carlino had in store for Leon, but she had a feeling his death wouldn't be quick. Chloe opened her eyes and turned to the man who she knew could have her killed and not feel any remorse about it. "I want to go home," she whispered.

"And what will you tell the authorities?" he asked.

"Nothing," she confirmed.

"And our investments?" he pressed.

"What investments?" she replied dutifully. "All I want is to go home. To live my life in peace. No offense, but I don't want anything to do with you or your business. I don't care what you do, as long as I'm not involved. I'm glad you aren't using women, because it really sucks when men think they can do whatever they want because they're bigger and stronger. Please. I know Ro has to be freaking out and that he's worried. I just want to go back to his house and pretend none of this happened."

Joseph didn't reply, just snapped his fingers and scared the crap out of her in the process. He looked over at the men on the other side of the table. "Ms. Harris would like to leave now. Please make sure she's escorted to the edge of the property. Tell the gentlemen who are even now preparing to make entry along the west side of the gate that they are free to take her and go. That we don't want any trouble."

Chloe's head whipped back to him. How in the world did he know someone was on his property? She hadn't seen anyone pass him a note or whisper to him during dinner.

Then she glanced down at his arm. He had one of those fancy smartwatches that could receive text messages as well as browse the internet. She'd seen him looking at it several times during dinner, but she hadn't thought much about it.

For the first time since she'd woken up in the bedroom upstairs, her spirits rose.

Joseph looked back to her and put his hand on the side of her face. "I'm sorry about your father, little one. He was a good man, and one we enjoyed working with. If I may give you some advice . . ." His voice trailed off, and Chloe could do nothing but nod.

"The amount of money you will come into on your thirty-fifth birthday isn't something to mess around with. Make sure you and those you love are protected so that something like this doesn't happen again. With your background, I'm sure you can figure out how to do that."

She nodded. She understood what he was saying. Money ultimately had killed her entire family. Ro had a lot, as well, but she never would've guessed. She didn't need a huge house and servants and other things like that. She just needed Ro. She'd figure out what to do about her inheritance so it wouldn't be a magnet for evil, one way or another.

"Thank you," she told Joseph.

"You're welcome. Now, up you go. Your man and his friends are getting impatient. Hurry along now."

Chloe stood, and the Smaldone sons were there to escort her. Without a backward glance at the two most powerful men in Denver, or at the doorway her brother had disappeared through, she eagerly followed the men toward the front door . . . and Ro.

Chapter Twenty

Ro flexed his fingers as he prepared to scale the large fence surrounding the Carlino estate. When Rex had told them that the man wasn't happy to learn about what Leon had been doing, everything clicked.

They couldn't find Leon Harris because Joseph Carlino had gotten to him first. He had a feeling Chloe wouldn't ever have to worry about her brother again. Which kind of sucked, because Ro had wanted to make the man pay himself.

He realized that the men who had come to his house were most likely working for Carlino as well. They were professionals, and there was no way they would've left him alive if they didn't *want* him alive.

The head of the Denver Mafia had snatched Chloe right out from under his nose, but Ro didn't know why, and that was what pushed him at the moment. He needed to make sure Chloe was safe. It didn't matter that pissing off the Denver Mafia wasn't exactly a smart move. Chloe wasn't a pawn to be used. If Carlino tried to use her to make her brother do something, he'd have a rude awakening when he found out there was no love lost between the siblings.

Just when he was ready to move, to storm Carlino's house and find Chloe, Gray said, "Hold. Movement at one o'clock."

Everyone crouched low at the metal fence surrounding the property and stilled, waiting to see who was approaching.

Ro blinked in disbelief as two men calmly walked straight toward them. They were wearing polo shirts and khaki pants and looked like they were on a nightly stroll.

Except for the fact they each had a hand on a woman's elbow. She was walking between them, trying to keep up with their long strides.

Chloe.

Ro growled low in his throat and had no conscious memory of moving. One second, he was crouched on the ground, and the next he was up and over the fence as if it didn't exist. He vaguely heard his teammates swearing and scrambling to follow him, but he had eyes and ears only for Chloe.

The two men stopped when they saw him and stood stock-still. They didn't reach for weapons and didn't make any threatening moves toward him or Chloe, but Ro wasn't going to take any chances that they weren't armed.

"Let her go," he said in a low, deadly voice when he was about ten feet from them. His pistol was up and aimed in the middle of one of the men's foreheads. At this distance, he definitely wouldn't miss. But neither man seemed ruffled to have not only his weapon, but four others from his teammates pointed at them.

"Of course," the man on the left said. "But first, a word."

"Are you all right?" Ro asked Chloe, not taking his eyes from the man who had spoken.

"I'm okay," she answered. Her voice was a bit shaky, but otherwise she was hanging in there. Ro had never been prouder.

"If you think we didn't know you were here, you're insane," the man on the right said. "We knew the second you stepped foot on the property. But Mr. Carlino doesn't have any beef with the Mountain Mercenaries. He and our father, Peter Smaldone, have taken it upon themselves to get rid of a pesky problem you seem to have acquired in the last week."

Ro heard someone behind him let out a breath of irritation. "You're *about* to have a beef with us if you don't let her come to me in the next three seconds," Ro told him.

With that, the man nodded, then dropped his hand from Chloe's elbow. His brother did the same. "Go on, Chloe," one of the Smaldone brothers told her. "You're free. Just remember what was said tonight."

Chloe nodded and took a hesitant step forward, as if afraid it was a trick and they'd grab her back and laugh. She took another step, and then, as if she realized they were truly letting her go, she ran toward him.

Ro wanted nothing more than to wrap both arms around her and carry her away from there, but instead he caught her with his free arm, then pushed her behind him and toward his teammates. He sighed in relief when she didn't protest the movement.

Keeping his weapon raised and his eyes on the two men, he asked, "Are we going to have a problem?"

They both shook their heads. "No. As far as Cosa Nostra is concerned, the Harris family is no longer a member."

"As easy as that?" Ro asked, the skepticism clear in his tone.

"Nothing comes easy," one of the men said. "But we don't do business with women."

The words weren't said in anger or scorn. They were stated as fact.

"And Leon?" Ro asked, needing to make sure the man wasn't going to be a problem in the future.

"Sex trafficking is a dangerous business," one of the men said. "It can be deadly. Which is why Cosa Nostra doesn't dabble in it."

Feeling something loosen inside of him, Ro lowered his weapon a fraction of an inch.

"Rex wanted to talk to the man," Gray said from behind him.

One of the men shrugged. "He's more than welcome to discuss the issue with our father."

Knowing they weren't going to get anything else out of the pair, Ro began to back up slowly. They'd come for Chloe, and now that they had her, it was time to go. They could stand there all night exchanging veiled references to things neither side wanted to admit, or they could have Rex call Carlino and get real answers. Ro knew which he preferred.

"There's a gate about five hundred feet to your right," one of the men called out. "It'd be easier for Ms. Harris rather than having to climb back over the way you came."

No one said a word, and the two men turned their backs on the group and headed for the house. It was extremely ballsy to turn their backs on five well-armed and pissed-off men, but they still hadn't hesitated.

Knowing the team had his back, Ro holstered his weapon, turned, and headed straight for Chloe. The second her arms went around him, he breathed a sigh of relief. The familiar scent of lilac wafted into his nose, and he buried his face in her hair.

"I love you," she told him without hesitation.

Ro stilled, then pulled back to look at her. "What?"

"I love you," she repeated. "I promised myself that I'd tell you if I ever got to see you again."

Ro could only stare at her in disbelief.

"I've been kept prisoner by my own brother, browbeaten by his girlfriend, forced to do things no woman ever wants to be forced to do, and then I was kidnapped, *twice*, and just had the weirdest dinner in the history of dinners. I'm scared and worried that Joseph Carlino and Peter Smaldone are going to decide they don't want to let me go, after all. But you want to know what kept me sane?"

"What, love?" Ro asked quietly.

"You. I knew you'd come for me."

And with that, Ro finally got his head out of his arse. "Too bloody right, I was coming for you. I love you, Chloe. So much it scares me. I didn't know it at the time, but my life changed the second I saw you standing in my driveway."

She smiled up at him and brushed a fingertip over the cut on his head. "Are you okay?"

"I'm perfect," Ro said. And he was. The moment he got her in his arms, his headache disappeared, and the ache in his stomach went away. All he needed was her. Always. Ro lowered his head to hers.

Before he could capture her lips with his own, Arrow asked irritably, "Are we going to go home, or stand around on the lawn of one of the heads of the Denver Mafia, watching Ro make out with his girlfriend?"

The others chuckled, and Ro grinned. "Ready to go home?" he asked Chloe.

"Absolutely."

Unfortunately, they didn't get to go straight home. Rex called when they were halfway back to Colorado Springs and ordered them to go straight to The Pit. Meat was still there waiting on them, and Chloe told the team everything that had happened to her from the time she was taken from Ro's house.

Ro wasn't happy to hear that she'd been drugged again, but did his best to stay relaxed so as not to stress out Chloe even more. She was currently sitting on his lap at the back of the pool hall, and he didn't think he'd be able to let her out of his sight anytime in the near future.

"He said I was free to go about my business as long as I didn't talk to anyone about their finances," she said, talking about Carlino.

"And you believe him?" Ball asked.

Chloe nodded. "Surprisingly, I do. They asked that I find another profession, but I'm okay with that. I don't think I want anything more to do with investments and taxes." She shuddered, and Ro tightened his hold on her.

"Leon had our dad killed. And Dad's lawyer. And who knows how many other people. He's my brother, and I should feel awful that I didn't try to plead for his life," Chloe said sadly. "But I don't. He was a terrible person who treated me like shit for years. But still, I feel like that makes me just as bad as those Mafia guys."

Ro's arms tightened around Chloe, and he opened his mouth to deny her words when Arrow beat him to it.

"Wrong," his friend said, his voice hard. "You are *nothing* like them or your brother. You do your best to be nice to everyone around you. Even without trying, you make friends easily. I haven't been around you all that much, and even *I* know you don't have a mean bone in your body. Rex even talked to your old boss at Springs Financial, and he said he never believed the rumors about you. He had no choice but to let you go because of the pressure his colleagues were putting on him . . . through Leon, of course. The bottom line is that what happened to your brother was because of his own actions. Not yours. With what he was doing, the dangerous life he was leading, it was only a matter of time before it came back to bite him in the ass."

Ro heard Chloe sniff, and she gave him all her weight as she leaned back against him. He tightened his arms around her and propped his chin on her shoulder. "He's gone," he said softly. "You don't have to worry about him ever again."

"What about Abbie? She hated me too."

"She overdosed," Black told her without hesitation. "We found her in your old room. We surmise that Carlino's goons locked her in. We don't know what they said to her, but whatever it was must have scared her enough to believe taking her own life was a better option than facing whatever they might've had planned for her."

"We should've realized immediately after finding her body that the Mafia was behind your kidnapping," Ro lamented. "Leon most likely wouldn't've locked her in that room."

"So I'm really free?" Chloe asked in disbelief.

"You're really free," Ro told her.

"Thank you for coming to look for me," she told him.

"Thank you for being strong enough to hold on until I found you," he returned.

"I love you."

"I love you too," Ro told her.

"Go home," Meat ordered. "The windows in your house are boarded up, and I took the liberty of having the place cleaned as well. It'll be dark until those windows can be replaced, but it's safe."

Ro nodded. "Are you okay with going back there?" he asked Chloe gently.

"I'll go anywhere as long as you're with me."

"There's no doubt about that," he told her, then stood, lifting her in his arms as he did. Without a word to the rest of his team, he strode through the back room of The Pit and out into the main bar area. He nodded at Dave on his way out and got a big smile from the aloof bartender in return.

He placed Chloe in the front seat of Meat's Hummer and hurried around to the other side. He wanted to get her home and in his bed. He needed to hold her. Today had been too close. He could've lost her, and they both knew it. They both needed some time to just be.

As he drove north toward his home in the Colorado Springs suburb, Ro felt happier than he'd been in a long time. It had been a whirlwind week, but a life-changing one.

Epilogue

Chloe smiled across the table at Allye. It was the morning of her thirty-fifth birthday, and she should've been feeling on top of the world . . . but she wasn't.

"How did your meeting with your lawyer go?" Allye asked. She knew all about the inheritance Chloe had come into that morning, but pure Allye, she hadn't pushed to know details about how much money she had or what she was going to do with it.

"Good," Chloe told her. "We put most of the money into an account that will dole out five million dollars a year to various charities."

"Holy crap," Allye breathed. "That's a lot of money. Are you sure you want to do that?"

"Absolutely," Chloe said without hesitation. "All that money has done is cause sadness. I don't need that much, and I'd rather it go to women who are trying to get back on their feet after being abused or being rescued from trafficking situations. I did a ton of research to try to find the best organizations where it would be used responsibly."

Chloe reached into her purse and pulled something out, then slid it across the table to Allye.

"What's this?"

"Check it out and see," Chloe told her with a small grin.

Allye picked up the piece of paper, and her eyes went wide when she understood what she was seeing. "What the hell? Chloe, no."

"Yes. I can't imagine anything better than giving that money to your dance school. Half of that is specifically earmarked to go to your program for special-needs kids."

Allye's eyes filled with tears. "I don't know what to say. This is too much."

"No, it's not. I have more money than I know what to do with. I want you to have it. I watched the videos you sent me of your kids at their latest recital at least twenty times. The joy in their eyes at being able to perform is priceless. The world needs more joy like that in it. The money that caused so many deaths and so much pain should be used for happiness."

Allye scooted her chair back and reached for Chloe, embracing her so tightly it was hard for her to breathe. They both shed some tears before calming down and sitting back down to eat.

"Tell me about Ro," Allye ordered.

Chloe sighed. "What about him?"

"What's up with you two? I mean, Gray told me you'd moved out into an apartment? What's that about?"

Chloe's eyes filled with tears, but she blinked them back. "Ro told me he thought it would be good for me."

Allye's eyes got huge in her face, and she stared at Chloe in disbelief. "Seriously?"

Chloe nodded. "I stayed with him for a couple weeks after everything happened, but I could tell something was up. He started working out in his garage more and more, and when I asked what was wrong, he said nothing. We slept together every night, and our love life was as good as ever, but then one day . . . he told me that he thought I should get my own place. Told me that I hadn't been free to live where I wanted and do what I wanted for so long that I should 'find myself' before we got any more serious."

"Any more serious? What the hell does that mean?" Allye asked.

Chloe shrugged. "I have no idea. I mean, I love him. And he told me he loved me back. But then he practically forced me to move out. I'm so confused. I only get to see him a couple of times a week now." She looked up at her new friend. "I miss him. And I'm so lonely."

Allye frowned. "You need to confront him. Ask him if he wants to be with you. You can't live like this."

"I know."

"So what's holding you back? This isn't like you."

"What if he says he doesn't love me anymore?" Chloe asked quietly. "I can't lose him too. Not after everything we went through."

"You did have a fast courtship," Allye mused. "Even faster than me and Gray . . . and that's saying something."

"It might've been fast, but it's been more real than anything else I've ever felt in my life," Chloe protested. "I love him. So much. And it hurts that he's pushing me away."

"Then ask him," Allye said, leaning forward. "Demand he talk to you. Ask him point-blank if he still loves you."

"What if he says no?" Chloe asked.

"Then at least you'll know. It'll suck, but you won't be wasting your time with him anymore," Allye said.

The thought of Ro telling her that he was mistaken and he didn't love her was enough to make Chloe double over in pain, but she stayed upright by sheer force of will. The more she thought about Allye's words, the more she knew her friend was right. It was time to confront Ro and ask him where they stood.

Ro ran a hand through his hair in agitation. He hadn't been able to concentrate on anything lately, and he knew it was because of Chloe. But what was done was done. He'd thought a lot about her situation and had come to the conclusion that he needed to give her some space.

He hated it. But for the last few years, she'd been under her brother's thumb. She'd had to lie to the world and pretend to be heartbroken when her brother's badly burned body was found in the rubble of his strip club.

Today was her thirty-fifth birthday, and she'd become a rich woman. She could do anything. Be anyone. He needed to give her the time and space to be the amazing woman he already knew her to be.

She'd called earlier and asked to see him. He couldn't deny her anything, so he said he'd meet her at her new apartment, but she'd insisted on coming to his house.

Having her there would be painful, but Ro would suck it up and hide how much he missed her. Everywhere he looked in his house, he saw her. What sucked the most was that the scent of her lilac lotion had finally dissipated. He no longer smelled her when he went to bed, and his bathroom was devoid of her scent as well.

Pacing back and forth, Ro waited for her to arrive.

His watch finally vibrated, letting him know someone was pulling into his driveway. After the night the Mafia had infiltrated his house, he'd had his security upgraded so if a squirrel so much as farted on his property, he'd be notified. He had the door open and was waiting for her by the time she pulled up in front of his house.

He'd gone with her to car-shop, and she'd ended up with a practical Honda Pilot. He'd wanted her to consider a Hummer, like Meat's, as it was almost impenetrable and would keep her safe on the road, but she'd refused, saying she wanted something less flashy, more normal.

Ro held his breath as Chloe stepped out of the vehicle. She was wearing a pair of tight jeans that molded to her body, and a flowy blouse with large flowers on it. Sunglasses shielded her eyes from him, which made him frown. He loved looking into her brown eyes. She couldn't hide her feelings from him, which was something he always counted on.

She walked toward him, though *walked* wasn't the best word. Stomped was more like it. She stood in front of him and put her hands on her hips. "We need to talk."

Ro swallowed the bile that rose up his throat at her words. It was never good when anyone said they wanted to "talk," the way she'd said it. Nodding, not trusting himself to speak, Ro gestured toward the open door.

He kept his eyes on her arse as she walked into his house ahead of him. Inhaling deeply, Ro felt his heart skip a beat as her familiar smell followed in her wake. He wanted to ask her to please go and roll around on his bed before she left so he'd have something to remember her by, but he kept quiet and merely followed along behind her meekly. She went straight to his living room and whipped off her sunglasses.

The pain he saw in her eyes nearly brought him to his knees.

"What's wrong?" he asked.

"What's wrong?" she asked incredulously. "Everything!"

"Tell me what I can do to help," he told her.

"Do you love me?" she asked almost belligerently.

Ro blinked. That wasn't what he was expecting to hear. "Yes. Of course I do."

"You haven't been acting like it," she said gruffly. "After Leon's funeral, you did everything but push me out the door. I didn't want to get an apartment, but you basically told me that you wanted me out of your house. I only see you a couple times a week, and even then you barely touch me. If you want to break up with me, you just need to tell me. Stop playing games, and come right out and do it."

"I don't want to break up with you," Ro stammered.

"Then why are you pushing me away?" Chloe asked quietly, as if all the bravado had left after she'd said what she needed to say.

Ro swallowed hard. He needed to tread lightly here. "You've been under your brother's control for years. Not free to go where you wanted, eat what you wanted, or do anything without him or his girlfriend watching over your shoulder. You're rich now. You're free. You can do anything you want. Go on a vacation to Hawaii, buy a flat in Paris, go on a cruise around the world. You should do those things. Get out. *Live.*"

Her brows came down in confusion. "But I don't *want* to do those things."

"How do you know if you don't try them?" Ro countered.

"Because. That's not me. Big cities scare me. I barely tolerate Denver. I don't tan, I burn, so why would I want to go to Hawaii? And I get seasick, so a cruise is definitely out."

Ro stared at her, at a loss for words.

"You're right. I *have* been at my brother's mercy for years. But I'm not eighteen, I'm thirty-five. I've lived on my own before, and I chose to stay here in Colorado Springs. I *like* it here. The last four years have been awful, but don't treat me like I'm a little kid, Ronan. As if I don't know what and who I want. Since the day you came and got me from Joseph Carlino's house, I've felt freer than I have in my entire life. I don't need money. I don't need fancy clothes and trips. All I need is *you*. At your side, I felt strong enough to do anything. But then you pushed me away. Made me feel as if you didn't want me around anymore. That hurt me more than anything my brother ever did."

Ro took a step back. It felt as if she'd hit him. Her words stung.

"I didn't want you to feel stifled by me. By our relationship."

Chloe rolled her eyes. "You're a bloody tosser."

Ro stared at her for a second, then his lips quirked up. But she didn't give him a chance to respond.

"I love you, Ronan Cross. Being with you makes me feel free. Strong. Until you started acting weird. At night, I thought everything was okay. You held me and made love to me so sweetly, and it felt right. But in the morning, you'd be cold and leave me alone the entire day. Then you forced me to get my own apartment when I didn't want to be away from you. I *hate* it there. My neighbors are loud, and the guy next door keeps inviting me over to the parties he throws every weekend."

"He does what?" Ro growled. "That arsehole."

"I need to know," Chloe said, her eyes swimming in tears. "Are you pushing me away because you're trying to end things, or what?"

Ro was done talking. He took the three steps required to get to her and pulled her roughly against his body. He put his hands on her face and held her gaze. "I love you, Chloe Harris. I want to marry you. Put my babies inside your belly and tie you to me so strongly you'll never be able to leave. I was afraid that since you had money now, you wouldn't need me anymore. That you'd get bored living up here in my out-of-the-way house. That you'd regret hooking up with me so quickly."

"Never," she whispered.

"Move in with me," he told her, placing one hand at the small of her back and the other on her nape. "I swear I'm done being a bloody tosser. I won't push you away again. If you start to feel stifled, tell me, and we'll go and do something. We'll fly to Paris, and I'll hold your hand as we explore. We'll fly to Hawaii and spend our time checking out aquariums, eating out, and other things that won't involve you getting too much sun. Name it, and I'll give it to you."

"You, Ro. I just want *you*."

"You have me," he told her, right before he dropped his lips onto hers. He kissed her as if he'd never get another chance. And she returned his kiss just as aggressively. Before he knew it, she was straddling him after he'd fallen back onto the couch. Without lifting her head, she began to undo the fastenings of his jeans.

Her urgency contagious, he pushed her hands away and took over. She broke their kiss long enough to swing a leg off him and pull off one leg of her jeans and panties. She didn't bother with the other, leaving the denim dangling.

"I need you," she told him.

"Shhh." Ro tried to soothe her, even though he was as hard as a pike and just as desperate to get inside her as she was to have him there. "I want to make sure you're ready for me."

"I'm ready," she said, pushing his jeans down enough to pull his dick out and rubbing the head up and down her soaking-wet slit.

With that, she broke his restraint. Putting one hand on her arse and the other on her waist, he held her above him easily. She moaned. "Please, Ro."

"I love you," he said, looking her in the eyes as he said it.

"I love you," she replied.

"You're moving back in. I need your lilac smell on my sheets and on my body every morning. I need you by my side and at my back. I want you to go to the doctor and have them remove that bloody birth-control thing so I can get you pregnant."

"Ro," she moaned, trying to sink down on top of him, but he refused to give her more of his cock. Not until she agreed.

"And we're gonna get married. Soon. If you want a big wedding, we'll do that. But you need to be able to plan it within a month. I'm not waiting any longer than that. I gave you a chance to be free of me, and you didn't take it. You're mine, Chloe. Whether you choose to take my name or not, you're mine. Body and soul."

"Yesssss. Please, Ro. Fuck me."

"No, Chloe. You fuck *me*." And with that, he let go of her, letting her sink all the way down on top of him.

They both moaned as he filled her. She was soaking wet, creaming all over his cock as she immediately began to move on top of him. They were both mostly still dressed—they'd only uncovered the necessary parts.

"God, I love you," Ro told her again, watching her bounce up and down on his cock.

She didn't respond, simply moaned. Her hands grasped his shoulders, and he felt her nails dig into his flesh even through his T-shirt.

A light sheen of perspiration covered her forehead, and he knew he'd never get enough of this.

He let her take what she needed as she ground her clit against his belly and moved over him. He held her steady throughout their love-making. When she stiffened in his arms and began to shudder with her orgasm, Ro took over. Slamming her down on top of him and thrusting up at the same time. He took her hard, showing her without words how sorry he was and how much he loved her.

It didn't take long; even as she was still clenching her inner muscles with her orgasm, he exploded, groaning as he shot pulse after pulse of come deep inside her, coating her with it.

She fell onto his chest and put her arms around his shoulders, holding on for dear life. Ro felt puffs of air against his neck as she tried to regain her senses. He wasn't much better off. Every time he was with her, it got better. He ran a hand over her head, petting her, and getting his fingers tangled in her long black hair in the process.

Eventually, she sat up. He could tell the hurt was still there. "Don't push me away again, Ro. I couldn't stand it. If you don't want to be with me, simply say so."

"I'll never not want you," he told her. "I wanted you so badly it scared me. I wanted to lock you in my house and never let you go. That's when I knew I had to. Remember the saying?"

She smiled then. The relief was so stark in her eyes, Ro vowed then and there to never do anything that would hurt her again. "If you love something, set it free. If it's meant to be, it'll come back."

"You came back," he told her unnecessarily.

"I did," Chloe agreed. "Thank you for giving me wings."

"You're welcome."

"Take me upstairs," she ordered. "I've missed your bed."

"With pleasure."

The next morning, Chloe woke up with Ro's arms around her and his face buried in her neck. He'd admitted that he'd ordered a bottle of her lotion online and had used it to masturbate at night. That he couldn't get off without smelling it now.

It had been a bit creepy and endearing all at the same time.

She thought about his words from the day before. He wanted to marry her. To have a family with her. She hadn't thought much about children, but suddenly she knew without a doubt that she wanted them with Ro. Neither had family left, no one that mattered. They could make their own family, and make sure their kids knew how much they were loved and cherished every day of their lives.

It wasn't too long ago that she'd wondered if she'd be under her brother's thumb forever. If she'd be forced to do things she didn't want to. Then Ro had shown up, like a miracle. She thought about the other women and kids they rescued as Mountain Mercenaries. She couldn't lie—his job scared her, but she'd never ask him to quit. No one deserved to be forced into a life of slavery. Sexual or otherwise.

Maybe she'd send an anonymous donation to Rex and his Mountain Mercenaries. She couldn't think of a better use for her money.

Ro stirred then, and she was smiling at him when he finally opened his eyes.

"Morning, love," he said sleepily. "You sleep all right?"

"Better than all right," she reassured him. "Can we go and get my stuff today?" she asked.

"Already planned on it," Ro said, then rolled until she was under him. "But first . . . I need you."

Chloe giggled. "You had me last night. Three times."

"That was last night. This is this morning," he said with a grin and dropped his head.

Chloe smiled and decided he was right.

∿

One Month Later

Archer Kane, known as "Arrow" to his friends on the Mountain Mercenaries team, stood at the electrical box next to a dilapidated house in a shit hole of a city in the Dominican Republic. Under the cover of darkness, his job was to cut the power to the house, allowing them to slip in, grab the little girl they'd come after, and leave, hopefully undetected.

Rex had arranged the mission after the girl's mother had contacted him. Her father, a douchebag of the highest order, had disappeared with the girl after his scheduled visitation. Rex had traced him to the city of Santo Domingo and to this run-down shack of a building.

There were only three of them on the mission, as they didn't want to attract unwanted attention. And besides, Ro was on his honeymoon with Chloe, and Meat had the flu, of all things. Arrow, Black, and Ball had volunteered, and Gray only agreed to stay back in Colorado Springs because Allye was performing with the Cleo Parker Robinson Dance Theatre in Denver in a special guest performance.

The few lights in the house blinked out, and Arrow nodded to his teammates. "Done."

"Let's do this," Black said.

The three men disappeared behind the back of the house and silently made entry through a window. They didn't make a sound, and other than a slight snoring, there weren't any other noises coming from the dark house.

Nodding his head to the left, Arrow indicated that he'd take the room there. Black and Ball nodded back and spread out to search the other rooms. Pushing the door open, Arrow held his breath, sighing in relief when the hinges didn't squeak.

He was wearing a pair of night-vision goggles, so it was easy to make out shapes in the small, dingy room.

He'd expected to find the missing little girl—but what he *hadn't* expected was the woman standing in front of her.

She was holding a knife, her hands shaking so hard, he was amazed she was able to hold the gun at all.

The view with his night-vision goggles was green and black and distorted, but the woman's hair was as light as his skin, telling him she was most likely blonde.

"Get out," she whispered in a low, harsh tone.

Arrow took a silent step to the right.

As he suspected, the tip of the knife didn't follow his movements. She couldn't see him, not like he could see her.

Instead of responding, he moved completely silently until he was by her side. Regretting what he had to do, Arrow brought an arm down, hard, on her own outstretched arms.

She didn't scream in pain, like he'd expected; instead, she grunted softly. But his actions had the desired effect. She dropped the knife, and it fell with a loud clang to the wooden planks beneath their feet.

Moving quickly, Arrow wrapped an arm around her chest and another around her neck.

Forcing her head up and immobilizing her, Arrow bent so his lips were by her ear. "Keep calm. We're not here for you. We're here to take the little girl home."

Shocking him further, the woman didn't fight, but instead sagged a little in his arms at hearing his words. "You're American?"

"Yes."

"You swear you're taking her back to the States? To her mom?"

"Yes."

And with that, Arrow could feel all the fight leave her. But then, almost immediately, she began to squirm. "What are you waiting for? You need to get out of here," she said urgently.

Arrow loosened his hold, though he was prepared to grab the woman again if she made any kind of threatening move toward him or the little girl cowering at her feet.

The woman immediately crouched down and began to feel for the child. He watched as she took the little girl's face in her hands and leaned in close to her. "You're safe now," she whispered. "This man is here to take you home to Mommy."

"Are you coming?" the little girl asked, her eyes huge in her face, her pupils fully dilated in the dark room.

The woman shook her head, then realized that it was too dark for her to be seen. "No. I can't go. You know that."

"I want you to come too!" the little girl complained, her voice a little too loud for comfort.

Arrow crouched down next to the pair and touched the girl's head. "My name is Arrow. I'm gonna get you home," he said.

The girl threw herself into the woman's arms so hard, she fell back on her ass. But again, not one extraneous sound left her lips. It must have hurt, but she didn't so much as wince. "Shhhh, Nina. You know we have to be quiet."

"So the bad men don't hear us," the little girl whispered solemnly.

"Exactly. Arrow is here to take you home. You need to be a big, brave girl now."

"Like you are when the bad men take you away?"

Arrow's eyes narrowed at that, but the woman didn't hesitate.

"Exactly like that. But Arrow won't hurt you. Will you?" she asked, turning in his direction. If he didn't know the room was pitch-black and she couldn't see anything, Arrow would've thought she could see as well as he could.

"That's right, Nina. Me and my friends will make sure the bad men won't touch one hair on your head ever again."

"I want Morgan to come too," she said, gripping the woman around the neck even tighter. "She doesn't want to stay with the bad men either. She told me."

The woman, Morgan, cleared her throat quietly to respond, but Arrow had heard enough. He put a hand on Morgan's upper arm and asked, "What's your name?"

He heard Black and Ball enter the room but didn't take his gaze from Morgan.

"Morgan Byrd," she said softly.

"Holy shit," Black said.

At the same time, Ball exclaimed, "Fuck."

Arrow could only stare at her in disbelief. "Morgan Byrd, from Atlanta?"

She blinked. "You know me?"

Arrow helped her stand, putting a hand under little Nina's butt when she refused to let go and wound her legs around Morgan's waist. "Know you?" Arrow asked. "Honey, *everyone* knows you. Your father has been all over the news since you disappeared a year ago."

He heard her breath hitch at that, but she got control over her emotions and nodded. "If it's not too much trouble, I'd love to come with you."

The fact of the matter was that it *was* trouble. They didn't have any identification for her. They had Nina's passport, and had planned on catching a commercial flight out of the country.

But things had changed.

Morgan Byrd was twenty-six . . . no, twenty-seven now. She'd disappeared a year or so ago. She'd simply vanished without a trace after a night out on the town in Atlanta, Georgia, with friends. There had been no ransom demand and no clues left behind as to who might've taken her or where she'd gone. There had been a ton of media attention right after her disappearance, which had waned, but her father made sure that the public never forgot about his missing daughter.

They'd come to the Dominican Republic to rescue a kidnapped little girl, but it looked like they'd be leaving with possibly the most famous missing person since Elizabeth Smart.

Arrow reached down and intertwined his fingers with hers. The way she clung to him, even though she hadn't gotten the smallest glimpse of what he or his teammates looked like, spoke volumes. She was terrified. Her fingers were small and dainty, much like she was. At about five feet three, she wasn't much taller than a little girl herself, but Arrow could feel the determination and strength in her grip.

"If things go bad, take Nina and go," Morgan said urgently.

"Morgan—" Arrow began, but she interrupted him.

"No. I mean it. You need to get her out of here. No matter what."

"Okay," Arrow agreed, lying through his teeth. He wasn't leaving her in this hellhole. No way.

She sighed in relief and squeezed his hand. "Okay."

As silently as they'd entered, they left the run-down house through the back window. Arrow had no idea how they were going to get Morgan out of the country, but he'd cross that bridge once they were at their safe house. The flight they'd planned on taking wasn't for another two days, giving them time to deal with any hiccups in their operation and to get Nina medical attention if needed. But the entire plan was now up in the air. He needed to talk to Black and Ball, and call Rex. They needed help.

He looked over at Morgan as they slunk along the disgusting and dangerous back alleys of Santo Domingo.

She looked nothing like the woman whose face had been on every television station. She'd lost a ton of weight, and her hair was matted. Her arms were covered in dirt, and she was wearing a filthy T-shirt.

She turned then, and met his gaze for the first time—and he inhaled sharply at what he saw there.

Emptiness.

Morgan Byrd had been through hell. Whatever had happened to her had almost broken her. But she was holding on. Barely.

Reaching out, Arrow couldn't stop himself from saying, "I've got you, Morgan. I'm going to get you home no matter what it takes."

She didn't respond, but the brief flare of hope in her eyes, quickly doused, was enough.

Acknowledgments

I would be remiss if I didn't acknowledge my amazing developmental editor, Kelli Collins. She meticulously takes notes on my characters and their idiosyncrasies and calls me on every stupid thing I have them say . . . and makes me change them. I swear if you all could read my first drafts, you'd be rolling your eyes so hard at me and the things I have my characters say and do. And Kelli never makes me feel like an idiot either . . . she's nice about telling me I've lost my mind.

I also want to thank everyone at Montlake for making the process of writing a book so easy. From the very beginning, they've been nothing but supportive and communicative, which is so important.

I have to give a shout-out to my husband, Mr. Stoker. He doesn't hesitate to tell people what his wife does for a living, and he's not ashamed or embarrassed to tell people I write romance (because there's nothing *to* be ashamed of!). He's read all my books and is seriously one of my biggest supporters, and that means the world to me.

And last, to all of *you*, my readers. Thank you for loving my characters as much as you do and for continuing to read my books. I'm so glad you enjoy reading the kinds of stories I like to write.

About the Author

Susan Stoker is a *New York Times*, *USA Today*, and *Wall Street Journal* bestselling author whose series include Ace Security, Badge of Honor: Texas Heroes, SEAL of Protection, Unsung Heroes: Delta Force, and Mountain Mercenaries. Married to a retired army noncommissioned officer, Stoker has lived all over the country—from Missouri to California to Colorado to Texas—and currently lives under the big skies of Tennessee. A true believer in happily ever after, Stoker enjoys writing novels in which romance turns to love. To learn more about the author and her work, visit her website, www.stokeraces.com, or find her on Facebook at www.facebook.com/authorsusanstoker.

Connect with Susan Online

Susan's Facebook Profile and Page

www.facebook.com/authorsstoker

www.facebook.com/authorsusanstoker

Follow Susan on Twitter

www.twitter.com/Susan_Stoker

Find Susan's Books on Goodreads

www.goodreads.com/SusanStoker

Email

Susan@StokerAces.com

Website

www.StokerAces.com